Broken Compass

Ivy Hale

Published by Ivy Hale, 2024.

BROKEN COMPASS

First edition. October 30, 2024.

ISBN: 979-8227970886

Written by Ivy Hale.

Chapter 1: The Last Goodbye

I stood on the edge of the sprawling red cliffs of Firestone Bay, the salty breeze tugging at my hair as I watched the waves crash violently against the rocks below. It was a place of solace and heartbreak, the backdrop of my childhood memories. Today, it felt different, charged with an energy I couldn't quite understand. My father had just been laid to rest, and as I traced my fingers over the engraved words on his headstone, the reality of my loss hit me hard. Little did I know, this day would mark the beginning of a journey that would shake my world to its core.

The wind howled, carrying with it the scent of brine and distant storms, whispering secrets from the ocean's depths. I could still hear the echoes of my father's laughter, a warm melody that used to fill our modest home with joy. Those memories played like a movie reel in my mind, vivid and bittersweet. I remembered his stories about the ocean, his deep voice weaving tales of daring sailors and mystical sea creatures. "The sea is full of magic, Mira," he'd say, his eyes twinkling with mischief. "You just have to know where to look." Now, standing at the cliff's edge, I felt the weight of that magic—a bittersweet longing for the impossible.

As I turned away from the grave, my heart heavy with grief, I noticed a flicker of movement on the shore. A figure, silhouetted against the crashing waves, stood where the water kissed the sand. Curiosity piqued, I stepped closer, careful not to slip on the loose pebbles that littered the cliff. The figure appeared to be a young man, his dark hair tousled by the wind, gazing out at the tumultuous sea as if searching for something lost in its depths.

"Hey!" I called out, my voice barely rising above the roar of the ocean. "Are you okay down there?"

He turned slowly, revealing a face that was strikingly handsome, marked by a hint of weariness. His blue eyes, as deep as the ocean itself, met mine with an intensity that sent a shiver down my spine. "I'm fine," he shouted back, though the slight quiver in his voice betrayed him. "Just needed some air."

I hesitated, my heart thrumming in my chest. "You sure? It's dangerous so close to the edge."

"Dangerous is my middle name," he replied, a smirk breaking through his otherwise serious demeanor. "Just taking a moment to breathe. Or, you know, contemplate life choices."

There was something about him—an allure mixed with a hint of vulnerability—that made me feel inexplicably drawn to his plight. It struck me then how alone I felt in my grief, as if I were an island amidst a sea of memories. "I get that," I said, my voice softer. "Sometimes the ocean is the only thing that understands."

He turned, really looking at me for the first time. "You lost someone, didn't you?"

My breath caught in my throat. "My father. Just today."

He nodded, an understanding passing between us. "I'm sorry. Losing someone is never easy. But sometimes, it's those moments that lead us to unexpected places."

As we stood there, the crashing waves mirroring the tumult within me, I felt an undeniable connection—an anchor in a storm. "I'm Mira," I said, extending a hand in a gesture of camaraderie.

"Liam," he replied, shaking my hand firmly. "And I'd say it's a pleasure to meet you, but I guess that would be a bit insensitive right now, wouldn't it?"

I chuckled lightly, the tension in my chest easing just a fraction. "A little bit, but I appreciate the honesty."

We stood in silence for a moment, watching the waves as they danced upon the shore, both of us lost in our thoughts. The wind whipped around us, a chaotic symphony of nature, pulling at the edges of our conversation like a tide refusing to recede. "What brings you to Firestone Bay?" I asked, intrigued by his presence.

"I'm just passing through," he said, turning his gaze back to the horizon. "Came to clear my head. Sometimes you need to get away from everything."

"Firestone Bay is a strange choice for that," I replied, trying to inject a bit of humor into our somber exchange. "Especially today. It's got more than its fair share of memories. You might drown in them."

He laughed, the sound rich and warm. "True, but every place has its ghosts. Might as well choose the ones that have a good view."

Liam's words lingered in the air between us, resonating with the unspoken truths we both carried. I felt an inexplicable pull to this stranger, a sense that he was more than just a passerby. Perhaps he was the reminder I needed that life continued beyond loss, even when it felt like the waves would crash forever against the cliffs of my heart.

"Do you want to join me?" I asked suddenly, surprising myself. "I mean, if you're not too busy contemplating life choices."

His expression shifted, a mixture of surprise and something warmer flickering across his features. "You sure? I don't want to intrude on your mourning process."

"It's not like I'm going to get any more depressed," I replied, waving a dismissive hand. "Besides, if there's one thing I've learned, it's that sharing grief makes it a little less heavy."

Liam hesitated for a moment, then nodded. "Alright, lead the way."

Together, we made our way down the jagged path that led from the cliffs to the sandy beach below, the weight of our shared sorrow binding us in a fragile thread of connection. As we walked, the sun dipped lower in the sky, painting the horizon in shades of orange and pink, casting a warm glow on the cool sand. It felt like a blessing amidst the turmoil, a silent promise that new beginnings could emerge from the ashes of heartache.

And as we reached the beach, I realized that perhaps today was not just a goodbye but also the unanticipated start of something I could never have foreseen—a journey that would stretch beyond the boundaries of my grief into the uncharted waters of new possibilities.

Liam and I settled on the cool, damp sand, the tide pulling back like an old friend reluctant to say goodbye. The ocean stretched before us, a vast expanse of blue and white, endless and wild, mirroring the chaos swirling inside my mind. I felt lighter here, away from the heaviness of my father's grave, as if the rhythm of the waves could wash away the weight of my sorrow, if only for a moment.

"So, are you a local?" Liam asked, drawing circles in the sand with his fingers. His casual demeanor belied the depth of our earlier conversation, the lightness of his voice a stark contrast to the somber reality we had just faced.

I let out a soft laugh, half amusement and half disbelief. "Local? Hardly. I'm just the ghost who haunts this place now. I grew up here, but it feels different now. Like I don't belong."

"Ghosts have a knack for lingering in places they loved," he said, a hint of empathy in his eyes. "Trust me, I get it. I've been running away from my own shadows."

I raised an eyebrow, intrigued. "Running? That's one way to keep life interesting. What are you running from?"

He paused, his expression flickering with something akin to pain. "A lot of things. Family expectations. A future I didn't choose. It's exhausting, really."

"Family can be a real pain," I replied, a wry smile playing on my lips. "My dad had a way of showing up just when I thought I had life figured out. Now, I'm not sure I can find my way without him."

The honesty in my voice startled me, and for a moment, I feared I had revealed too much. But Liam didn't look away. Instead, he nodded, as if my confession resonated with him in ways I couldn't yet understand. "Maybe that's the trick," he said. "Finding your own path, even when the map's gone. Or better yet, creating a new one."

His words settled around us like a blanket, warming the chilly air. I couldn't help but admire his perspective. "And how exactly does one create a map? With crayons and glitter?"

"Sure," he said, a grin breaking through. "Who says we can't have a little fun while figuring out life's messes? Besides, I hear glitter is quite effective in distracting from the more serious stuff."

As I laughed, I felt the knot in my chest begin to loosen. Perhaps this unexpected friendship, borne of shared grief and laughter, was what I needed to navigate this uncharted territory. "So, tell me about your glitter," I prompted, leaning closer. "What's the most ridiculous thing you've done in the name of escape?"

He chuckled, scratching his chin thoughtfully. "Oh, that would have to be the time I dyed my hair bright purple right before a family reunion. My grandmother nearly had a heart attack. But, you know, it felt liberating, like a tiny rebellion."

I could hardly contain my laughter. "Purple? Really? That's bold."

"It was," he said, his eyes sparkling with mischief. "But there's something liberating about shaking things up. Sometimes, it's the little acts of defiance that remind you you're alive."

"I could use a little defiance in my life," I admitted, staring out at the frothy waves crashing against the shore. "Maybe I should dye my hair bright blue. Or maybe I'll just start with something more manageable, like a new wardrobe."

"Blue would suit you," he said, glancing at me with a playful smirk. "Though, I'd suggest avoiding the glitter. You might end up stuck in a situation where you can't escape without looking like a disco ball."

We shared another laugh, the sound mingling with the rhythmic crashing of the waves, and for the first time in hours, I felt a flicker of something resembling hope. Just as I was beginning to feel at ease, a loud shout echoed from the direction of the cliff.

"Mira! Where are you?"

My heart sank as I recognized the voice of my younger brother, Jake. He'd been a whirlwind of energy since our father's death, needing constant reassurance that the world hadn't crumbled into chaos. "I'm down here!" I called back, standing up and brushing the sand from my jeans.

Jake appeared at the top of the path, his face a mix of concern and irritation. "You've been gone forever! Mom is looking for you. She's...well, you know how she gets."

"Yeah, yeah," I replied, rolling my eyes. "She worries too much."

"Because we just buried Dad," Jake retorted, his voice tight. "Maybe you should worry about that instead of whatever you're doing down there."

Liam remained seated, watching the exchange with a mix of amusement and concern. I felt a sudden rush of embarrassment, a reminder that while I was finding a sliver of connection and humor, my family was still very much grappling with the reality of our loss.

"Alright, alright," I said, lifting my hands in mock surrender. "I'm coming. It's just a little fresh air."

"Fresh air that I'm sure will turn into a long, drawn-out conversation," Jake grumbled as he started back up the path. "You know how Mom gets about these things."

"Yeah, I do," I muttered under my breath, feeling a twinge of irritation. "And how about you let me have my moment? Just this once?"

He paused, glancing back at me with an exasperated sigh. "I'm just looking out for you, Mira. Someone has to."

"Yeah, and I appreciate it," I replied, forcing a smile to lighten the mood. "But I'm not made of glass, you know."

"Just be careful, alright?" he called as he reached the top of the cliff.

I looked back at Liam, who was now standing, brushing the sand off his pants. "Looks like the world is calling," he said, his tone slightly teasing.

"Unfortunately," I replied, feeling a pang of disappointment. "I was just starting to enjoy the escape."

"Escape doesn't have to end here," he said, a hint of determination in his voice. "You know where to find me if you need another dose of purple hair inspiration or a distraction from the chaos."

I smiled, warmth flooding my chest at the thought. "I might just take you up on that."

With one last glance at the ocean, I turned to follow Jake up the path, my heart heavy with the weight of reality but somehow lighter with the promise of new beginnings. Liam's laughter lingered in the air, an unexpected reminder that amidst loss, life continued to weave its intricate tapestry, and perhaps, just perhaps, I was beginning to find my thread.

I made my way back up the steep path, my heart still echoing with the remnants of our conversation. The landscape around me seemed to shift with every step, each rock and scraggly shrub whispering secrets of the past. My brother waited impatiently, tapping his foot as if trying to summon me back to reality with sheer determination. "You really took your time, didn't you?" he said, crossing his arms over his chest.

"Not everyone is in a hurry to confront the aftermath of a funeral, Jake," I shot back lightly, though the tension in my voice belied my attempt at humor. I had felt like I was running from grief, but now it was catching up with me like a relentless tide.

As we reached the top, I saw my mother standing by our car, her expression a mix of worry and frustration. The wind whipped her hair around her face, making her look almost ethereal. "Mira! Thank goodness. I was about to send a search party," she said, the relief in her voice palpable.

"I'm fine, Mom. Just needed a moment," I replied, forcing a smile that didn't quite reach my eyes.

Her gaze softened, but I could still see the worry etched in the lines around her mouth. "I understand, but we have to keep moving. I don't want to linger here too long."

I nodded, feeling the weight of her unspoken fears. Losing Dad had shattered something fundamental within our family, leaving jagged edges that refused to heal. We climbed into the car, and as I settled into my seat, the air inside felt heavy with unexpressed emotions. Jake fiddled with his phone, pretending to be engrossed in the screen, while I stared out at the cliffs one last time.

As we drove away, I couldn't shake the feeling that I was leaving something vital behind, something that had just begun to awaken in the hours I spent with Liam. My thoughts wandered back to him, his laughter mingling with the crashing waves, creating a melody I wished I could bottle up and carry with me.

The car ride was filled with awkward silence, punctuated only by the soft hum of the engine and my mother's occasional glances in the rearview mirror. She was trying to gauge our moods, I could tell, and I felt a pang of guilt for making her worry. "Maybe we should stop for ice cream," she suggested after a while, attempting to lighten the atmosphere.

"I'm in," Jake said, his face brightening.

"Fine, but only if they have chocolate chip cookie dough," I added, trying to embrace the semblance of normalcy that my mother was so desperately trying to create.

We pulled into the small ice cream shop, a local favorite, its bright blue and white exterior standing out against the backdrop of the grey sky. I watched as families bustled in and out, their laughter mingling with the sounds of jingling bells above the door. The scene felt surreal, as if I were watching life unfold from behind a glass barrier.

While my mother ordered, Jake and I claimed a small table outside. The cool breeze carried the scent of freshly baked waffle cones, reminding me of happier days spent here with Dad, sharing ridiculous flavors and arguing over the best toppings. "Remember when you insisted on putting gummy bears on everything?" Jake teased, a spark of mischief lighting his eyes.

"I still think gummy bears are a perfectly acceptable topping," I shot back, grinning despite the sadness weighing on my heart. "It's the blend of chewy and creamy. A culinary masterpiece!"

"Sure, if you're a five-year-old," he laughed, rolling his eyes.

We shared a moment of levity that felt like a breath of fresh air in the suffocating grief. As our ice creams were served, I took a moment to savor the coolness against my tongue, letting the sweetness wash over me. But as I looked over at Jake, his smile faltered, and I felt a familiar heaviness return. "You alright?" I asked, my voice gentle.

He shrugged, his gaze distant. "I guess. Just... I miss him, you know?"

"I know," I whispered, my throat tightening. "We all do."

Just then, my phone buzzed in my pocket, pulling me from the moment. I fished it out, glancing at the screen to see a message from an unknown number. Curiosity tinged with apprehension danced in my stomach as I read the text: Meet me at the old boathouse. I have something important to tell you.

My heart raced. Who could this be? I looked up at Jake and Mom, but they were too engrossed in their own world to notice my sudden shift in focus. I typed a quick reply, my fingers trembling as I responded: Who is this?

The reply came almost instantly: Someone who knows what happened. Someone who can help.

I felt a chill run down my spine. The last thing I wanted to deal with right now was more drama, especially with the already tumultuous emotions swirling within my family. Yet the intrigue tugged at me, a siren call I found hard to resist. "I need to go," I said abruptly, my voice stronger than I felt.

Mom looked up, her brow furrowed in confusion. "Go where?"

"To the boathouse," I replied, adrenaline coursing through me.

"Now?" she exclaimed, her tone shifting to one of concern. "You can't be serious! It's been a long day."

"Mom, please. I'll be fine," I insisted, already feeling the urgency of the message pulling me forward.

Jake leaned in, his voice a low whisper. "What's going on?"

"Just... something I need to check out," I replied, avoiding his gaze.

"Are you sure?" he asked, worry etching lines across his young face.

I nodded, the decision solidifying within me. "I'll be quick. I promise."

With one last glance at my brother and mother, I grabbed my bag and headed back to the car. As I drove toward the boathouse, the road twisted through the familiar trees, their branches reaching out like grasping hands. My heart raced in anticipation, mixing with a nagging sense of dread.

The boathouse loomed ahead, its weathered wooden frame standing sentinel against the encroaching dusk. I parked, the engine's hum dying into an unsettling silence. Stepping out of the car, I hesitated, the stillness wrapping around me like a shroud. I walked toward the entrance, each step echoing in the hushed surroundings.

Just as I reached for the door, it swung open, revealing a shadowed figure inside. My breath caught, a jolt of recognition piercing through the tension. "Liam?" I whispered, unable to mask my surprise.

He stepped forward, the fading light revealing the contours of his face. "You came."

"What's going on?" I demanded, glancing around, half-expecting an ambush.

He hesitated, his expression unreadable. "There's something you need to know about your father... and the reason he's gone."

A chill crept down my spine, the weight of his words settling around us like fog. "What do you mean?"

Before he could answer, a sudden noise shattered the silence—a sharp crack from behind me, followed by the unmistakable sound of footsteps drawing near. My heart raced as I turned, adrenaline surging through my veins. I was not alone, and whatever was coming next would change everything.

Chapter 2: The Encounter

The cobblestone streets of Firestone Bay wound like an unsteady heartbeat, their edges softened by the creeping vines that clung tenaciously to the weathered brick walls. As I ambled down the alley, a chill swept in from the sea, whispering promises of salt and freedom. The air was fragrant with the tang of ocean waves crashing against the jagged rocks, mingling with the sweet scent of blooming jasmine that tumbled over the garden fences. I had always found comfort in these familiar aromas, reminders of a childhood spent chasing dreams along the shore. Yet today, even the scents felt heavy, laden with unspoken memories and unprocessed grief.

Lost in my thoughts, I hardly noticed him at first—Hunter Blackwood. He was leaning casually against a lamppost, the golden glow illuminating the contours of his face, giving him an almost ethereal quality. I had once thought of him as infuriatingly handsome, but that notion seemed almost trivial now, stripped bare by the years and the weight of our past. His dark hair tousled by the wind framed a face marked by a certain ruggedness, a hint of vulnerability beneath the confidence he wore like a second skin.

Our rivalry had been the stuff of legends back in high school. While others were swept up in the trivial pursuits of teenage life—dances, promposals, and parties—we had battled for the top spot in every class, for the approval of teachers and parents alike. We were the stars of our own competitive show, but beneath the surface, the animosity was a tangled web of admiration, envy, and something I couldn't quite name. The tension between us had always felt like electricity, crackling in the air whenever we were in the same room.

As our eyes met, a flicker of recognition sparked between us, igniting memories of late nights spent studying, the shared glances over exam papers, and the countless times we had pushed each other to our limits. But this was no longer a battle of wits; it was a reunion of two weary souls who had each tasted the bitter fruit of loss.

"Fancy running into you here," he said, his voice smooth like aged whiskey, yet there was an edge to it—like he was unsure whether to extend a truce or reignite the war. I could hear the undertone of sarcasm that felt both familiar and unsettling.

"Likewise," I replied, crossing my arms defensively, my heart thudding in my chest. "I didn't expect to see you, Hunter. I thought you'd be off conquering the world or something."

A ghost of a smile flitted across his lips, but it didn't reach his eyes. "Conquering the world? Nah, I left that to the superheroes. Just trying to find my place in it, like everyone else."

His honesty cut through the tension like a knife, a stark reminder that beneath the bravado we had once flaunted, we were just two people trying to navigate a life that had dealt us both heavy hands.

I glanced away, unable to meet the depth of his gaze for too long, feeling the weight of the unspoken tragedies that hung between us like a shroud. "Things have changed, haven't they?" I murmured, my voice barely above a whisper, the realization settling heavy in the pit of my stomach. The high school dramas felt like echoes of a lifetime ago, replaced by the harsh reality of adulthood.

Hunter shifted slightly, pushing himself off the lamppost. The movement brought him closer, an involuntary magnetism that drew my attention back to him. "Yeah, they have," he admitted, running a hand through his tousled hair, a gesture that felt both casual and intimate. "I guess we can't avoid the storms forever."

I nodded, the weight of his words resonating deeply. "Storms are part of life," I replied, feeling a surge of warmth in the vulnerability he displayed. "Some leave wreckage in their wake, and others... they just teach us how to rebuild."

His expression shifted, and for a moment, the walls we had constructed around ourselves began to crack. "What are you rebuilding?" he asked, his tone softer now, almost curious.

"Just... my life," I answered honestly, surprised by my own openness. "After everything, I thought I knew what I wanted, but it turns out I was just lost. I'm trying to figure it out one step at a time."

"Lost is familiar territory," he replied, a hint of sadness threading through his voice. "I think we all are in some way."

The conversation took on a life of its own, and I found myself captivated by the way he spoke—how the lines of his face softened when he allowed himself to be vulnerable, how his eyes, usually so guarded, opened just a fraction to let me in. I could sense that the years had not dulled the sharpness of his wit, nor had they extinguished the fire that had always burned within him. Instead, they had tempered it, revealing the layers of a man shaped by hardship and loss.

"I heard about your mom," he said finally, the words hanging heavy in the air between us. "I'm... I'm really sorry."

The sincerity of his apology hit me harder than I expected, and I felt the sting of tears threaten to spill over. "Thank you," I managed, feeling raw and exposed under the weight of his sympathy. "It's been hard, but I'm trying to keep moving forward."

He nodded, his expression shifting to one of understanding. "It's okay to feel lost. Sometimes, it's in the darkness that we find the light."

For a moment, we stood in silence, our shared grief weaving an invisible thread between us, pulling us closer together in our mutual struggle. The playful rivalry we once knew felt like a distant memory, replaced by an unexpected camaraderie born from shared experiences.

I caught a glimpse of something in his eyes—a flicker of hope, perhaps, or the promise of friendship rekindled. The realization hit me then, that beneath the layers of our past lay a potential for something different. Something deeper. Something worth exploring.

A gust of wind swirled around us, carrying with it the scent of sea salt and adventure, but the air was heavy with unsaid things, and it felt almost electric. I couldn't help but notice how much he had changed—or perhaps how much I had. Hunter wore his heart on his sleeve now, though it was obscured by a tough exterior that had been polished by trials I could only imagine. My fingers twitched at my sides, wanting to reach out and bridge the distance, but caution held me back, tethered to the frayed edges of my pride.

"So, what brings you back to Firestone?" he asked, a teasing lilt in his voice, as if we were simply engaging in the usual back-and-forth we had always been known for. "Hiding from your fans?"

"I doubt they'd notice my absence," I shot back, trying to inject some levity into the moment. "Most of them are still lost in their high school romances while I'm just... existing."

He laughed, the sound deep and genuine, a stark contrast to the strained atmosphere of our previous encounters. "Ah, existence. The great leveler. It's what we're all doing, I suppose. At least you're not doing it in a cubicle."

I couldn't help but smile at his playful jab. "You're right. I'd much rather exist amidst the chaos of the world than be trapped behind a desk."

His gaze sharpened, as if trying to decode the layers beneath my words. "So, what chaos are you indulging in? Any wild adventures I should know about?"

"Just a few," I replied, feeling a sense of daring as I glanced up at him. "A trip to Paris that turned into an unexpected scavenger hunt. A hike that ended with me getting lost and nearly adopted by a family of goats."

"Goats?" he repeated, eyebrows arching with interest. "Now that's a story I'd pay to hear. Did you negotiate your way out, or did you simply charm them into letting you go?"

"I might have offered them some snacks," I said, laughing. "They seemed more interested in the potato chips I had in my backpack than in me, to be honest."

Hunter chuckled, the warmth in his eyes brightening as he leaned against the lamppost again, this time with a relaxed posture. "Sounds like you've been busy charming more than just goats, huh? Are there any prospects on the horizon? Romantic interests, perhaps?"

The question caught me off guard, my laughter dying in my throat. "Romantic interests? You mean beyond my new goat friends?"

"I'm just trying to gauge whether you've completely sworn off human interaction," he teased, his tone light, but there was something more serious beneath it.

I shrugged, feigning nonchalance while my heart raced. "Let's just say the dating scene is as appealing as a cold cup of coffee right now."

His lips twitched with amusement, a knowing look passing between us. "That bad, huh? Or are you just holding out for a charming rival to sweep you off your feet?"

"Charming rivals are in short supply," I replied, unable to suppress a smirk. "Besides, I'm busy saving my energy for more pressing matters, like not getting lost in a sea of grocery aisles."

Hunter's laughter rang out again, rich and melodic. "It sounds like you're better at evading relationships than actual goats. Maybe you need a partner in crime, someone to help keep you grounded while you navigate the chaos of life."

The suggestion hung in the air, charged with possibility. I met his gaze, the playful banter slipping into something more profound.

"And what makes you the perfect candidate for this role? Last I checked, you were still busy being a 'perpetual mystery.'"

"I've had my share of adventures too, you know," he replied, a shadow passing over his features. "Sometimes those mysteries hide deeper truths. But I guess that's part of being human."

Silence enveloped us, the weight of unacknowledged struggles settling like dust in a sunbeam. It was a delicate balance of vulnerability and bravado, each of us standing on the precipice of confiding in the other yet reluctant to jump.

I took a step back, breaking the tension. "Maybe we should stop hiding behind our metaphors and get back to reality. We're adults now, after all."

"Adults, yes, but still terribly good at avoiding the heart of the matter," he replied, his smile faltering as he regarded me seriously. "I'm not just here to chat about old high school rivalries or goat adventures. There's a reason I came back, and it's more than just nostalgia."

Curiosity piqued, I leaned in slightly, my interest piqued like a cat sensing movement in the bushes. "And that reason would be...?"

He hesitated, uncertainty clouding his expression. "I don't want to share everything just yet, but let's say I'm here to confront some unfinished business. Life has a way of reminding you of things you thought were buried."

My heart thudded in my chest, an unsteady rhythm echoing the unsteady ground beneath us. "Unfinished business can be a double-edged sword. It can lead to healing or... complications."

"I'm well aware of the complications," he said, his voice low and serious. "And I could use a friend. Or maybe even a rival who's willing to tackle this head-on."

The shift in our dynamic struck me like a bolt of lightning, illuminating the dark corners of what had been our tangled history. There was an unspoken challenge in his words, an invitation to join him in navigating the murky waters of our past. I felt the pull of something both terrifying and exhilarating, a chance to rekindle our rivalry in a way that might foster something unexpected.

"I'm not one to shy away from a challenge," I said, meeting his gaze with newfound determination. "But if we're going to do this, let's do it without the pretense of past grudges. We're both just trying to find our way."

"Deal," he replied, extending a hand, his grin returning as he shook off the heaviness. "Let's embrace the chaos together, then. Who knows? We might just end up being the best of allies—or at least the worst of enemies."

I took his hand, feeling the warmth of his grip seep into my bones. In that moment, the weight of rivalry shifted to something lighter, an uncharted territory stretching before us, and I couldn't help but feel a spark of excitement at the thought of facing whatever lay ahead together. As we stood there, our laughter mingling with the salty breeze, it felt as if the tide had finally turned.

The playful banter we had exchanged hung in the air like a forgotten melody, one that echoed through the narrow alleys and the salty tang of the ocean breeze. Standing there, hand in hand, I could feel the tide of emotions shift beneath us. It was as if the universe conspired to blend the past with the present, igniting old flames while simultaneously dousing them in the reality of who we had become.

"Just so we're clear," Hunter said, pulling his hand back with a reluctant smile, "if we're going to tackle this unfinished business, I get to choose the first challenge."

I raised an eyebrow, intrigued. "And what challenge do you have in mind? A race to the pier? Or perhaps a pie-eating contest?"

His laughter danced in the air, a sound that felt too warm for the brisk autumn afternoon. "I was thinking something a little more... intense. How about we start by revisiting our old haunts? We could take a trip down memory lane. You know, relive the good ol' days before the world went crazy."

"Relive the good ol' days?" I echoed, skeptical. "You mean the days of sabotaged science projects and academic rivalry?"

"Exactly. We could visit the library, that sacred battleground of ours. I dare you to outwit me there. Winner gets bragging rights—forever."

I felt the thrill of competition bubble up within me, a long-lost sensation that had sparked countless late-night study sessions. "You think you can still beat me? It's been years since we've had a proper contest."

"Years, yes, but I've had a lot of time to hone my skills," he shot back, a playful glint in his eyes. "And I might have done some reading on strategic warfare in the meantime."

The challenge hung enticingly between us, and as the sun dipped lower in the sky, casting golden hues across the cobblestones, I found myself swept up in the idea of revisiting our past. "Fine," I relented, the spark of competition igniting my spirit. "Let's see if you've really got what it takes."

We set off, the familiar streets of Firestone Bay transforming under our feet, each step drawing us deeper into a past that felt at once foreign and comforting. We passed by the quaint cafés, their windows glowing with warm light and laughter spilling into the street. The memories flooded back, fragments of laughter and late-night study sessions, our heated debates echoing in my mind.

As we approached the library, a towering structure of brick and ivy, nostalgia washed over me like a wave. It loomed before us, a fortress of knowledge that had witnessed our every triumph and failure. Hunter pushed the heavy wooden door open, and we stepped inside, the scent of aged paper and leather binding enveloping us like a warm embrace.

"Ah, home sweet home," he mused, glancing around with a mixture of reverence and mischief. "Let the games begin."

I grinned, excitement bubbling within me as I recalled the many hours spent buried in books, racing against the clock to outsmart one another. "First rule of engagement: no cheating!"

"Who, me? Cheat?" He feigned innocence, raising an eyebrow in mock surprise. "I'm offended you would even suggest it."

"Please, I'm sure you've got a few tricks up your sleeve," I shot back, moving deeper into the library. The musty air was filled with whispers of the past, the heavy silence only broken by the soft rustling of pages.

The competition unfolded with each turn of the page. We debated obscure authors, recounted historical facts, and unraveled the complexities of literature until laughter echoed off the shelves. For a while, it felt like the years had melted away, and we were once again those bright-eyed students with unyielding dreams, consumed by the desire to outshine each other.

As we drew closer to the heart of the library, I caught sight of a faded poster taped to a bulletin board, its edges curling with age. "What's this?" I asked, stepping closer to examine the old flyer.

Hunter sidled up beside me, curiosity piqued. "Looks like an event from years ago. 'Mysterious Disappearances in Firestone Bay'?"

I scanned the details, a shiver creeping down my spine. "I've heard whispers about that. People vanishing without a trace... It's just a rumor, right?"

Hunter frowned, his brow furrowing with concern. "I thought it was just talk. But if it's happening again..."

Before I could respond, the door swung open with a creak, drawing our attention. A gust of wind rushed in, followed by a figure clad in shadows, face obscured by a hood. My heart raced, a sudden tension pulsing through the air.

"Who are you?" I demanded, instinctively stepping in front of Hunter, my protective instincts kicking in.

The figure paused, and for a heartbeat, silence reigned in the library. "I have a message," the voice was low and gravelly, sending chills racing down my spine. "The disappearances are not just rumors. They're coming for you."

Hunter stiffened beside me, his eyes narrowing as he assessed the threat. "What do you mean?"

"Someone knows about your past," the figure continued, eyes glinting beneath the shadow of the hood. "And they won't stop until they get what they want. Stay away from the water."

With that cryptic warning, the figure spun on their heel and disappeared as quickly as they had come, leaving behind an unsettling silence that buzzed in my ears.

"What just happened?" I gasped, turning to Hunter, who looked equally shaken.

"I don't know," he replied, his voice taut with tension. "But we need to figure out what's going on before it's too late."

My heart thudded in my chest, an unfamiliar sense of dread pooling within me. "This can't be happening. We were just having fun, revisiting old ghosts... not facing new ones."

"Fun just took a backseat," Hunter said, glancing toward the door, anxiety etched on his features. "But we can't let this stop us. We're in this together, remember?"

As we stood there, the shadows of the library closing in around us, a sense of impending danger loomed like a storm cloud. I didn't know what awaited us beyond those walls, but one thing was clear: we were about to embark on a journey that would test our resolve, our friendship, and the very fabric of our lives. The past had returned with a vengeance, and it was time to confront the darkness that lay ahead.

Chapter 3: Unraveled Threads

The salty air was thick with tension, clinging to my skin like the damp fog that rolled off the churning waves of Firestone Bay. Each step I took on the creaking wooden pier felt heavier, as if the weight of my father's unspoken secrets pressed down on me, urging me to retreat into the comforting embrace of ignorance. Yet, the truth was a tempest I couldn't escape, swirling relentlessly in the back of my mind, compelling me to seek answers.

I had stumbled upon the letters buried in the depths of my father's study, tucked away in a battered leather-bound journal. Their pages, yellowed and fragile, whispered tales of deceit and shadowy dealings that had unfolded long before I was born. Each letter was a thread unraveling a larger tapestry, revealing a man I hardly recognized—the father who had always been my steadfast anchor now appeared shrouded in an unsettling ambiguity. As I read the words scrawled in hurried handwriting, I felt a chill creep up my spine, sending a shiver of dread coursing through my veins.

"What are you doing with that?" The voice cut through the stillness of the room like a knife, drawing my attention from the letters that spoke of danger and desperation. Hunter stood in the doorway, framed by the soft glow of the hallway light. His tousled hair caught the golden rays, casting a halo around him, but the storm brewing in his dark eyes told a different story.

"Just some old letters," I replied, trying to sound nonchalant despite the frantic beating of my heart. "They're from my dad."

His brows furrowed, and I could see the gears turning in his mind as he approached me, each step echoing the tension thickening between us. "You shouldn't be reading those. You don't know what they could lead to."

"Is that your way of saying I should leave the past buried?" I shot back, my frustration bubbling to the surface. I had always admired

Hunter's protectiveness, but right now, it felt suffocating. His aura was magnetic, yet it repelled me when he tried to impose his will on me.

"Some things are meant to stay hidden, Avery," he said, his voice low, almost pleading. The way he said my name sent a jolt through me, a stark reminder of the electric connection that crackled between us. I had tried to deny it, tried to push it away, but here it was again, hovering in the air like an uninvited guest.

"I need to know," I insisted, my resolve hardening. "If my dad kept these from me, there must be a reason." I folded the letters back into the journal and met his gaze, unwilling to back down. "You can't just decide what I can and can't handle."

"I'm not trying to decide for you, Avery," he replied, frustration lacing his tone. "I just don't want you to get hurt." His eyes softened for a moment, the storm giving way to a flicker of something more vulnerable. "You have no idea what you're playing with."

"Neither do you," I shot back, the words spilling from my lips before I could rein them in. The tension thickened, wrapping around us like a suffocating shroud. I could feel the spark between us igniting, a firestorm of emotions swirling in the confined space of the study.

The silence that followed felt heavy, pregnant with unspoken words and longing glances. I had always been drawn to Hunter, his mysterious past and fiercely loyal nature stirring something deep within me. But this push and pull between us, this incessant battle over control, was a dance I had grown weary of.

"Why can't you just trust me?" I whispered, the heat of the moment settling in my chest like a weight I couldn't shake.

"Trust?" He scoffed, running a hand through his hair, an exasperated gesture that only heightened my annoyance. "You think trust is built on a foundation of secrets? Secrets that could put you in danger?"

"I'm not some fragile little thing that needs protecting, Hunter!" My voice rose, fueled by frustration and a flicker of hurt. "I can handle this. I want to handle this."

"Yeah? What if you uncover something that changes everything?" he challenged, his voice rising to meet my intensity. "What if you find something that can't be undone? Do you really think you're ready for that?"

A moment of silence passed between us, heavy and charged, as I grappled with his words. The truth was, I didn't know what I was ready for. But I was tired of feeling like a pawn in a game I didn't understand.

"I'll take that chance," I finally replied, my voice steady. "I'd rather face whatever it is than live in the dark."

His expression softened, the sharp edges of his anger blurring into something more complex, layered with frustration and an undeniable attraction. "You're infuriating, you know that?"

"I've been told," I retorted, unable to suppress a smirk. "But you seem to like it."

A reluctant smile tugged at the corners of his lips, a momentary truce in our escalating war of wills. It was a small victory, yet it felt monumental—a reminder that beneath the tension, there was an unshakeable bond between us. But that bond was also the reason I had to keep digging. Hunter might be fiercely protective, but I wouldn't let his fears dictate my choices.

With a determined heart, I turned away from him and back to the letters. There were more secrets to uncover, and I would face them head-on, regardless of the consequences. The truth was out there, waiting for me in the shadows, and I was ready to unravel it thread by thread, no matter the cost.

The next morning arrived shrouded in a heavy fog that blanketed Firestone Bay like a thick quilt, dulling the sharp edges of reality and cloaking the world in muted grays. I stared out the window of my father's study, the water swirling restlessly beneath the overcast sky. It mirrored the chaos brewing within me—each ripple a reflection of the secrets I was determined to unveil. The letters had left a mark on me, haunting my thoughts as I traced the strange connections hidden within their ink.

With a deep breath, I gathered my resolve. Today, I would confront Hunter. I could already envision him leaning against his truck, the very picture of casual indifference, but I knew better. Beneath that façade was a man who bore the weight of a thousand storms, and I was determined to navigate through it, even if it meant sailing through turbulent waters.

The drive to the dock was filled with an anxious energy, a feeling that the air itself crackled with potential. The moment I parked, I could see him. Hunter stood by the edge of the pier, his posture relaxed but with that familiar intensity about him. The wind whipped through his dark hair, giving him an almost ethereal quality, as though he were part of the very landscape itself. My stomach flipped, but I shook it off. This wasn't about us. This was about the truth.

"Avery," he called, his voice cutting through the silence, drawing me toward him like a moth to a flame. "You're up early."

"Some of us have work to do," I shot back, a smirk playing on my lips as I approached. "And by work, I mean digging through my father's past."

His brow furrowed, concern replacing the playful banter. "Are you sure that's a good idea? You don't know what you're getting into."

"And you don't know what I've already uncovered," I replied, crossing my arms defiantly. "I found letters that suggest he was involved in something... something shady."

Hunter's expression darkened, the worry lines on his forehead deepening. "Shady? Avery, you don't know what you're talking about."

I could see the urge to protect me written all over him, but it only fueled my determination. "I do know what I'm talking about. If he was involved in something dangerous, I need to understand why."

"Understanding could lead you down a path you can't come back from." His voice was low, almost a growl, but the intensity of it sent a thrill through me. He was fierce, unyielding, yet there was something tender lurking beneath the surface, something I wanted to coax out into the open.

"Then help me," I challenged, taking a step closer. "Don't push me away. You're the only one who might know something."

For a heartbeat, silence hung between us, thick with unspoken thoughts. The way he stared at me, dark eyes smoldering, felt like a promise waiting to be fulfilled. Then, without breaking our gaze, he sighed, running a hand through his hair in that familiar frustrated way. "Fine. But you need to promise me that you'll be careful."

"Careful is my middle name," I quipped, unable to resist teasing him.

"More like reckless," he muttered, but I caught the hint of a smile tugging at his lips, the tension between us easing just a fraction.

We decided to head to the local café, a cozy little spot nestled at the end of the pier, where the smell of fresh coffee mingled with the salty breeze. As we walked side by side, the familiar banter began to flow, easing the weight of our earlier argument. Hunter teased me about my choice of breakfast, a particularly adventurous decision involving eggs benedict and a side of avocado toast.

"Isn't that a little too fancy for a girl who's hunting for dark family secrets?" he smirked, sliding into a booth across from me.

I feigned offense, placing my hand over my heart. "How dare you! Just because I'm unraveling a family mystery doesn't mean I can't enjoy a little culinary sophistication."

"I just worry you'll get lost in the sauce," he chuckled, his laughter brightening the room. It was moments like this, with his playful jabs and infectious laughter, that reminded me why I was drawn to him. Beneath the serious demeanor lay a man with a quick wit and a genuine heart.

Our food arrived, and as we dug in, I couldn't help but notice the way Hunter watched me, his gaze flicking between my eyes and my plate. "So, what's next?" he asked, his voice a low rumble.

I swallowed a bite of toast, the creamy avocado melting on my tongue. "I need to confront the last person who had contact with my dad before he passed. There's a name mentioned in the letters, someone I think I can find in town."

"Are you sure that's wise?" he questioned, his eyes narrowing slightly, a hint of worry creeping back in. "You don't know what kind of person you're dealing with."

"Neither do you, but I'm not backing down," I countered. "This is about my father, and I owe it to him to figure this out."

He leaned forward, resting his elbows on the table, the playful banter replaced with a serious tone. "Avery, I know you're strong, but you don't have to do this alone. Let me help you."

For a moment, I considered his offer, the sincerity in his eyes stirring something deep within me. "I appreciate that, really, but I need to do this on my own."

"I get that, but promise me you'll call if things get too intense," he urged, his voice laced with an urgency that made my heart race. "I don't want you caught off guard."

"I promise," I said, and there it was again—the pull between us, the gravity of a connection that felt so real and so terrifying all at once.

With our conversation winding down, I glanced outside, catching sight of a shadow moving along the pier. My heart skipped as the familiar figure of an older man approached—a man I hadn't seen in years, yet his presence felt like a jolt of electricity. He was the last person I expected to see, but there he was, stepping out of the mist like a ghost from my past.

"Looks like you've got company," Hunter muttered, following my gaze, his earlier lightness slipping away.

The man paused a few feet from our table, his expression inscrutable as he scanned the café, finally locking eyes with me. I took a deep breath, ready to embrace whatever questions awaited me. Today had promised to be a quest for truth, and if this was part of the journey, I was more than ready to face it.

The café door swung open with a soft chime, pulling my attention away from the older man who loomed like a specter at the edge of my memory. His familiar silhouette brought a rush of conflicting emotions—nostalgia tangled with unease. Hunter, sitting across from me, leaned forward, his brows knit in concern. "You know him?"

"Not really," I replied, my voice barely above a whisper, the memories flooding back. This was Richard, my father's business partner, a man whose presence had been a constant but distant shadow during my childhood. He had always seemed gruff, more concerned with numbers than feelings. Seeing him now sent a chill down my spine.

Richard stepped closer, the aroma of salt and coffee mingling in the air as he approached our table. "Avery," he said, his voice gravelly, laden with years of burden. "I was hoping to find you."

"Why?" The word slipped out, edged with suspicion. I wasn't sure I was ready to face whatever answers he might provide, especially with the whirlwind of revelations swirling around me.

He hesitated, glancing at Hunter, who remained silently protective, arms crossed over his chest. "It's about your father."

A cold rush of adrenaline surged through me, and I felt my heart quicken. "What do you know?"

"Can we talk privately?" Richard glanced around the café, clearly uncomfortable with the bustling atmosphere. "There are things that need to be said, and they can't be discussed here."

Hunter shifted beside me, clearly on guard. "Whatever you have to say can be said in front of me."

Richard waved a hand dismissively. "This isn't about you, kid. This is about Avery. If you care about her at all, you'll let us talk."

I looked between the two men, feeling the tension thrumming in the air, a taut wire ready to snap. "Fine," I said, my voice firm, even as a small part of me trembled at the thought of stepping away from Hunter's side. "Let's go outside."

As we moved to the back of the café, the scent of brewing coffee faded, replaced by the sharp, salty tang of the ocean. The fog was beginning to lift, revealing a stunning vista of churning waves crashing against jagged rocks. I took a deep breath, steeling myself for whatever revelations Richard had in store.

"Your father," Richard began, rubbing the back of his neck, "was involved in some things that could put you in danger."

"Danger?" My heart raced. "What kind of things?"

He hesitated, clearly weighing his words. "He had dealings with some... unsavory people. I tried to keep him out of it, but he didn't listen."

I felt my stomach drop, the ground beneath me unsteady. "What do you mean? What kind of dealings?"

Richard looked away, as if he were grappling with the ghosts of the past. "I can't go into details. It's too dangerous. But I need you to understand—whatever you're digging into, it's not just family secrets. It's far more complicated than that."

Hunter's presence beside me was reassuring, yet I felt the walls closing in. "You still haven't told me what happened to my father," I pressed, my voice rising. "If there's something I need to know, I deserve to hear it."

Richard sighed, his eyes heavy with regret. "Your father got mixed up with people who don't play by the rules. I wanted to protect you from this life, Avery. He thought he could handle it, but it spiraled out of control. It was only a matter of time before it caught up with him."

"Caught up with him?" My voice trembled. "You mean... he was killed?"

The word hung in the air, a palpable weight. Richard's silence confirmed my fears, crashing down like a wave breaking on the shore.

"I wish I could tell you more, but I don't want to put you in any further danger," he said, his voice gravelly with emotion.

"I've already put myself in danger," I shot back, frustration bubbling within me. "I need to know everything."

Richard stepped closer, his voice dropping to a conspiratorial whisper. "There's something else you should know—there's a man who has been watching you, someone connected to your father's past."

The world tilted on its axis. "Watching me? Who?"

"His name is Marcus. I don't know the extent of his involvement, but he has a stake in this situation. He's dangerous, Avery. If he finds out what you're doing..."

Hunter's hand on my arm felt like a lifeline, grounding me in the storm of revelations. "We'll handle this together," he said quietly, but I could see the storm brewing in his eyes, a reflection of my own turmoil.

"Together?" Richard scoffed, shaking his head. "You have no idea what you're dealing with. This isn't just a game. Marcus is ruthless, and he'll do anything to protect his interests."

"What are his interests?" I demanded, desperate for clarity. "What does he want from me?"

Richard opened his mouth, but before he could respond, a shadow loomed behind him. A figure emerged from the mist, stepping into the fading sunlight. My breath caught as I recognized the familiar silhouette—Marcus, a man I had never met but whose presence felt ominously palpable.

"Ah, Avery," he said, his voice smooth and unsettling. "I've been looking for you."

My heart raced as I stepped back, instinctively drawing closer to Hunter, who stood rigid beside me, a barrier between me and the approaching danger. The air crackled with tension, and I could feel the world narrowing, the stakes climbing higher with each passing second.

"What do you want?" I managed to say, my voice barely above a whisper.

Marcus smiled, but it was devoid of warmth, his eyes glinting with a predatory gleam. "Oh, we have much to discuss. Secrets tend to bind us, don't they? And I believe you're in possession of something very valuable."

Before I could react, the ground beneath me felt unstable, and I suddenly understood the precariousness of the situation. In that moment, as the shadow of danger loomed larger, I realized that the threads of my life were unraveling, and the truth I sought might just lead me down a path from which I couldn't return.

Chapter 4: Secrets and Shadows

The town of Firestone Bay had its secrets, woven into the very fabric of its existence, much like the tangled seaweed that clung stubbornly to the rocks at low tide. As I stood outside Hunter's house, a blend of dread and anticipation twisted in my stomach, the warmth of the evening wrapping around me like an old blanket. The house was not imposing, but there was something about its facade—the weathered wood and the salt-tinged air—that felt alive, as if it held a pulse that synchronized with my own racing heart. Light spilled from the windows, a warm golden hue that contrasted sharply with the encroaching shadows of dusk, inviting yet intimidating.

I had never planned on coming here, certainly not on the pretext of unearthing truths I wasn't sure I was ready to face. Hunter was an enigma, a solitary figure who loomed large in the whispers of the townsfolk. They spoke of him in hushed tones, often laced with a mix of admiration and caution. "He's got a past," they would say, "and some say it's best left buried." Yet, here I was, grappling with my own tangled history, compelled to seek him out for answers about my father's life before it became an unturned page in a book I desperately needed to read.

As the door creaked open, Hunter's expression shifted from annoyance to mild surprise. The irritation etched across his face softened momentarily, revealing a vulnerability beneath his rugged exterior. "What are you doing here, Ash?" he asked, his voice deep and gravelly, like stones rolling over one another in a riverbed. I could feel the weight of his gaze as it swept over me, taking in my determination, my uncertainty, and perhaps the hint of desperation lurking beneath.

"Hunter, I need to talk to you," I said, stepping into the threshold, the warmth of his home enveloping me, a stark contrast to the cool air outside. The familiar scent of pine and a hint of something floral wafted through the open space, grounding me in the moment despite the chaos swirling in my mind. I could hear the faint crackling of a fire, its glow casting flickering shadows on the walls, and for a moment, I allowed myself to be lulled into the comfort of this haven.

His brow furrowed as he motioned for me to follow him to the living room. I took in the room's cozy clutter—books stacked haphazardly on a wooden coffee table, an old guitar leaning against the wall, and the vibrant tapestry of art on the walls that told stories without uttering a single word. It was a space that felt both intimate and revealing, echoing with the history of a man who had clearly chosen solitude over the noise of the outside world.

"About what?" he asked, settling into a worn armchair opposite me, his posture guarded. I opened my mouth, but the words caught in my throat, tangled in the web of emotions swirling within me. Instead, I leaned forward, studying him closely, the way the firelight danced across his chiseled features, highlighting the faint scars that told tales of past battles—both seen and unseen.

"I need to know about my dad," I finally said, the weight of my own words settling heavily between us. "I've heard things, Hunter. Things that don't add up." There it was, my lifeline thrown into the unknown waters, the kind of plunge that felt exhilarating and terrifying all at once. Hunter's expression shifted, a flicker of recognition flaring in his eyes before it was masked by something deeper, something darker.

"I can't help you," he said bluntly, his tone brusque. The edge in his voice cut through the warmth of the room, leaving a chill that crept down my spine. My heart raced in protest, an instinctual response to his rejection. But I was not one to back down easily.

"Why not?" I shot back, determination igniting the embers of my defiance. "You know something. I can feel it." The air thickened with tension, a palpable energy crackling between us as if the very walls were leaning in to eavesdrop on our confrontation. Hunter's jaw tightened, and for a moment, I thought he might dismiss me outright. But then his defenses seemed to falter, and the mask slipped just enough for me to glimpse the conflict raging beneath the surface.

"Ash, it's not that simple," he replied, his voice softer now, laced with an urgency that hinted at buried fears. "There are things you don't understand. Things that could put you in danger." The seriousness of his words sent a shiver down my spine, awakening a mix of fear and curiosity. I had never been one to shy away from danger; my life felt like a storm waiting to break, and I wanted to navigate the chaos rather than run from it.

"What are you afraid of?" I pressed, my voice steady despite the storm brewing inside me. "You think I can't handle the truth? I've lived in a town that thrives on secrets. What could be worse?" The challenge hung between us, a gauntlet thrown down at his feet. His gaze pierced into mine, searching for something—perhaps courage, or foolishness, or a blend of both.

"I'm afraid of losing you," he finally admitted, the raw honesty of his confession unraveling the tension like a thread pulled loose from a tightly woven tapestry. His vulnerability disarmed me, exposing the deeper layers of a man I had only seen from the periphery. I felt a rush of warmth bloom within me, a flame igniting in response to his admission. The walls I had built around my heart began to crack, revealing the tender spots that had long remained hidden.

"Then help me," I whispered, leaning forward, my heart pounding like a drumbeat urging him to surrender to the truth. "Let's face it together."

His gaze flickered, uncertainty warring with resolve. The silence that followed stretched long and taut between us, thick with unspoken promises and lingering doubts. And in that moment, I knew we were teetering on the edge of something monumental, a precipice that could either lead us to freedom or plunge us into the abyss of our pasts.

The flickering flames in the fireplace cast dancing shadows on the walls, transforming the cozy living room into a stage set for a drama that neither of us had rehearsed. Hunter's gaze remained fixed on me, the tension between us thickening like the smoke curling upwards from the embers. I could see his mind racing, weighing his options, trying to gauge just how much he was willing to share. It was a battle of wills, and I refused to back down.

"Look," I started, breaking the charged silence, "I get it. You have your reasons for keeping things quiet, but I'm not asking for the world. I just need a piece of the puzzle." I leaned forward, my hands resting on my knees, willing him to see the determination etched across my face. "My father wasn't just some shadowy figure in my life; he was a person with a history, and if you know anything about it, I deserve to know."

He sighed, the weight of my words pressing against him. "It's not that simple, Ash. Your father's life was... complicated. You think you're ready to hear about it, but—"

"But what?" I interjected, my voice rising slightly. "You're afraid I'll break? That I'll shatter like glass when I hear something I don't want to? I've been piecing together fragments of my life for too long, and I'm done living in the shadows." My heart raced, the urgency of my words pushing me to the edge of vulnerability. Hunter's expression softened, and I caught a glimpse of the boy behind the man—someone grappling with his own demons.

"Fine," he finally said, the resolve in his voice wavering. "But you have to promise me you won't get involved. This isn't just about your father; it's about things that run deeper than you can imagine."

I nodded, eager to grasp any thread of understanding. "I promise. Just tell me what you know."

He leaned back in his chair, arms crossed, the shadows playing across his rugged features. "Your father was a part of something—a group that operated in the shadows, making decisions that affected the town in ways most people don't realize. It wasn't all good."

"Why didn't anyone tell me?" I shot back, feeling the fire within me flare. "Why the secrecy?"

Hunter's eyes darkened, and he leaned forward, his voice barely above a whisper. "Because some secrets are meant to protect those we care about. And sometimes, those secrets can put us in danger."

I felt a chill race down my spine. "Danger? What kind of danger?"

"Let's just say not everyone who was involved has moved on," he replied, his gaze shifting momentarily to the window, as if expecting someone to come through the door. "There are people in this town who still hold grudges. And if they find out you're digging into your father's past..." He let the sentence hang, the unspoken threat lingering in the air like a storm cloud ready to burst.

A knot of apprehension tightened in my chest. "You think they would come after me?"

"Possibly," he admitted, the gravity of his words settling between us like a dense fog. "It's not just about you anymore. This goes back generations. There are layers to this history you can't begin to comprehend."

I took a deep breath, forcing my mind to stay calm amidst the rising tide of emotion. "Then help me understand. If my father was involved in something dangerous, doesn't that mean I have a right to know? Shouldn't I be prepared?"

Hunter's gaze softened, and for a brief moment, I saw the flicker of sympathy in his eyes. "You think knowing will prepare you? It might just put a target on your back."

"Then let me decide what's worth the risk," I insisted, my voice steady. "I can't live with half-truths any longer."

He hesitated, the conflict playing out on his face like a vivid tableau. "Alright," he said finally, "but you need to promise me one thing. If things get too dangerous, you have to walk away. Promise me."

"I promise," I said, the words feeling like a contract that sealed our unspoken agreement. With that, he began to recount the fragments of my father's life—the shadows that danced around his legacy.

"He was part of a group that believed they could control the flow of information in this town, make decisions that would influence the course of events without anyone knowing," Hunter explained. "They were idealists, but they operated in the dark. And when you play with shadows, you get burned."

I listened intently, the pieces beginning to fit together in my mind. The stories I had heard growing up—the odd glances exchanged, the hushed whispers in grocery store aisles—were starting to make sense. "What happened to them?" I asked, trying to grasp the implications of his words.

"Some left town. Some... didn't fare as well," he replied, the shadow of sadness passing across his face. "Your father was one of the few who tried to break away, but it came at a cost. He didn't just lose friends; he lost everything."

"What do you mean, everything?" My heart raced, fear mixing with an intense desire to understand. "Was he in danger?"

"Yes," Hunter said slowly. "And that danger never truly left him. It followed him here, to Firestone Bay. That's why he kept you away from all this. He wanted to protect you."

"Protect me from what?" I pressed, the frustration bubbling beneath the surface. "What could be worse than the uncertainty I've lived with all these years?"

He opened his mouth to respond but then paused, his gaze flickering toward the window again. "There are things you can't see,

Ash. Secrets that run deeper than blood. You might think you want to know, but—"

Suddenly, a loud crash outside interrupted us, followed by the sound of something heavy thudding against the door. Hunter's eyes widened, and I felt my breath catch in my throat. The room, once a sanctuary of warmth, transformed into a space filled with trepidation.

"What was that?" I asked, my heart pounding in my chest.

Hunter shot to his feet, urgency replacing his earlier calm. "Stay here!" he commanded, his voice sharp as he moved toward the door. I wanted to protest, to demand that he take me with him, but something in his eyes told me that whatever was outside was a danger he wanted to shield me from.

As he reached for the doorknob, I felt a rush of adrenaline. The shadows around us seemed to stretch and darken, and the air crackled with tension. "Hunter, wait!" I shouted, but it was too late. The door swung open, revealing the storm that had brewed outside, and I knew that whatever came next would irrevocably alter the course of our lives.

The door swung open, revealing not just the outside world but an uninvited guest whose sudden presence sent a jolt of electricity through the air. A figure stood there, silhouetted against the fading light, a tall shape cloaked in shadows. I squinted, trying to discern who it was as the evening darkness pressed in closer. Hunter's muscles tensed beside me, and I could almost feel the palpable change in the atmosphere—a shift from curiosity to dread.

"Ash," he said, his voice low and steady, "stay back."

The stranger took a step forward, and the warm glow from the house illuminated a face I recognized. It was Jake, the town's local handyman, who always seemed to know too much about everything happening in Firestone Bay. The sight of him sent a shiver down my spine, not just because of the shock of his sudden appearance, but also due to the look in his eyes—intense, almost frantic.

"What are you doing here, Jake?" Hunter demanded, his irritation surfacing once more. "You know it's not safe to come here."

"I know, I know!" Jake panted, his breath coming in sharp bursts. "But it's urgent. You have to listen." He glanced over his shoulder, the fear in his eyes betraying the urgency of his message. "They're back. They've come for you, Ash."

The room spun, and the gravity of his words slammed into me like a wave. "Who's back?" I asked, feeling the adrenaline surge through me, turning my limbs to steel. "What do you mean?"

Jake's eyes darted between Hunter and me, his demeanor shifting from urgency to palpable dread. "The group your father was involved with—those who wanted to keep things quiet. They think you've been asking questions, digging into the past. They're looking for anyone who might know something."

A chill washed over me, and I felt the walls closing in, the weight of the secrets I had sought spilling out like dark ink on a page. "Why now? What do they want with me?"

Hunter stepped closer, his presence a reassuring anchor amid the turmoil. "Jake, what do you know? Who is it that's coming after her?"

"The old members," Jake replied, his voice barely above a whisper. "They're restless, and they believe Ash is the key to digging up old truths they want buried. They won't stop until they find her."

"Then we need to leave," Hunter said, decisively, his hand reaching out to grab my arm, urgency tinging his tone. "We can't stay here."

I hesitated, fear gnawing at my insides, but something deeper than instinct pushed back against the urge to flee. "No," I said firmly, pulling my arm away. "I need to understand what's happening. If they want me, it means I'm connected to whatever my father was involved in. I can't run from that."

Hunter's eyes flared with frustration, but I could see the flicker of respect for my resolve. "Ash, this isn't just about you anymore. If they find you, it puts everyone at risk. We need to come up with a plan."

"Like what?" I shot back, my own determination rising to meet his. "Do we sit here and wait for them to knock down the door? I refuse to be a victim in my own life. I need answers."

"Think about what you're saying!" Hunter exclaimed, his voice rising in intensity. "You have no idea what you're dealing with!"

"And you think hiding away will protect me?" I countered, the heat of our exchange illuminating the tension that had simmered beneath the surface since I first stepped into his world. "If they're already onto me, the only way to confront this is head-on. I refuse to let them control my life."

Jake's expression shifted to one of reluctant admiration, but he still looked terrified. "You're playing with fire, Ash. I don't know if you fully grasp the danger involved."

Hunter's face darkened, shadows flickering across his features as he stood between us, embodying the protective instinct that had drawn me to him from the start. "Then we do this together," he said, his voice steadied by determination. "But if it gets too risky, we go. Agreed?"

"Agreed," I said, swallowing the lump in my throat. I felt the weight of our pact settle between us, fragile yet solid, like a bridge forged in fire.

"Alright," Jake said, glancing nervously toward the door. "We don't have much time. They're mobilizing. I overheard them talking about you at the market."

I felt a knot of dread tighten in my stomach. "What do you mean they were talking about me?"

"Someone saw you with Hunter. They think you're working together, trying to uncover the past. They won't hesitate to do whatever it takes to keep their secrets safe."

The implications of his words sent a wave of nausea crashing over me. I glanced at Hunter, whose brow had furrowed deeper in thought, the light of the fire dancing off his tense jawline. "We need to move. Get to the old boathouse. It's secluded. If we can lay low until the storm passes, we might have a chance to figure this out."

"Storm?" I echoed, confusion swirling in my mind.

"Figuratively speaking, I hope," Hunter said with a hint of dark humor, but I could see the seriousness in his eyes. "Grab whatever you need and let's go. I'll take the lead."

I nodded, adrenaline surging as I moved toward the small backpack I had tossed aside earlier. As I hastily stuffed it with essentials, my mind raced with thoughts of what lay ahead. The boathouse—my father had often taken me there as a child, a sanctuary where we had spent lazy afternoons fishing and swapping stories, far removed from the whispers of the town. But now it felt like a refuge tinged with unease, a hiding place that might harbor both safety and danger.

"What about your car?" I asked, glancing at Hunter as he surveyed the room, assessing potential escape routes.

"Too obvious," he replied, his eyes darkening. "We'll take the back roads. They'll be watching the main roads, but we'll stay under the radar."

I finished packing and stood, feeling a mix of fear and determination. "Let's go then. The sooner we get moving, the better."

We moved swiftly, the urgency of our mission propelling us into action. As we stepped outside, the night air hit me like a cold splash of water, clearing my mind yet heightening my senses. The moon hung low, casting an eerie glow across the landscape, and every rustle of leaves seemed to echo with the weight of impending danger.

"Stay close," Hunter instructed as we began our trek down the narrow path that led to the boathouse. Jake took up position behind us, his breath quickening with every step. I could sense the tension coiling tighter, a spring ready to snap.

As we made our way through the dense underbrush, my heart thudded in my chest, an incessant reminder of the stakes at hand. Every sound, every whisper of the wind, felt amplified, and I couldn't shake the feeling of being watched. The world around us held its breath, the silence pressing in as we navigated through the thickening shadows.

Then, out of nowhere, a sharp crack echoed through the night, piercing the silence like a gunshot. We all froze, instinctively turning toward the source of the sound. My pulse quickened, and I glanced at Hunter, who held up a hand, signaling us to remain silent.

"What was that?" I whispered, my voice trembling.

Before Hunter could respond, a shadow detached itself from the trees, moving with purpose toward us. The figure emerged, illuminated momentarily by the moonlight, and my breath caught in my throat. It was a familiar face—one I had hoped never to see again.

"Hello, Ash," the figure said, a smirk creeping across his lips, a taunting glimmer in his eyes. "Miss me?"

Chapter 5: The Revelation

The night air buzzed with an energy that mirrored the crackling of the bonfire, casting flickering shadows around us. I sat cross-legged on the ground, the warmth of the flames wrapping around me like a comforting embrace, while Hunter leaned against an ancient oak tree, his silhouette strong against the glow. The forest around us was alive, the chirping of crickets and rustle of leaves creating a symphony that felt both enchanting and foreboding.

Hunter's eyes, bright and revealing in the firelight, searched mine as he opened up about the loss that had carved deep lines into his life. "She was my sister," he said, his voice steady but the hint of pain unmistakable. "We were inseparable. The day I lost her... it felt like the ground had been pulled from under me." He paused, the weight of his words hanging between us, thick and palpable. "It was an accident—something completely preventable. The world just kept spinning while I stood still, trapped in my own grief."

I could feel the air shift, charged with an understanding that transcended words. I had my own scars, each one a testament to battles fought in silence. "I get that," I replied, my voice barely above a whisper. "I lost my mother two years ago. One moment she was there, and the next... it was like watching the sun disappear behind clouds that never parted." The memory hit me hard, an unexpected wave of sorrow crashing against the dam I had carefully constructed. "I had to grow up so fast. It felt like everyone expected me to be okay, to just move on."

Our gazes locked, and for a heartbeat, the world around us faded away, leaving only the two of us wrapped in our shared grief. The fire crackled, sending sparks dancing into the night, as if celebrating the fragile intimacy we were building. "It's the silence after the storm that gets you," he continued, a knowing look in his eyes. "The kind that echoes, reminding you of what you've lost and what you can never reclaim."

With each revelation, the barriers that had previously defined us began to dissolve. I found myself leaning closer to him, as though drawn by an invisible force, an irresistible magnetism that sparked in the pit of my stomach. I had always been the girl with walls built high, fortress-like in my isolation, but in that moment, I felt those defenses start to waver. "We're not alone in this, are we?" I asked softly, the vulnerability lacing my words making me hold my breath in anticipation of his reply.

"No," Hunter said, his voice barely a whisper, "but it feels like we're the only two left who care about finding the truth." His gaze hardened for a moment, as if recalling a memory that chilled him. "There are others out there, but I don't trust them. Not after what I've seen."

The tension in the air shifted, charging the atmosphere with an urgency that sent shivers down my spine. Just as I thought we were stepping into a space of warmth and safety, the threat loomed larger, more tangible. I could sense the darkness lurking just beyond the perimeter of our firelight, shadows whispering secrets in a language I couldn't quite decipher. I took a deep breath, steadying myself against the swell of emotion threatening to overwhelm me.

"What do you mean?" I asked, tilting my head slightly, my curiosity piqued despite the apprehension brewing inside me.

"There are people who want to keep the past buried," he replied, his expression darkening. "They believe that knowledge is dangerous. They don't want us digging too deep." The fire crackled again, casting erratic shadows across his face, making him look both fierce and haunted. "And if we keep pushing, they'll come for us."

A chilling breeze swept through the clearing, and a shiver raced down my spine, igniting the adrenaline that had been simmering beneath the surface. "So what do we do?" I asked, my voice firmer than I felt. "Do we back down? Let them win?"

Hunter's gaze bore into mine, unwavering and fierce. "No. We push back. We dig deeper. We find the truth, no matter the cost." The conviction in his voice ignited a fire within me, the embers of determination flickering to life. There was something about his resolve that inspired me, that pushed me beyond the limitations I had imposed on myself.

But just as I felt that surge of courage, the atmosphere shifted once more. My phone buzzed against the ground, a jarring interruption that sliced through the fragile cocoon of safety we had spun around ourselves. I reached for it, glancing at the screen, my heart plummeting at the sight of the message.

"Don't trust him."

The words were stark, cold, and devoid of any context. My breath caught in my throat, and I looked up at Hunter, who had also tensed, his expression shifting from warmth to suspicion in the blink of an eye. "Who sent that?" he asked, his voice edged with concern.

"I... I don't know," I stammered, my mind racing. The sudden twist sent tendrils of unease spiraling through me. Had someone been watching us? Had we already stirred up something far darker than we could comprehend?

The fire crackled ominously as I fumbled to respond, my heart hammering in my chest. The warning rang in my ears, drowning out the sounds of the forest. I glanced around, the shadows suddenly feeling much less inviting, the secrets of the night lurking just beyond the glow of our sanctuary.

"We need to be careful," Hunter said, his voice low and serious, the warmth of our earlier connection feeling like a distant memory. "We can't let fear control us, but we can't be reckless either. We need a plan."

I nodded, swallowing hard against the wave of anxiety washing over me. It was clear that the deeper we delved into our pasts, the more tangled and dangerous our present became. But with the stakes rising higher than ever, one thing was certain: I couldn't turn back now. With Hunter at my side, we were on a path that could lead to both enlightenment and peril, and I was ready to uncover whatever truths awaited us—no matter the cost.

The fire flickered ominously, casting erratic shadows that danced on the trees surrounding us. A primal instinct urged me to lean closer to Hunter, the warmth of his body offering a comfort that belied the coldness of the message. I tucked my phone away, my heart racing as I fought to maintain my composure. The earlier intimacy felt fragile now, like a delicate web easily swept away by a gust of wind.

"Do you think it's a prank?" I asked, trying to sound casual, even though the knot in my stomach told me otherwise. "Maybe someone's just trying to mess with us."

Hunter shook his head, the seriousness of his expression grounding me. "No one plays pranks with that kind of warning. It's too pointed, too personal. Someone knows about us, and they want to keep us off balance."

I swallowed hard, the fire's glow suddenly feeling more sinister than welcoming. "So what do we do? Should we just sit here and wait for the other shoe to drop? Because I'm not a fan of that plan."

His lips quirked into a half-smile, the tension in his features easing slightly. "No, I have a better idea. Let's not give them the satisfaction of seeing us rattle. We'll keep digging, but we'll be smarter about it. No more late-night bonfires with heartfelt confessions."

"Great," I said, crossing my arms defiantly. "Because I really enjoy deep conversations under a sky full of stars. Who needs therapy when you can bond over existential dread, right?" I forced a chuckle, trying to lighten the mood, but the weight of uncertainty still loomed large.

"Exactly! I'm sure the stars would be thrilled to witness our emotional unraveling." He leaned forward, resting his elbows on his knees, his gaze steady on mine. "How about we start by figuring out who sent that message? We need to gather intel without making it obvious we're onto someone."

The fire crackled in agreement, sending a few sparks spiraling into the night sky as if urging us onward. "Right," I said, buoyed by his determination. "We need a plan. And I have a few ideas about where we might start. What if we—"

Before I could finish, a rustling in the underbrush sent my heart racing. My pulse quickened, and I instinctively reached for Hunter's arm, gripping it tightly. "What was that?"

He tensed, his body transforming from relaxed to alert in an instant. "I don't know. Stay close." His voice dropped to a whisper, and I felt the atmosphere shift, turning the air electric with anticipation.

The rustling grew louder, accompanied by an unmistakable crunching of leaves. My breath hitched, and I peered into the darkness, half-expecting a wild animal or perhaps a lurking figure to emerge. But instead, from the shadows, a small, disheveled dog trotted into view, tail wagging and tongue lolling out as though we were the best thing it had encountered in ages.

"Great, a woodland creature to brighten our grim evening," Hunter said, a smile breaking through the tension. He knelt, extending a hand toward the scruffy pup, who immediately bounded over to him, showering him with sloppy dog kisses. "Where did you come from, little guy?"

I couldn't help but laugh, the tension melting away. "You know, if we have to deal with ominous warnings, I'd rather do it with a companion like that." The dog seemed unfazed by our earlier anxiety, wagging its tail as if it had come to rescue us from the gloom.

Hunter stroked the dog's fur, glancing up at me with a mischievous glint in his eyes. "What should we name him? He looks like a 'Mochi' to me."

"Mochi?" I snorted. "Like the rice cake? What a name for a tough little survivor."

"Hey, don't underestimate Mochi! He's clearly seen some things," Hunter replied, feigning seriousness as the dog rolled over, begging for more attention. "I bet he's full of wisdom."

With a laugh, I leaned down to scratch Mochi behind the ears, feeling the warmth of joy bubble up within me. "I guess every hero needs a sidekick, right? Let's just hope he doesn't lead us into a trap."

Hunter stood, brushing off his hands as he regarded Mochi with newfound admiration. "Alright, sidekick. You're part of our team now. Just try not to chew on any critical documents or bite any enemies."

We exchanged a look, and the camaraderie that had been strained by worry felt more genuine now, bolstered by the unexpected addition of our furry companion. "Okay, where were we?" I asked, trying to regain the thread of our earlier conversation.

"I think we were brainstorming ways to gather intel without drawing attention to ourselves," he reminded me, his demeanor shifting back to business. "What about going undercover at the local hangouts? You know, places where the people who might know something could be?"

"Are you suggesting we become sleuths?" I raised an eyebrow, skepticism lacing my voice. "Because I'm not sure I'm cut out for that. I barely keep my plants alive."

"Come on, it'll be fun! Think of it as a little adventure." He grinned, and I couldn't help but mirror his enthusiasm. "Plus, Mochi will make a great distraction if anyone gets suspicious."

I hesitated for a moment, considering the idea. The thought of prowling around town, gathering whispers while trying not to attract attention was both thrilling and terrifying. "Alright, but if we get caught, I'm blaming you. This was your idea, after all."

He chuckled, the sound lightening the air. "Deal. We'll meet back here tomorrow night, and then we'll set our plan in motion. Just remember to look inconspicuous. That's critical for effective sleuthing."

"Inconspicuous? You mean like blending in with the crowd or wearing dark sunglasses at night?" I replied, smirking at the image of us trying to look casual while desperately failing.

"Exactly!" Hunter's laughter echoed through the trees, a sweet sound that mingled with the night air, leaving me momentarily disarmed. "Who could resist two quirky characters and a scruffy dog?"

"Maybe we should add capes to our disguise," I suggested, giggling at the absurdity of it all. "You know, for dramatic flair."

"Absolutely," he said, his eyes sparkling with mischief. "We'll be the most memorable undercover agents this town has ever seen."

As the fire dwindled, our laughter filled the clearing, wrapping around us like a protective barrier against the uncertainty that lay ahead. With Mochi nestled comfortably at our feet, I felt a surge of resolve. This new adventure might lead us into danger, but it would also forge a path of discovery, and for the first time in a long while, I was ready to embrace whatever came next. Together, we would peel back the layers of secrets that shrouded our lives, even if it meant stepping into the shadows along the way.

With the laughter of the night still echoing in my mind, I found myself caught between the thrill of our plan and the unease that lingered in the air. Hunter and I had established a camaraderie that felt almost effortless, an inexplicable bond forged in shared grief and unexpected humor. The warmth of our connection enveloped me, but the warning from the message hung over us like a storm cloud, darkening the otherwise brilliant night.

As we prepared to leave the clearing, I felt the cool night air wrap around me, sending a shiver down my spine. "Do you think we should take Mochi with us tomorrow?" I asked, glancing down at our newfound companion, who was now curled up, fast asleep at our feet.

Hunter shrugged, the corners of his mouth lifting in a half-smile. "Absolutely. He'll make the perfect decoy. If anyone starts getting nosy, we can just say we're dog-sitting." His expression turned serious for a moment, and he added, "Besides, I think he needs us more than we need him."

I nodded, looking at Mochi's blissful face. There was something undeniably comforting about the little dog, a simple reminder that in the midst of chaos, there could still be warmth and loyalty. As I stood up, brushing the dirt off my jeans, I couldn't shake the feeling that our lives were about to change dramatically. I glanced at Hunter, who was already gathering his things, and the realization struck me: we were stepping into a world filled with unknowns, where danger lurked in the shadows.

"Are you sure you're ready for this?" I asked, searching his face for any hint of doubt. "Once we dive into this, there's no going back."

His gaze met mine, steady and resolute. "I've never been more certain about anything in my life. Besides, I'd rather face whatever's out there with you than go it alone." His words sparked a flicker of hope in my chest, the kind that ignites courage even in the face of uncertainty.

With Mochi nestled comfortably in my arms, we made our way through the woods, the path illuminated by the soft glow of the moonlight. The trees swayed gently, whispering secrets that I wished I could decipher. As we reached the edge of the forest, I could see the faint lights of the town shimmering in the distance, a reminder of the lives we were temporarily leaving behind.

"Let's meet at the coffee shop tomorrow afternoon," I suggested. "It's a good spot to blend in, and we can scope out the crowd without raising suspicion."

"Perfect. Just be ready to act like you're not secretly plotting world domination." He winked, the levity in his voice making me laugh despite the seriousness of our situation.

"Right, I'll work on my 'I'm just a regular citizen' face," I replied, rolling my eyes playfully.

"Trust me, you'll nail it. Just remember to keep Mochi on his best behavior."

"Not sure how well he'll handle that," I said, scratching the pup behind the ears. "But I have a feeling he's got a few tricks up his furry sleeves."

As we parted ways, I felt the weight of the night settle over me. With every step towards home, the air grew thicker, heavy with anticipation and uncertainty. The comforting normalcy of my bedroom seemed worlds away, and I knew that by tomorrow evening, my life would look entirely different. The thought of facing whatever dangers awaited us filled me with both excitement and trepidation.

The next day unfolded in a blur of mundane tasks—school, homework, and half-hearted conversations with friends. Each moment felt like a countdown, leading to the inevitable confrontation with the unknown. As the clock inched closer to our meeting time, I could barely concentrate on anything else, my mind racing with possibilities and scenarios. I imagined the coffee shop bustling with activity, unaware of the storm brewing just beneath the surface.

When the clock finally struck four, I grabbed my bag and headed out, determined to stick to our plan. The sun cast a golden hue over the town, illuminating familiar streets that now felt tainted with unease. As I approached the coffee shop, the comforting aroma of roasted beans wafted through the air, but the anticipation curling in my stomach made it hard to appreciate.

Pushing open the door, I scanned the room for Hunter. He was seated in a corner booth, his brow furrowed in concentration as he tapped away at his phone. I made my way over, feeling a rush of relief wash over me as I slid into the seat across from him. "You're here early," I remarked, trying to sound casual.

"Had to check a few things before we got started," he replied, glancing up with a grin. "And I ordered you a vanilla latte—your favorite."

"Look at you, winning points already," I said, accepting the cup gratefully. "What's on the agenda for today?"

He leaned forward, lowering his voice as if the walls might have ears. "I did some digging on local chat rooms and forums. There are whispers about something happening in town—people going missing, odd occurrences. It's all very vague, but it feels connected to what we've been uncovering."

I took a sip of my latte, letting the sweetness calm my nerves. "Missing people? That's... unsettling."

He nodded, his expression serious. "Exactly. And it's not just isolated incidents; it seems to be happening more frequently. We need to figure out if there's a pattern, something that ties it all together."

As we delved deeper into our conversation, I felt the weight of the world pressing against us. With each revelation, the stakes grew higher, and I could feel the tension crackling in the air between us. Just as we began to piece together a timeline, the door swung open, and a familiar face stepped inside.

My heart sank as I recognized Jessica, my classmate and someone I'd never particularly gotten along with. She scanned the room, her gaze locking onto us as a knowing smirk danced across her lips. I felt Hunter tense beside me, the atmosphere shifting instantly.

"Oh, look who's playing detective," she drawled, her voice dripping with mockery as she approached our table. "Is this a little secret club I wasn't invited to?"

"Just enjoying coffee, Jess," I said, trying to sound unbothered. "Nothing too exciting."

She leaned in closer, her eyes glinting with curiosity. "Sure, that's what they all say before the plot thickens." Her gaze flicked to Hunter, a hint of challenge lingering in the air. "What's your angle here, Hunter? You're not just slumming it with the misfits for the fun of it, are you?"

The tension thickened, wrapping around us like a vice. I could feel my heart racing, a mix of anger and anxiety bubbling to the surface. "We're not up to anything, Jessica. Why don't you just leave us alone?"

She smiled, a predatory gleam in her eyes. "Why would I do that? This is way too interesting."

Just then, Hunter's phone buzzed loudly on the table, breaking the tense silence. He glanced at the screen, his expression shifting from irritation to alarm. "We need to go. Now."

"What? Why?" I asked, my voice barely above a whisper.

"Just trust me," he replied, his eyes locked onto Jessica, who now seemed to sense the urgency in the air. "Get Mochi. We can't be here."

In an instant, everything shifted. Jessica's smile faded, replaced by a look of confusion and something more sinister as she realized we were serious. "You're not leaving this table without explaining," she said, stepping closer, her tone shifting from playful to confrontational.

And that's when the lights flickered ominously, plunging the shop into a momentary darkness. The buzz of conversation halted, a collective gasp echoing through the air. I clutched my coffee cup, the warm ceramic suddenly feeling cold against my palm.

When the lights returned, everything had changed. The bustling café was now shrouded in a heavy silence, and my heart raced as I looked around. People were staring, and in the back corner, a figure loomed, watching us intently.

I locked eyes with Hunter, and the unspoken message was clear: whatever was happening, it was bigger than us, and we were running out of time.

Chapter 6: Caught in the Crossfire

The air was thick with salt and suspicion as I stood on the sun-bleached dock of Firestone Bay, the creaking wood beneath my feet whispering secrets to the rolling waves. I squinted against the harsh afternoon sun, its golden rays glimmering off the water, revealing the undulating beauty of the bay that now felt more like a trap than a paradise. Hunter leaned against the railing beside me, his silhouette framed against the horizon, a striking figure with tousled hair and piercing eyes that seemed to hold both the ocean's depth and the stormy skies above. We were tethered together by a fragile thread of trust, one that frayed with every ominous occurrence that darkened our lives.

Just last week, I'd found a note tucked beneath the door of my little beach cottage, the paper yellowed and crisp as if it had been waiting for me since the dawn of time. "Stay away from the truth, or you'll regret it." The words burned into my mind, a sinister promise that hung over my head like a guillotine. I could feel Hunter's presence beside me, his protective energy crackling in the charged air. We had become each other's shields, but the growing uncertainty gnawed at my insides. With every hushed conversation in town, every sidelong glance from strangers, I sensed we were mere pawns in a game much larger than ourselves.

"I think they're watching us," I said, my voice barely more than a breath, the fear lacing my words. I glanced around, half-expecting to see someone lurking behind the tall pines that lined the coast, their gaze fixed on us with malevolent intent.

"Let them watch," Hunter replied, his tone brimming with an unyielding resolve that made my heart race. "We won't be intimidated."

A chill danced along my spine. His confidence was reassuring, yet it only added to the weight of the unsolved mysteries that loomed over us. Firestone Bay, with its charming cottages and the symphony of waves crashing against the shore, had transformed into a haunting labyrinth of deceit and fear. The locals who once smiled and waved now kept their heads down, hurriedly crossing the streets as if dodging invisible threats.

"Did you see that guy yesterday?" I continued, feeling the adrenaline kick in. "The one who just stood there, staring at us from the coffee shop?"

"I did," he said, his jaw tightening. "It's not just you. We need to be careful. If someone wants to keep the truth buried, they won't hesitate to make sure we stay quiet."

My heart raced as I recalled the icy grip of dread that had coiled around me when I spotted the man. He was nondescript, clad in a faded flannel shirt, but his eyes—those cold, calculating eyes—had sent an unmistakable message. He wasn't just an observer; he was a player in this twisted game.

The memory of that moment stuck with me as we headed back to my cottage. The sun began to dip below the horizon, casting an amber hue across the sky that belied the darkness creeping into our lives. The scent of the ocean mixed with the damp earth as we entered the cozy abode, the familiar space now feeling more like a fortress under siege.

"Let's go over what we know," Hunter suggested, his voice steady despite the tension that hung between us. We settled at the small kitchen table, the wood worn and polished from years of family meals and laughter. I pulled out the scattered papers filled with notes, maps, and articles about the town's history, each page steeped in secrets that tied us together.

As we pieced together the fragments, I felt the distance between us shift. The air crackled with an electric tension, each stolen glance, each accidental brush of hands igniting a spark that blurred the line between fear and something deeper. "If we can connect the dots, we might figure out why we're being targeted," I said, my fingers tracing the edge of a particularly yellowed newspaper clipping that detailed the town's dark past.

Hunter leaned closer, his warm breath grazing my cheek as he pointed to a name that leaped off the page—"Clara Dempsey." I had heard whispers about her, a woman who had disappeared under mysterious circumstances decades ago, her case never solved. "She was involved in something big. Something that might tie into whatever is happening now."

My pulse quickened at the thought. "Do you think someone is trying to protect her secrets? Or is it something more?"

"Maybe both," he replied, his eyes locking onto mine with a ferocity that sent a shiver down my spine. "If Clara had information that could expose someone, they might want to make sure it stays buried. And we're getting too close to finding it."

As the darkness settled over the bay, cloaking us in shadows, the reality of our situation loomed large. The air around us felt charged, heavy with unspoken words and buried emotions. I couldn't help but feel the walls closing in, each tick of the clock amplifying the threat we faced.

Just then, a sudden crash echoed from outside, causing us both to jump. "What was that?" I asked, fear threading through my voice.

"Stay here," Hunter instructed, his expression hardening as he moved toward the door. "I'll check it out."

"No, I'm coming with you," I insisted, stubbornness fueling my determination. We were in this together, and I wouldn't let him face whatever lay beyond the threshold alone.

With a nod of reluctant agreement, we stepped outside into the cool night air, the moon casting an eerie glow over the bay. Shadows danced along the path, and I couldn't shake the feeling of being watched. As we moved closer to the source of the noise, adrenaline surged through my veins. Whatever was out there was just as determined to keep us from unearthing the truth as we were to confront it.

The darkness enveloped us, a shroud of mystery and danger, and in that moment, I realized that the shadows weren't just a backdrop; they were a reflection of the turmoil brewing within my heart. I was no longer merely a pawn in this game; I was a player, ready to face whatever darkness lay ahead, with Hunter by my side.

The moon hung high over Firestone Bay, casting a silvery glow that shimmered on the dark waters, a stark contrast to the storm brewing within me. Hunter and I stood in the narrow space between my cottage and the thick line of trees that framed the yard. The sudden crash we had heard moments ago echoed ominously in my mind, a sound that seemed to ripple through the stillness of the night.

"What do you think it was?" I whispered, glancing at Hunter, who remained tense, his body coiled like a spring ready to snap.

"Could be a raccoon or something," he replied, but his tone lacked conviction. The tension in the air was palpable, and I could feel it tightening around us like a vise.

"Or it could be someone trying to send us a message," I countered, shivering despite the warmth of the evening. My instincts screamed at me to retreat, to bolt back into the safety of the cottage, but there was a fierceness within me that urged me forward. I would not be intimidated; not now, not ever.

With a slow, deliberate motion, Hunter stepped closer to the edge of the trees, his eyes scanning the darkness. I held my breath, wishing I had a flashlight to pierce through the shadows, but I had long learned that light often drew attention. Instead, I gripped the small penknife I kept in my pocket, a comfort more than a weapon.

"Stay behind me," Hunter said softly, and I could hear the underlying tension in his voice. There was an air of protectiveness about him, an instinctual drive to shield me from whatever lay hidden in the dark.

"I can take care of myself, you know," I shot back, forcing a brave smile that didn't quite reach my eyes. "But I'll let you lead since you seem to have a flair for drama."

He chuckled, the sound low and warm, a welcome distraction from the knot of anxiety twisting in my stomach. "Drama, huh? You think I'm the one being dramatic?"

"I mean, you do look good in a heroic light," I teased, nudging him playfully. "Just promise me you won't jump out of the bushes like some sort of superhero."

"I can't make any promises." He grinned, and the moment of levity felt like a small beacon of hope amidst the uncertainty that surrounded us.

As we cautiously moved forward, I felt the weight of every rustling leaf and snapping twig beneath our feet. The trees loomed like ancient sentinels, their gnarled branches twisting against the backdrop of the night sky. I could hear the distant lapping of waves, the soft whispers of the ocean urging us on. Each step we took felt significant, laden with the weight of the unknown.

Suddenly, a rustle in the underbrush sent my heart racing. My grip tightened around the knife as Hunter halted, his posture shifting from relaxed to alert in an instant. "What was that?"

"Not sure," I replied, peering into the darkness. "Maybe it's just a raccoon after all."

Before I could finish my sentence, a figure emerged from the shadows, tall and imposing. My breath caught in my throat, and Hunter stepped in front of me, his body a solid wall of determination.

"Who's there?" Hunter called out, his voice steady but laced with an underlying tension.

The figure took a step forward, revealing a familiar face that sent a wave of confusion washing over me. It was Derek, a childhood friend who had vanished from my life years ago, only to resurface now, in the middle of this chaos. His wild hair and worn jeans looked like a time capsule from our teenage years, but the worry etched into his features spoke of a harsher reality.

"Derek? What are you doing here?" I stammered, half-relieved and half-terrified.

"I came to warn you," he said, glancing nervously over his shoulder as if he expected shadows to spring to life. "Things are getting worse in town. People are looking for you, for both of you."

"What do you mean?" Hunter interjected, his protective stance unyielding. "Why would anyone be looking for us?"

"Because of Clara," Derek said, his voice dropping to a conspiratorial whisper. "People think you're digging too deep into things that should stay buried."

My stomach twisted at the mention of Clara Dempsey, her name carrying the weight of lost history and buried truths. "We're not looking for trouble," I said, but even as the words left my lips, I knew they were inadequate. Trouble had found us, whether we sought it or not.

"Doesn't matter if you're looking for it or not," Derek replied. "People don't like it when the past resurfaces. They'll do anything to keep it buried."

Hunter's expression hardened, the shadows of concern flickering in his eyes. "We're not going to let them intimidate us. We need to know what happened to Clara."

Derek shook his head, an expression of desperation crossing his face. "You don't understand. There are those who have made it their mission to ensure that the truth remains hidden. It's not just the town's history at stake; it's their livelihoods."

"Then we'll expose them," I said fiercely, emboldened by the adrenaline coursing through me. "They can't silence us forever."

Derek exchanged glances with Hunter, uncertainty etched on both their faces. "You're playing with fire," Derek warned. "But if you're determined, you need to be careful. You're already in the crosshairs, and one wrong move could bring the whole town down on you."

"Careful is my middle name," I said with a confidence I didn't entirely feel. "Well, not literally, but you get the point."

As the tension hung thick in the air, I could see that Derek's fear was genuine. He didn't just come to warn us—he cared. "Meet me tomorrow at the old pier," he said urgently. "I have more to tell you. But for now, get inside. It's not safe out here."

With that, he vanished back into the shadows, leaving us to digest the weight of his words. I turned to Hunter, who looked pensive, his brows knitted in thought.

"Do you trust him?" Hunter asked, his voice low.

"I think he's scared," I replied. "And scared people can be dangerous. But he wouldn't have come if he didn't think we needed to know something."

Hunter nodded, his expression thoughtful. "Let's get inside. We need to strategize."

As we stepped back into the cottage, the familiar scent of ocean air and wooden beams welcomed us, but now it felt like a sanctuary under siege. The flickering light of the single lamp cast long shadows that danced across the walls, a reminder that we were not just dealing with the shadows of the past but also those of the present.

The night unfolded like a coiled spring, filled with uncertainty and potential danger. But amidst the chaos, I felt the threads of determination weaving through me. Hunter and I were no longer just navigating the murky waters of Firestone Bay; we were diving headfirst into a world of secrets and lies, and I was resolute in uncovering the truth—no matter the cost.

Morning light crept through the curtains, casting soft, golden rays that danced across the worn floorboards of my cottage. I awoke with a jolt, the remnants of last night's anxiety still clinging to me like a wet blanket. The encounter with Derek replayed in my mind, each detail sharp and disquieting. I pushed myself up, shaking off the remnants of sleep and the swirling uncertainties of the night. Today was going to be pivotal, and the weight of that realization settled on my shoulders.

Hunter was already awake, leaning against the kitchen counter, his tall frame relaxed but alert. He glanced up as I entered the room, and I caught the faintest hint of a smile tugging at the corners of his mouth. "Good morning, Sunshine," he said, his voice low and teasing. "Ready to dive into the chaos?"

"Chaos? Oh, you mean the delightful storm we've stirred up?" I shot back, pouring myself a cup of coffee and savoring the rich aroma. "Who knew uncovering the past could be so... invigorating?"

His laughter echoed in the small space, a warm sound that filled the air and made my heart flutter. "Invigorating is one way to put it. I'd prefer 'suicidally reckless,' but to each their own."

We shared a moment of levity, the tension momentarily forgotten, but I could feel the current of unease still lingering beneath the surface. I leaned against the counter, swirling the coffee in my cup, and asked, "So, what's the plan for today? Confronting our pasts while dodging the present?"

"Exactly. We meet Derek at the pier and see what else he knows about Clara," he replied, his expression growing serious. "But I think we need to take precautions. If someone's watching us, we can't afford to be reckless."

"Reckless? You mean like how we broke into the library last week?" I grinned, recalling the thrill of sifting through dusty archives, hoping to uncover a shred of evidence that would help unravel Clara's story.

"Exactly like that," Hunter said, his lips twitching in amusement. "I don't want to end up as a cautionary tale for the next generation of thrill-seekers."

"Cautionary tales do have a nice ring to them, though. 'Here lies Hunter, the brave fool who poked the bear.'"

He chuckled again, and for a moment, the shadows hovering around us felt less oppressive. Yet, as we finished our coffee, the heaviness returned, a reminder of the peril that lingered just beyond our walls.

After getting dressed, we walked in silence, the quiet of the morning punctuated by the rhythmic sound of waves crashing against the shore. The salty air was refreshing, yet every step felt like a countdown, a reminder of the ticking clock that pushed us closer to the unknown.

The old pier loomed ahead, weathered and worn, its wooden slats creaking underfoot as we approached. It was a place steeped in memories, both joyful and haunting. Derek waited at the edge, his hands shoved deep into his pockets, his posture tense as he scanned the horizon, the restless sea reflecting the turmoil in his expression.

"Hey," I called out as we neared, and he turned, relief washing over his features momentarily before concern settled back in.

"You made it," he said, glancing around as if expecting someone else to emerge from the shadows. "We need to talk quickly."

"What did you find out?" Hunter's voice was firm, his eyes narrowed with determination.

Derek hesitated, the weight of his words palpable in the air. "It's worse than I thought. The town is restless, and the people who've been watching you are getting more desperate. They think you're getting too close to uncovering what happened to Clara."

"Why does it matter so much? It's history," I said, frustration bubbling to the surface. "People die. Secrets are buried. Why can't they just let it go?"

"Because Clara wasn't just a local. She had ties, connections to powerful people. And the truth? It could expose a lot more than just an old case."

"What does that mean?" Hunter pressed, a frown deepening on his brow.

"It means that whoever is watching you isn't just some random troublemaker. They're part of something bigger. They'll stop at nothing to keep their secrets safe."

I felt a chill creep down my spine as Derek's words sank in. The stakes were higher than we had anticipated, and the danger was no longer abstract; it was real, looming like a thunderstorm on the horizon.

"Then we need to be smart about this," I said, my voice steadier than I felt. "If we can find out who's behind this, maybe we can turn the tide."

"Turn the tide?" Derek laughed darkly. "You're dealing with a tide that has swallowed others whole. We need to tread carefully."

"I refuse to let fear dictate our actions," Hunter replied, determination lacing his voice. "If we have to fight back, we will. But we need to gather more information first."

As we discussed our next steps, a movement caught my eye near the tree line. A figure emerged, their features obscured by the shadows of the thick foliage. My heart raced as I squinted, recognizing the familiar silhouette.

"Who's that?" I asked, my voice barely above a whisper.

Derek's face paled as he turned to look. "I don't know... but it doesn't look friendly."

Before we could react, the figure stepped into the light, revealing a woman whose striking features were marked by a fierce intensity.

She was older, her hair streaked with silver but her eyes burned with an unmistakable fire.

"You shouldn't be here," she said, her voice low and threatening, sending a jolt of adrenaline through me. "You've put yourselves in danger, and I can't let that happen."

"Who are you?" Hunter demanded, stepping in front of me, his stance protective.

The woman took a step closer, her gaze unwavering. "I'm someone who knows the truth about Clara. And you're playing a dangerous game."

Derek stiffened, glancing at Hunter and me, his eyes wide. "We need to get out of here."

"Not until we know what she wants," Hunter replied, his voice steady but his grip tightening.

"I'm here to help," the woman said, her expression softening just enough to reveal a glimmer of vulnerability beneath her tough exterior. "But you need to understand: the past doesn't just fade away. It has a way of clawing back, especially when you stir the pot."

As the tension in the air thickened, I felt a pull toward this mysterious woman, an urge to know what secrets she held. But before I could voice my thoughts, a loud crack echoed through the trees, and the world tilted on its axis.

"What was that?" I gasped, my heart racing as I turned toward the sound, fear tightening around my chest like a vice.

"We need to move!" Derek urged, panic flooding his voice.

Before we could react, a figure lunged from the trees, and in that moment, everything blurred into chaos. My breath caught in my throat as I realized we were caught in a web of danger far more intricate than we could have imagined. As darkness descended, I felt the ground shift beneath my feet, and I was left teetering on the brink, unsure of what fate awaited us in the shadows.

Chapter 7: The Turning Point

The storm raged outside, a wild cacophony that mirrored the tumult inside my heart. Thunder cracked like a whip, its echo rumbling through the walls of Hunter's home, shaking the very foundations of our unspoken tension. We had gathered in the dimly lit living room, the flickering candlelight casting dancing shadows on the walls, as if they too were part of our unsteady alliance. Hunter, with his tousled hair and stormy gray eyes, sat across from me, his brows furrowed in that familiar way, a blend of frustration and something deeper, more vulnerable.

The rain hammered against the glass like a chorus of desperate hands begging for entry, and I could feel the tension in the air thickening, wrapping around us like a tightening noose. It was a night fraught with uncertainty, each gust of wind howling like a beast unleashed, reminding me of the wildness that lingered in my own chest. For weeks, we had danced around our feelings, each verbal jab a distraction from the undeniable pull we had toward one another. But now, with the storm raging and our walls worn thin, I felt the time had come to break the silence.

"Why do you always have to be so infuriating?" I blurted out, my voice barely above a whisper, but the truth of it rang like a bell in the silence that followed. Hunter's eyes sparked, a glimmer of challenge flaring to life. "Me? Look who's talking," he retorted, leaning forward, the candlelight illuminating the sharp angles of his face, making him look even more dangerously handsome. "You're the one who spends half the time acting like I'm a stray cat you can't stand but secretly want to cuddle."

I opened my mouth to retort, but the truth stung more than I anticipated. His words cut through my defenses, exposing the raw nerve I had carefully hidden. I wanted to scoff, to throw a witty comeback back at him, but instead, a quiet desperation seeped into my voice. "Maybe I'm just trying to figure you out. You're infuriatingly charming one minute and then a complete jerk the next."

Hunter ran a hand through his hair, frustration mingling with amusement as he regarded me. "And you're like a puzzle missing half the pieces, always making me guess." The air between us crackled with unspoken words, our fears swirling in the storm like leaves caught in a tempest. I could feel the weight of my admission hanging between us, thick and heavy, a palpable tension that begged to be released.

The winds howled louder, an almost sinister presence outside, urging me to push past the fear that gripped my heart. "You know," I said slowly, my voice trembling as I took a step closer, "for so long, I thought hating you was easier than acknowledging how I feel." There was a moment of stillness, the chaos outside fading into a backdrop, our breaths harmonizing in a suspended rhythm.

"Maybe we should stop fighting it," he murmured, his voice low and gravelly, each word igniting something deep within me. "Maybe it's time we admit what's been brewing under all that animosity." The sincerity in his tone made my heart race. There was a tremor in the air, a mixture of fear and thrill that pulsed like a heartbeat, echoing in the silence that followed.

Just as I opened my mouth to respond, the world outside erupted. A deafening crash, the sound of something colossal succumbing to the storm, reverberated through the room, jolting us back to reality. My heart raced, not just from the confession hanging between us but from the sudden urgency of our situation. The moment felt suspended, poised on a precipice, and then the chaos of the world came crashing back in, breaking the delicate tension that had been building.

"Was that—?" I began, but Hunter was already moving toward the window, his silhouette stark against the flickering light. The view outside was a swirling mass of rain and wind, the trees bending dangerously low as if they were bowing to some unseen force. My gut twisted with a sense of foreboding.

"Stay here," he commanded, his voice steady despite the fear flickering in his eyes. I nodded, though the instinct to follow him surged within me. But he turned, and in that instant, the air crackled anew, the unsaid words hovering between us like a fragile spider's web, suddenly too delicate for the storm raging outside.

As Hunter stepped outside, the wind whipped around him, a chaotic dance of nature that threatened to swallow him whole. I pressed my face to the cold glass, the storm's roar drowning out the wild thumping of my heart. The sight of him standing firm against the tempest, his figure a beacon of strength in the chaos, sent a jolt through me. The tension, once a mere whisper of frustration and longing, exploded into something fierce and undeniable.

The wind howled as if it were an ominous harbinger, and I realized that our world was about to shift, irrevocably. Whatever came next would not only test our resolve but lay bare the truths we had been too afraid to confront. As the rain lashed against the windows, I clung to the hope that perhaps, through the storm, we could find a way to weather the tempest together.

The door slammed shut behind Hunter, and I was left alone with the tempest that raged outside, its fury matching the storm brewing within me. I paced the living room, the faint scent of candle wax mixing with the damp, earthy smell of the rain-soaked world beyond. Thunder rolled like an angry drum, rattling the windows and shaking the floorboards beneath my feet. I could hardly catch my breath, adrenaline coursing through my veins as I replayed our moment—the heat of his lips, the intensity of his gaze—as if those sensations could ground me amid the chaos.

What had just happened felt monumental, like a line drawn in the sand, one that I had been too afraid to cross until the very last moment. My heart raced, a wild creature seeking escape, while my mind spiraled in a whirlwind of confusion. Had I really opened up? Had we truly crossed that invisible boundary, the one that had kept us at odds for so long? My stomach flipped at the thought, both exhilarating and terrifying.

Outside, the wind picked up, rattling the trees like marionettes in a sinister play. The power flickered ominously, and I glanced around, wondering if I should grab a flashlight or find Hunter before he ventured too far. Just as I reached for the lamp, the lights flickered and then went out, plunging the room into darkness. The storm seemed to howl louder, a cacophony of nature that swallowed every thought I tried to grasp.

"Hunter?" I called, my voice small against the vastness of the storm. I strained to hear any response, the chaos outside drowning out my heartbeat. A pang of worry crept in, twisting my stomach as I realized I didn't know what danger lurked beyond the threshold.

The seconds felt like hours until I heard a thud followed by a curse. I rushed toward the front door, heart pounding as I flung it open. The wind howled, and rain lashed against my skin like icy needles. Hunter stood there, drenched and slightly dazed, his shirt clinging to his frame, making him look all the more formidable yet vulnerable.

"What were you thinking?" I shouted over the wind, half-exasperated, half-relieved.

"I thought I heard something," he replied, shaking his head as water cascaded down his face, slicking back his hair. He stepped inside, pushing the door closed behind him with a determined shove. "But all I found was my own stupidity."

I rolled my eyes, but there was a smirk tugging at my lips. "Well, at least you've got that covered."

Hunter took a step closer, his expression shifting from playful to serious in an instant. "You don't get it, do you? This storm isn't just bad weather—it's a warning." His voice dropped, the usual bravado replaced by a gravity that sent a shiver down my spine.

"What do you mean?" I pressed, suddenly aware that his stormy demeanor was no mere metaphor for the weather outside.

He sighed, running a hand through his hair again, sending rivulets of water cascading down his neck. "I've been sensing something... different. The way you and I have been dancing around each other, it's not just a fight; it's something bigger. We're caught in something we don't fully understand."

I frowned, crossing my arms against the chill that was seeping in, both from the storm and his words. "Bigger? Like a supernatural storm? Because if that's the case, I'm going to need a raincoat and a survival guide."

He chuckled, the sound rough but warm, cutting through the tension for just a moment. "No, not like that. Just... be careful. This storm feels like more than just wind and rain."

As he spoke, the lights flickered back on, illuminating the room in soft yellow hues. I could see the concern etched on his face, the deep lines in his brow signaling a mix of emotions I wasn't entirely sure I was prepared to navigate. My heart raced at the thought of something darker lurking beneath our surface tensions.

Before I could respond, another deafening crash echoed from outside, followed by a collective rumble that shook the ground beneath us. My heart jumped into my throat. "What was that?"

Hunter was already at the window, peering through the rain-streaked glass. "I don't know, but it sounded close."

Without thinking, I moved to join him, my instincts screaming for action. The outside world was a chaos of shadows and shifting silhouettes, the trees bending under the storm's wrath. And then I saw it—a flash of something moving, something large darting between the trees. My breath caught in my throat.

"Hunter, look!" I pointed, the urgency in my voice betraying my fear. "There's something out there."

He leaned closer to the window, squinting through the downpour. "I can't see—wait, are you sure it's not just the wind playing tricks on us?"

"Not this time!" I insisted, my voice rising above the storm. "It's too big to be just wind."

Before he could respond, the power flickered again, plunging us back into darkness. I felt Hunter's hand find mine, squeezing tightly as if grounding himself in my presence. The storm's fury grew, a low rumble of thunder vibrating through the house, and a gut instinct told me that whatever we were about to face was not simply a figment of our imaginations.

When the lights returned, my heart raced as I glanced back at Hunter. "What do we do?"

He hesitated for a moment, searching my eyes as if trying to gauge whether I was ready for whatever came next. "We check it out." His voice was steady, but I could hear the underlying tension.

"Check it out?" I echoed incredulously. "Are you out of your mind? What if it's something dangerous?"

"Or something we need to confront," he countered, determination hardening his features. "You and I have been running from our own feelings for too long. Maybe it's time we face them, together. But first, we need to see what's happening out there."

My pulse quickened at his words, the thrill of the moment mixing with my lingering apprehension. "You really think we can handle this? Together?"

Hunter's grip tightened around my hand, a solid promise amidst the chaos. "I know we can."

With a deep breath, I nodded, stepping closer to him as we prepared to face whatever lay beyond the safety of the door. The storm continued to rage, but something in Hunter's presence sparked a newfound courage within me. The night was far from over, and as we stepped into the chaos, I realized we were about to uncover not just the secrets of the storm, but the hidden truths of our own hearts.

The door creaked open, a reluctant invitation into the storm that howled like an enraged spirit outside. Hunter and I stepped into the chaos, our breaths mingling with the cool air that swirled around us, charged with tension and anticipation. The rain pelted down, creating a symphony of nature that drowned out our doubts. I could barely see in the dim light, but I felt his presence beside me—strong and steady, a pillar against the swirling storm.

"What if it's just the wind?" I ventured, more to convince myself than anything. I had been filled with dread since the first crash, but there was something stirring in Hunter's eyes that urged me to push through the uncertainty.

"Trust me," he replied, glancing back at me, his voice firm yet filled with a gentleness that was entirely disarming. "We've faced worse—like that time you tried to cook dinner, remember?"

I stifled a laugh, momentarily distracted from the brewing tension outside. "Hey, that was a culinary adventure! Besides, who knew onions could explode?"

"Explode is a strong word," he teased, grinning in that way that made my heart flutter. But then the smile faded as we heard another ominous crack, closer this time, followed by a sudden thud that resonated through the trees, sending a chill down my spine. The moment of levity evaporated, leaving only the weight of apprehension in its wake.

We moved cautiously toward the edge of the property, the storm enveloping us in a cold embrace. The trees swayed, their branches clawing at the sky as if they were desperate to escape the tempest. My pulse raced with every step we took, the atmosphere thickening with an electric charge that heightened my senses. Hunter's grip on my hand tightened, our fingers intertwined as we navigated through the thick brush, each sound amplified in the night.

"I wish I had brought a flashlight," I murmured, squinting into the darkness, the shadows shifting ominously.

"Who needs a flashlight when you have the power of courage?" he quipped, but the slight tremor in his voice betrayed the bravado.

"Courage, huh? Let me remember that next time I'm in a dark alley. I'll just shout 'courage' and hope for the best," I shot back, trying to keep the atmosphere light even as my heart hammered in my chest.

Then, as we reached a clearing, we both froze, taking in the scene before us. A large tree had been uprooted, its roots sprawling like grotesque fingers clawing at the earth. But it wasn't the fallen tree that caught our attention; it was the shadowy figure moving just beyond it.

"What in the world..." I whispered, my voice barely carrying over the wind. The figure stood still, cloaked in darkness, as if it were woven into the fabric of the night itself.

Hunter stepped forward, his posture alert. "Stay back," he ordered, his voice low and firm, but I could see the uncertainty in his eyes.

"Maybe it's just a lost deer or something," I suggested, though a part of me felt the tension in the air shift, like a rubber band stretched to its breaking point.

"Or maybe it's something else entirely," he murmured, eyes narrowing as he peered into the gloom.

Suddenly, the figure moved, darting behind the fallen tree, its speed uncanny. My heart raced. "Did you see that?"

"Yeah," Hunter replied, the line of his jaw set tight. "We need to go."

But just as he turned to lead me back, a howl sliced through the air—a sound so raw and primal it made my blood run cold. It wasn't the kind of howl you'd hear from a typical wolf; it was deeper, resonating with a haunting familiarity that sent shivers down my spine.

"Was that...?" I couldn't finish my thought, the reality settling over us like a fog.

Before we could react, the figure lunged from behind the tree, a dark silhouette that blurred with the shadows, leaping toward us with a speed that made my heart leap into my throat. Hunter instinctively pulled me behind him, shielding me as the figure landed with a grace that belied its sheer size.

The creature stood before us, eyes glinting like polished stones, reflecting the dim light. It was neither wolf nor man, but something in between—muscles rippling under dark fur, a snarl curling its lips. My breath caught as I felt the weight of ancient, primal magic thrumming in the air.

"Hunter!" I gasped, panic bubbling within me as the creature took a cautious step forward, its gaze locked onto Hunter. The storm raged on, but the world had narrowed to this moment, the tension stretching like a taut wire ready to snap.

"Don't move," Hunter warned, his voice steady, though I could see the resolve flicker in his eyes. "It's just as scared as we are."

The creature growled low, a sound that vibrated through my bones, and for a heartbeat, time stood still. I could feel my heart racing, a wild drumbeat echoing the chaos around us. Fear coursed through my veins, but beneath that fear was an undeniable curiosity. What was it? What did it want?

Before I could process the danger fully, the creature lunged again, but this time it didn't come for us. Instead, it veered to the side, as if sensing a shift in the winds, and let out a warning growl that echoed into the stormy night.

"What is it doing?" I breathed, my voice trembling.

"I don't know, but we need to get out of here!" Hunter urged, but just as he turned to pull me away, another figure emerged from the shadows, this one larger and far more imposing. The air thickened with tension, a palpable force that crackled between us.

The creature paused, its snarl morphing into something that looked like desperation, a deep instinct to protect or flee overwhelming it. The new figure advanced, an ethereal glow surrounding it that illuminated the darkness in a way that was both beautiful and terrifying.

I stood frozen, my heart racing as I struggled to process what was unfolding before me. This was no ordinary storm; it was a convergence of forces I couldn't comprehend. And just as the realization hit me—just as the first tendrils of understanding began to weave their way through my mind—the air shifted again. The storm surged, and with it came a blinding flash of light, illuminating everything for a fleeting moment.

In that instant, I saw the true nature of the beings before us—neither fully beast nor human, but something ancient and powerful. As the light flickered and the shadows danced, I caught Hunter's gaze, a storm of emotions reflected in his eyes, before the world plunged back into darkness.

And then the howl rang out again, louder and more insistent than before, leaving me breathless as the night closed in, drawing us toward an unimaginable fate.

Chapter 8: The Unraveling

The remnants of the storm hung heavy in the air, the world outside wrapped in an eerie calm. Light filtered through the fractured clouds, casting an unsettling glow over everything it touched. Each breath I took felt charged, as if the atmosphere itself pulsed with secrets just waiting to be unearthed. Hunter stood beside me, his silhouette stark against the horizon. The man I had once viewed as an adversary now felt more like a reluctant partner in this tangled mess we found ourselves in. We exchanged wary glances, each of us aware that our alliance was tenuous at best, and I wondered how we had arrived at this point.

The night had stripped us bare, unveiling truths that had long been buried. The echoes of whispered confessions and the thrill of our shared danger hummed in my veins, a potent reminder that in the midst of chaos, something beautiful had begun to bloom. Yet, as I glanced at Hunter, the hardened lines of his jaw betrayed a man grappling with demons of his own. He shifted his weight, the tension in his shoulders radiating a palpable unease.

"I don't like this," he said, his voice low and gravelly, tinged with a vulnerability that caught me off guard. "The storm's gone, but something feels...off."

"You think?" I shot back, more sharply than intended, though his concern mirrored my own. It was as if we were both threading the same frayed rope, desperately trying to tie it back together before it unraveled completely. "You didn't have to face the night alone. We both did this together."

He let out a soft chuckle, but it didn't reach his eyes. "Together, huh? That's a nice way of saying you dragged me along for the ride."

"Hey, you could have left me there," I pointed out, folding my arms across my chest as if it could shield me from the raw vulnerability swirling between us. "But you didn't. So, congratulations, Hunter. We're stuck together."

Our banter danced on the edge of something deeper, a tension that crackled and popped, holding the promise of more. But the moment slipped away, lost to the shadows creeping back into our lives. I knew we were running out of time. Each passing second pulled us further into the web of secrets, the shadows from our pasts extending their grasp, threatening to ensnare us both.

"We need to figure out who's behind this," he finally said, his brow furrowing as he stared out into the horizon, where the remnants of the storm lingered like fading memories. "Someone wants to keep us quiet, and that means we've stepped on someone's toes. Someone powerful."

A shiver coursed through me, not from the chill in the air but from the realization that our troubles were far from over. "You think it's related to my family? My father's business dealings?"

Hunter nodded slowly. "It's possible. You said your father had enemies. Maybe they're more than just disgruntled associates."

The thought sent a chill down my spine. Memories of whispered conversations and hurried phone calls flooded my mind, fragments of my father's world I had never wanted to fully understand. "But what does that mean for us? For me?"

"It means we need to dig deeper," he said, his tone resolute. "We can't run away. If we do, they'll win."

A knot twisted in my stomach, an instinctual fear battling the burgeoning connection I felt towards him. "And if we dig too deep? What if we unearth something that puts us both in danger?"

"We'll face it together," he replied, his gaze steady, anchoring me in the storm of uncertainty swirling in my mind. The sincerity in his voice ignited a spark of courage within me, propelling me forward.

"Okay. Together," I echoed, the word carrying more weight than I intended. It was an invitation and a promise wrapped in one.

With a shared determination, we set off toward the heart of the chaos. As we drove through the remnants of the storm, the landscape shifted around us, from the serene beauty of the countryside to the grim reality of the city. The streetlights flickered in and out of focus, casting haunting shadows on the pavement, and I couldn't shake the feeling that eyes were watching us, hidden behind the veil of normalcy.

"What do you think is going to happen next?" I asked, breaking the silence that had settled like a thick fog.

Hunter's lips curved into a wry smile. "More of the unexpected, I imagine. Isn't that how life works? You think you're in control, and then it pulls the rug out from under you."

I couldn't help but laugh, despite the gravity of our situation. "Well, at least we can be prepared for chaos."

"Or we can embrace it," he said, his grin infectious. "Sometimes chaos is where the best stories are born."

As we navigated the twisting streets, I couldn't help but feel a swell of something I hadn't expected—hope. Beneath the uncertainty lay a thrilling undercurrent, one that seemed to pulse in time with my racing heart. The storm had stripped away the facade, and now we stood on the precipice of something new.

But as we turned the corner, a figure emerged from the shadows. The air grew thick with tension, and an uneasy silence enveloped us, the promise of danger looming just beyond the edge of the streetlight's glow.

The figure standing at the edge of the streetlight's glow wasn't just a figment of my overactive imagination; it was real, and it radiated an energy that sent a shiver down my spine. A tall man, cloaked in shadows, his features obscured but his posture tense and alert, he seemed like a specter materializing from the remnants of our chaotic night.

"Stop the car," Hunter instructed, his voice low and urgent, piercing through the thick silence that had enveloped us.

"What? Why?" I shot back, anxiety creeping into my tone as I gripped the steering wheel. The urge to bolt was strong, but curiosity anchored me in place.

"Because I think that's our friend from the other night," he replied, his eyes narrowing as he studied the stranger.

My heart raced. The last encounter had left me rattled; I still felt the echoes of that confrontation in my bones. "Are you sure? What if it's not him? What if it's worse?"

"Trust me," he said, the intensity in his gaze locking onto mine. "If it's who I think it is, we need answers."

I took a deep breath, the weight of his words settling heavily on my chest, and slowly pressed the brakes. The tires squealed softly against the damp pavement, and I felt the car lurch to a stop. The figure shifted, taking a cautious step toward us, revealing a face both familiar and unsettling.

"Do you two always stop to chat with shady strangers?" he asked, a hint of sarcasm lacing his words. The moonlight caught his features—sharp cheekbones, tousled hair, and an expression that straddled amusement and irritation. It was the man from that night, a face I hadn't expected to see again, yet here he was, leaning against my driver's side door as if he owned the street.

"You've got a knack for timing," Hunter replied, his voice steady despite the tension crackling in the air.

"Yeah, well, I'd hate to miss out on all the fun," the stranger shot back, a smirk dancing on his lips. "And believe me, it seems like you two have had quite the whirlwind. Care to fill me in?"

I exchanged a glance with Hunter, feeling the electricity between us. This was no ordinary encounter; this was the beginning of something that could either illuminate our path or throw us into deeper shadows. "We don't have time for games. We're looking for answers," I said, my tone firmer than I felt.

"Answers?" The stranger chuckled softly, his amusement palpable. "You're diving into a pool of secrets, sweetheart. The deeper you go, the murkier it gets. Are you sure you want to wade in?"

"What do you know?" Hunter pressed, his voice edged with impatience. "This isn't a joke. People's lives are at stake."

"Tell me about it," he replied, his smile fading as a flicker of seriousness crossed his face. "But first, let's step away from the car. It's not safe here."

"Not safe?" I echoed, incredulity seeping into my words. "You're the one who just popped out of nowhere!"

"Precisely," he replied, and with a wave of his hand, gestured us to follow. "You'd be surprised at how many eyes are on you right now."

Against my better judgment, I turned off the engine and climbed out of the car, Hunter closely following behind me. The air felt charged, thick with an unnameable tension. We trailed behind the stranger as he led us to a secluded alleyway, far from prying eyes. The sounds of the city faded, replaced by the soft rustle of leaves and the distant hum of life continuing obliviously around us.

"Alright, spill it," Hunter urged, crossing his arms defensively as he stood beside me. "What do you know about the threats we're facing?"

"More than you think," the stranger replied, leaning against the wall, arms crossed casually as if discussing the weather instead of life and death. "My name's Asher, and trust me, you're both in deep. This isn't just a game; it's personal."

"Personal how?" I demanded, frustration bubbling just beneath the surface.

Asher glanced around, his demeanor shifting slightly as if he sensed someone watching. "You don't know the half of it. You're linked to something much larger than you realize. Your family's history, Hunter's... it all intertwines. Someone wants to keep you in the dark for a reason."

"Then enlighten us," I shot back, desperate for clarity.

"I can't just lay it all out. You need to trust me. But you're both in danger, and the clock is ticking." His gaze darted to the street, and I could see a flicker of fear behind his bravado. "There are eyes everywhere, and if you want to uncover the truth, you'll need allies—real allies."

"Who?" Hunter interjected, his voice cutting through the mounting tension. "You expect us to trust you just because you showed up?"

"Fair point," Asher conceded with a half-shrug. "But I'm not the enemy. You'll want to connect with those who know the game better. The underground is alive with whispers. Seek out Aveline; she knows more than anyone else."

"Aveline?" I repeated, the name tinged with a mix of curiosity and skepticism. "Why her?"

"She's been around long enough to have seen it all. She can help you navigate the mess you've stumbled into. But be careful—she doesn't take kindly to amateurs."

Hunter shot me a sidelong glance, a silent conversation passing between us. "And if we refuse?"

"Then you play into the hands of those who want to silence you," Asher replied, his tone grave. "Your choice, but I wouldn't dilly-dally. You've already drawn attention, and it won't be long before they come for you again."

Asher's words hung heavily in the air, and as we exchanged apprehensive glances, the reality of our situation settled in. This was no longer just about uncovering secrets; it was about survival. I felt a sense of urgency gripping me, but alongside it, a flicker of something unexpected—a strange exhilaration at the thought of venturing into the unknown, of digging deeper into the chaos that had become my life.

"Alright," I said, taking a deep breath, a mix of trepidation and resolve coursing through me. "We'll find Aveline."

"Good choice," Asher replied, a sly grin returning to his face. "But remember, the truth has a way of revealing itself in the most unexpected places. Just be ready for what you uncover."

With that, he stepped back into the shadows, leaving us standing at the brink of a new reality, our fates entwined in a web of secrets, danger, and an undeniable bond forged in the fire of shared peril.

The shadows from the alley swallowed us whole as Asher melted back into the darkness, leaving Hunter and me standing in a world that felt simultaneously larger and more confined. The distant hum of the city faded, replaced by the rhythmic thump of my heart. My mind raced with a medley of questions, doubts, and a flickering hope that perhaps this Aveline could shed some light on the chaos swirling around us.

"Do you think we can trust him?" Hunter asked, his voice low, filled with that familiar mix of caution and intrigue. I noticed how the tension in his shoulders relaxed slightly, as if the act of asking had freed him, if only a little.

"Trust is a luxury we can't afford," I replied, the wryness in my tone masking my own uncertainty. "But he does seem to know more than we do. That has to count for something, right?"

"True," Hunter admitted, his eyes scanning the street. "But this Aveline... do we have any idea where to find her?"

I thought for a moment, the gears in my brain churning. "Asher mentioned the underground. Maybe we should check out the old market on Willow Street. It's known for being a hotspot for anything off the grid."

"Sounds like a plan," he said, already moving toward the car. The familiar weight of dread settled back in my stomach, but there was a flicker of excitement buried beneath it. The thrill of stepping into the unknown tugged at me, an adrenaline rush I hadn't felt in too long.

The drive to Willow Street was quiet, punctuated only by the low rumble of the engine and the soft hum of tires on asphalt. I couldn't help but steal glances at Hunter, who sat in the passenger seat, his brow furrowed in thought. There was an intensity about him, a fierce determination that sent my heart racing and my thoughts tumbling into a chaotic mix of admiration and something deeper.

As we pulled into the parking lot of the old market, I couldn't shake the feeling that we were about to step into a world beyond our understanding. The air crackled with anticipation, thick with the scent of spices, damp earth, and a hint of something metallic that made me instinctively shiver.

The market bustled with life, vendors shouting over one another, hawking their wares. Lanterns hung from the rafters, casting warm, flickering light that danced across the rough-hewn wooden stalls. Everything felt alive—alive and teeming with secrets.

"Stick close," Hunter said, his voice low and firm as we stepped out of the car. "We don't know who we can trust here."

"Trust issues seem to be the theme of the day," I quipped, attempting to inject some levity into the mounting tension.

"Consider it a necessary survival skill," he replied with a smirk that did little to quell my rising unease.

We moved through the crowd, our senses assaulted by the vibrant chaos around us. A woman selling handmade trinkets caught my eye, her fingers expertly weaving bright threads into delicate patterns. A man nearby offered steaming cups of something fragrant, his smile wide as he beckoned passersby to indulge. Yet, beneath this vibrant surface lay an undercurrent of something darker, a whisper of danger threading through the fabric of everyday life.

"Where do we even start?" I asked, feeling a twinge of uncertainty creeping in.

"Let's ask around. Aveline should have a reputation; someone here will know her," Hunter suggested, scanning the crowd.

As we moved deeper into the market, we approached a stall piled high with various artifacts—a jumble of old books, strange charms, and glass orbs that sparkled enticingly. The vendor, a wiry man with a scraggly beard, looked up as we approached, his eyes flickering with curiosity.

"Looking for something special?" he asked, his tone friendly but with an edge that suggested he was well-acquainted with the business of secrets.

"We're searching for Aveline," Hunter said, cutting straight to the chase. "Do you know where we can find her?"

The vendor's expression shifted, his friendly facade momentarily slipping. "Aveline? You'd do well to tread carefully when asking about her. Not everyone in these parts appreciates curiosity."

I felt Hunter stiffen beside me, a muscle in his jaw tightening as he leaned forward. "We're not here to cause trouble. We need her help."

"Help? Everyone needs help until they realize they don't want to pay the price." The vendor's eyes glimmered, his smile stretching thin as he gestured to a darkened corner of the market. "If you insist on seeking her out, you'll find her down there. Just remember, once you enter her world, there's no turning back."

"Great, more ominous warnings," I muttered under my breath, sharing an incredulous glance with Hunter.

"Let's go," he said, determination evident in his stride as we moved toward the suggested path. The shadows loomed larger as we turned the corner, the market's cheerful noise fading into a muted hum.

As we descended deeper into the bowels of the market, the air thickened with tension. The passage was dimly lit, and I felt a cold shiver of apprehension race down my spine. "Is it just me, or does this place feel like the setting of a horror movie?" I whispered, trying to mask my unease with humor.

"Just keep your eyes open," Hunter replied, his voice steady. "We're getting closer."

The corridor opened up into a small, dimly lit room, where the atmosphere shifted dramatically. Aveline sat at a table in the corner, her back to us, surrounded by an array of curious artifacts—bones, crystals, and tattered books that seemed to pulse with an energy all their own. She exuded a presence that was both commanding and unsettling, the kind that made you acutely aware of your own heartbeat.

"Welcome," she said without turning, her voice smooth and laced with intrigue. "I've been expecting you."

My breath caught in my throat, and I exchanged a glance with Hunter, who looked equally taken aback. "You have?" I asked, my voice barely a whisper.

"Oh yes," she replied, finally turning to face us. Her eyes glimmered with a knowing light, as if she could see the very essence of our struggles. "You've stirred the waters, and now you must navigate the currents."

Just as the tension in the room peaked, the faint sound of footsteps echoed behind us, drawing closer. My heart raced, the instinct to flee tugging at me, but the door suddenly slammed shut, trapping us inside.

"What the hell?" I gasped, turning to Hunter, whose expression had shifted from curiosity to alarm.

Aveline's lips curled into a knowing smile, the kind that sent a shiver down my spine. "You've attracted attention, and now it's time to confront the shadows lurking in the corners of your lives."

Before I could process her words, the door rattled violently, and I realized that we were no longer just seekers of truth; we were now prey in a game far larger than we had anticipated.

Chapter 9: Shadows of the Past

The damp chill of autumn settled over Firestone Bay like a heavy shroud, its presence felt in the way the trees bowed under the weight of their fiery leaves. I had always adored this season—its vibrant hues, the smell of woodsmoke drifting through the air, and the promise of new beginnings tinged with nostalgia. Yet, this year, something felt different. The air carried an unease, a whisper of danger that stirred my instincts. As I walked along the winding path that hugged the shoreline, the waves crashed against the rocks, their fury matching the tumult inside me.

Hunter walked beside me, his stride long and purposeful, a stark contrast to the uncertainty brewing within my heart. The light from the setting sun painted the horizon in shades of gold and crimson, illuminating his features in a way that made my breath hitch. He glanced at me, his expression a mix of concern and determination. "You okay?" he asked, his voice low and comforting, like a warm blanket against the cool breeze.

"Yeah," I replied, forcing a smile that didn't quite reach my eyes. "Just thinking." The truth was, I was drowning in thoughts—dark, swirling currents that threatened to pull me under. The journal I had discovered among my father's belongings lay heavily in my bag, its pages filled with cryptic notes and half-formed ideas about a legend that seemed to haunt Firestone Bay like a specter.

As we reached a rocky outcrop, I stopped, my gaze drifting to the turbulent sea. "Do you believe in ghosts?" I asked suddenly, the question hanging in the air between us like an uninvited guest.

Hunter shrugged, his hands shoved deep into the pockets of his worn jacket. "Depends on the ghost. If it's just some sad soul looking for closure, I can get that. But if it's a vengeful spirit...that's another story." His eyes sparkled with mischief, a hint of his usual humor returning. "I prefer my ghosts to be the friendly type, you know? Maybe one who can help me with my math homework."

A laugh escaped me, but it quickly faded as memories of my father flooded my mind. "My dad wrote about a spirit. He thought it was connected to our family, something...terrible that happened long ago." The words slipped out before I could stop them, their weight heavy in the air.

"What do you mean?" Hunter stepped closer, his interest piqued, the lightheartedness replaced with a gravity that mirrored my own.

I took a deep breath, the salty air filling my lungs, grounding me. "There's this legend about a figure that haunts Firestone Bay, seeking vengeance for wrongs that were never made right. It's like...a curse, I guess. My father believed it was tied to his past." I fished the journal out of my bag, its leather cover worn and cracked, the edges frayed from time. As I opened it, a chill prickled at my skin. "He wrote about it in detail, almost like he was trying to warn me."

Hunter leaned over to read the pages, his brow furrowing as he scanned the neat handwriting. "This is...intense. Your dad seemed to think it was more than just a local myth."

"Yeah. He believed it was real. And I can't shake the feeling that whatever happened back then is somehow connected to his death." My voice trembled slightly, the weight of my father's unsolved murder pressing down on me like a stone. "I need to know the truth, Hunter. I need to understand why he wrote this."

"I'll help you." His response was immediate, firm. "Whatever it takes, we'll figure this out together."

I looked at him, gratitude washing over me like a wave. Hunter had a way of making me feel less alone in the face of the unknown, a lifeline in a sea of confusion. But even with his support, an unsettling sense of dread curled around my heart. What if uncovering the past only led to more pain?

The sun dipped below the horizon, casting long shadows that danced over the rocks, and I felt an inexplicable pull toward the darkened woods that lined the path back home. "There's something about the woods," I murmured, the words escaping before I could catch them. "They seem to call to me, like they're hiding something."

Hunter followed my gaze, his expression serious. "We should be careful. The forest is full of stories, both good and bad. It's where the legend began, isn't it?"

"Exactly." The thought sent a shiver down my spine, igniting a flicker of courage within me. "Maybe we need to go there, to uncover the truth."

With a nod, we began our trek toward the looming trees, their branches swaying like skeletal fingers in the twilight. The air thickened around us, and the sounds of the ocean faded into a haunting silence, leaving only the crunch of leaves beneath our feet. I clutched the journal tightly, its pages whispering secrets of the past, the shadows of forgotten memories lurking just beyond the trees.

As we crossed into the forest, a sudden rustle sent my heart racing. My breath quickened, and I turned to Hunter, whose eyes were sharp and alert. "Did you hear that?"

"Yeah." He paused, scanning the darkness. "Stay close."

I nodded, my heart pounding in sync with the crunch of twigs underfoot. Whatever lay ahead, I knew we were no longer just uncovering the past; we were stepping into a tale woven with danger, secrets, and perhaps even ghosts. The woods closed in around us, shadows deepening, and I couldn't shake the feeling that the past was waiting for us, eager to reclaim its hold.

The woods enveloped us like a thick fog, the dense trees towering above, their branches interlocking like fingers in a secret handshake. Shadows danced around us, twisting and curling as the last remnants of daylight faded into the horizon. I could feel the weight of history pressing down, the stories whispered among the rustling leaves echoing my father's words from the journal. Every step I took felt like a summons, a call to unearth truths long buried beneath layers of time and silence.

Hunter walked just a step behind me, his presence a comforting anchor amidst the gathering darkness. "I think I left my flashlight in the car," he quipped, a slight grin playing on his lips as he tried to lighten the mood. "But hey, what's a little darkness when you've got a journal filled with ghost stories?"

"Quite the adventure you're signing up for," I shot back, managing a small laugh despite the tension coiling in my stomach. "What if we encounter a vengeful spirit that demands a dance-off? You better be prepared to show off those moves you've been hiding."

He chuckled softly, but his eyes betrayed a flicker of seriousness. "As long as it doesn't end with us becoming its minions, I'll risk it."

As we moved deeper into the forest, the sounds of nature faded, replaced by an unsettling stillness that prickled at the back of my neck. I could feel the air shift, heavy with unspoken stories and unshed tears, and I wondered if we were being watched. The thought sent a shiver racing down my spine, and I wrapped my arms around myself, seeking comfort in the warmth of my jacket.

The path wound ahead, barely visible under the thick blanket of fallen leaves. Each crunch beneath our feet echoed, a reminder of our intrusion into a world that had remained untouched for far too long. I thought about the legends I'd read in my father's journal—about the spirit that roamed these woods, seeking retribution against those who had wronged it. The chilling tale gnawed at my thoughts, weaving its way into my imagination, each twist more vivid than the last.

"Do you think the stories are true?" I asked, breaking the silence that hung between us like a weight. "About the spirit?"

"Honestly? I'd say there's usually a grain of truth in every ghost story," Hunter replied, his tone turning thoughtful. "People don't just make up legends for the sake of it. There's always a reason behind them. Whether it's a tragic event or a dark family secret, something has to fuel the fire."

The moon began to rise, casting an ethereal glow that filtered through the treetops, illuminating the path ahead. I could almost hear the whisper of the past, calling to me from the depths of the forest. "Maybe we're not just looking for the truth about my dad," I mused aloud. "Maybe we're looking for something bigger. Something that could change everything."

"Or get us into serious trouble," Hunter countered, a smirk tugging at his lips. "But hey, I'm all in for an adventure, as long as it doesn't involve us becoming ghost snacks."

I rolled my eyes but couldn't help but smile. "You're impossible."

Suddenly, a rustling noise cut through our banter, snapping me to attention. My heart raced as I turned to face the direction of the sound, my breath catching in my throat. "Did you hear that?"

Hunter nodded, his playful demeanor vanishing. "Yeah, I did."

We stood still, the tension thickening around us. I held my breath, listening intently. The rustling continued, growing closer, sending my heart thudding louder in my chest. I could feel a rush of adrenaline surging through my veins, the fight-or-flight instinct igniting within me.

"Maybe it's just a deer," I suggested, trying to reassure myself.

"Or a rabid raccoon," Hunter added, his voice low.

"Let's hope for the deer," I whispered, my eyes wide as I scanned the darkness. Just as I was about to suggest we move back toward the safety of the path, a figure emerged from the shadows. My heart dropped as I recognized the unmistakable silhouette of a person.

"What are you doing here?" came a voice that sent a chill down my spine. It was Ava, a girl from my school who always seemed to orbit around trouble like a moth to a flame. She stepped closer, her dark hair framing her face, a wild look in her eyes. "You two shouldn't be out here. It's dangerous."

"Dangerous? Like vengeful spirits dangerous?" Hunter asked, his tone laced with disbelief.

"Something like that." Ava's eyes darted around, as if she were scanning the trees for hidden threats. "This place has a reputation. You really don't want to get mixed up in it."

"What do you know about it?" I pressed, my curiosity piqued despite the unease bubbling within me.

Ava smirked, clearly enjoying the attention. "Let's just say my family has a long history with Firestone Bay. Things aren't always as they seem, and some stories are better left untold."

Hunter stepped closer, his protective instinct kicking in. "Are you saying you know something about the spirit?"

"Maybe I do. Maybe I don't." She crossed her arms defiantly. "But if you're looking for answers, you might want to consider that you're digging in places best left alone."

"Why do you care?" I shot back, frustration rising within me. "What's your angle in all of this?"

Ava's expression shifted, a flicker of vulnerability crossing her face before it hardened again. "I just don't want you to end up like... well, like others who've come here. People disappear, you know? They're drawn in by the stories and never return."

Hunter glanced at me, his expression filled with concern. "We need to go. This isn't a game."

I hesitated, torn between my desire for answers and the warning ringing in my ears. But the lingering pull of the forest, combined with Ava's cryptic words, made it impossible to walk away now. "Wait," I said, "if there's something you know, tell us."

Ava sighed, her bravado fading slightly. "Fine. Just... promise me you'll be careful. This spirit, it isn't just a story. There's something real behind it. And if you awaken it, you might not be able to put it back to sleep."

A knot twisted in my stomach as her words sank in. Hunter's hand brushed against mine, grounding me in the moment. "We'll be careful," I assured her, though I felt anything but confident. "But we have to know the truth."

"Then let's see what the darkness holds," Ava said, her tone shifting from caution to intrigue. She stepped back, motioning for us to follow. "Just remember, once you start digging, there's no turning back."

And with that, we plunged deeper into the shadows, the trees closing in around us, each step taking us further from safety and deeper into the tangled web of Firestone Bay's haunting past.

The deeper we ventured into the woods, the more the atmosphere thickened, transforming from mere shadows into tangible whispers of a past that refused to remain buried. The night wrapped itself around us like a heavy cloak, and I could feel the forest pulsating with a life of its own. The air grew colder, sending a shiver down my spine as I glanced at Hunter, whose steady presence felt like a fragile lifeline.

"Are you sure this is a good idea?" he asked, his tone a mixture of concern and curiosity as he followed Ava, who led us deeper along the barely discernible path. The leaves crunched beneath our feet, each sound amplifying the tension coiling in my chest.

"I don't know, but we can't turn back now," I replied, my resolve hardening. "Not when there's so much at stake."

Ava turned to face us, her expression shifting from playful to serious. "Just remember, this isn't a fairy tale. What you're looking for isn't just answers; it could bring things back that should stay in the dark."

"Like a grumpy ghost with a vendetta?" Hunter quipped, trying to inject a bit of levity. "Sounds like a bad sequel to a horror movie."

"More like the plot of a horror movie that needs a better script," Ava shot back, her eyes glinting with mischief. "But really, you don't understand. People have been hurt—things happen that aren't easily explained."

As we trudged deeper into the underbrush, the trees began to close in around us, their gnarled roots twisting like the very secrets we were trying to unravel. The moonlight filtered through the branches, casting eerie patterns on the forest floor, and for a moment, I could almost imagine I heard a soft, mournful wail drifting through the air. I shivered and glanced at Hunter, who met my gaze with a look of determination.

"Stay close," he murmured, his voice low, almost protective.

We rounded a bend, and there it was—a clearing bathed in the silver glow of the moon, at its center a massive stone altar overgrown with ivy and moss, ancient and foreboding. It looked like something out of a legend, a place where sacrifices might have been made. My heart raced as I approached it, the journal's pages flipping through my mind like a whirlwind, detailing how this very altar had been the site of an unspeakable act decades ago.

"This is it," I whispered, awed and terrified. "This is where it all began."

Ava stepped forward, examining the altar. "This is where the stories say the spirit was bound. Whatever happened here ties directly to the curse." Her voice dropped to a whisper, filled with a reverence that sent chills coursing through me. "People who came seeking answers often vanished without a trace. It's as if the forest simply absorbed them."

"Absorbed them?" I repeated incredulously. "You can't be serious."

She nodded, her expression grave. "The woods have a way of taking what they want. They're alive in a way most don't understand."

Hunter scanned the clearing, his brows furrowing as he took in the unsettling scenery. "I'm beginning to think we should've brought snacks instead of ghost stories."

A soft laugh escaped me, but it quickly faded when I caught sight of something shimmering in the moonlight, half-buried among the roots of the altar. I knelt to investigate, brushing aside leaves and dirt until my fingers brushed against cold metal. I pulled it free, revealing an ornate locket, intricately designed with a pattern that seemed eerily familiar.

"Look at this," I said, holding it up for them to see. "It must belong to someone from the town."

Ava's eyes widened as she stepped closer, her expression a mix of awe and recognition. "That's—" She paused, as if weighing her words. "That belonged to Eliza Harrington, one of the first victims of the curse. She disappeared on her wedding day, right here in this clearing."

The air turned electric as the implications settled over us like a heavy fog. "Do you think it could be a clue?" I asked, turning the locket over in my hands, a sense of dread coiling in my stomach. "What if she's still here? What if she's the spirit?"

Hunter reached out to take the locket, examining it closely. "If Eliza was drawn here and her locket ended up buried at the altar, maybe she was trying to send a message. Maybe she's looking for help."

Ava's expression shifted, concern washing over her features. "But what if she's not? What if she's trapped? Or worse, what if whatever bound her here is still waiting for others?"

Suddenly, a gust of wind swept through the clearing, causing the trees to sway and creak ominously. The sound echoed like a warning, and I felt an instinctual urge to flee, but my feet felt rooted to the ground. Hunter tightened his grip on my arm, his presence anchoring me.

"We can't leave now," I insisted, my voice shaking. "We have to find out what this means. It's too big to ignore."

"Okay, but let's not summon a vengeful ghost in the process," Hunter replied, his eyes darting around, wary of the encroaching shadows.

Ava knelt beside me, her expression transforming from apprehension to determination. "If Eliza is still here, we need to find out how to help her. The journal might have more clues, something we can use to understand what happened."

As I rummaged through my bag for my father's journal, the ground beneath us trembled slightly, a low rumble that seemed to come from the very heart of the earth. I froze, my breath hitching in my throat as the noise intensified, resonating through my bones. The trees groaned, and the shadows thickened, swirling around us like dark smoke.

"Did you feel that?" I gasped, my pulse racing.

Hunter nodded, his expression serious. "We need to go. Now."

Just then, a figure emerged from the darkness, silhouetted against the moonlight. My heart raced, panic flooding my veins. It was too late to escape.

"Who dares disturb the past?" The voice was low and haunting, reverberating through the clearing. It sent chills cascading down my spine, freezing me in place.

I glanced at Hunter, whose eyes were wide with shock and fear, and Ava, who seemed to have turned into a statue, her expression a mix of terror and recognition.

"Run!" Hunter shouted, breaking the spell.

But before we could react, the figure stepped forward, revealing a pale face with hauntingly familiar features. "You should not have come here. You've awakened what was meant to remain asleep."

A scream tore through the stillness of the night, a scream that didn't come from any of us. Instead, it echoed around us, merging with the sound of the wind, engulfing us in a chorus of despair.

And in that moment, standing at the edge of an ancient truth, I realized the past wasn't just alive—it was hungry.

Chapter 10: Unearthed Memories

The journal led me to old photographs, faded snapshots of a happier time that suddenly felt tainted. Each image whispered stories of laughter and sun-drenched days, yet now they hung heavy in the air, their innocence tainted by the specter of lost moments. I had stumbled upon this trove of memories hidden beneath a loose floorboard in my grandmother's attic, a treasure that felt more like a curse. The sepia-toned faces grinned back at me, their joy stark against my present reality. Each photograph pulled at my heart, memories long buried beginning to resurface like tides creeping up the shore.

As I shared my discoveries with Hunter, an unspoken understanding passed between us, threading our fates together in a way that felt both thrilling and terrifying. He had become an unexpected confidant, a light in the shadowy corners of my mind. His dark hair tousled in the ocean breeze, and those striking eyes seemed to reflect the very depth of the sea itself. As we walked side by side, the weight of our shared history, both the painful and the joyous, settled around us, binding us tighter with every step.

The old lighthouse stood like a sentinel, a local landmark steeped in lore, its crumbling stones bathed in a golden glow as the sun began its descent. This was a place of secrets, its walls echoing the voices of those who had come before, each whisper resonating with the tales of lost sailors and unrequited loves. The salty air buzzed with unspoken tension as we approached, the sound of the waves crashing against the rocks below mingling with the pounding of my heart.

"Do you believe in ghosts?" Hunter asked, breaking the silence, his voice low and teasing. The corner of his mouth curled into a smile, a hint of mischief glimmering in his eyes.

"Only if they're charming and dashing," I replied, my own grin breaking through the weight of nostalgia. "Otherwise, they can keep their haunting to themselves."

He chuckled, the sound warming the cool evening air, and I caught a glimpse of the boy he once was—a carefree spirit before life's harsh realities had begun to weigh us down. We continued our ascent, the winding staircase spiraling upwards, each step a mixture of anticipation and dread. The walls were rough against my fingertips, a reminder of the passage of time that had weathered both the lighthouse and our souls.

As we climbed higher, the salty breeze wrapped around us, the scent of brine and the promise of rain lingering just out of reach. The higher we ascended, the more the weight of our emotions bore down on us, an electric current charging the atmosphere. We reached the lantern room, the glass panes glimmering in the fading light, and stepped out onto the balcony. Standing at the edge, overlooking the turbulent sea, I felt a rush of exhilaration and fear mingling in my chest. The waves roared below, wild and untamed, mirroring the storm brewing inside me.

"Can you hear it?" Hunter leaned against the railing, his eyes locked onto the horizon, where the sun dipped low, casting a fiery orange hue over the restless waves. "It's as if the ocean is calling, isn't it?"

I nodded, captivated by the beauty and the chaos before us. But as the light began to wane, I became aware of an unsettling sensation, a prickle at the back of my neck. Just as I leaned closer to Hunter, drawn to the warmth radiating from him like the sun, a shadow passed over the lighthouse, darkening the vibrant scene before me. My heart raced, a chill creeping down my spine as I turned, scanning the surroundings.

"What is it?" Hunter asked, his voice barely above a whisper, eyes narrowing as he searched for the source of my unease.

"I... I don't know," I stammered, a tangle of instinct and dread coiling in my gut. The shadow had vanished, leaving nothing but the wind whipping around us, yet the feeling of being watched lingered like a ghost.

"Let's get inside," he suggested, an edge to his tone now. I could see the flicker of concern in his eyes, a mirror to my own trepidation. We stepped back into the safety of the lighthouse, but the sense of vulnerability clung to us like a second skin.

Inside, the air was thick with history, the kind of weight that settled deep in your bones. As I turned to Hunter, our gazes locked, and an unspoken question passed between us. Did he feel it too? The magnetic pull of connection that had surged between us in the lighthouse's embrace, now undercut by the fear that slithered beneath the surface?

"What do you think it was?" I asked, trying to break the tension, but my voice trembled slightly, betraying my efforts to sound casual.

Hunter shrugged, his expression a mixture of curiosity and concern. "Could be nothing, or it could be the spirits keeping an eye on us. I'd say we're not the only ones who've come here to unearth memories."

"Charming," I replied, my tone sarcastic, but inside I felt a shiver of acknowledgment. Memories, after all, can haunt just as much as any specter. The past has a way of creeping into the present, reshaping what we thought we knew. "Let's not stay too long, then."

As we descended the stairs, the weight of unvoiced fears hung between us. The lighthouse, once a beacon of adventure, now felt like a labyrinth of our entangled pasts, leading us into a darkness we were not yet ready to face. I could feel the threads of our history weaving together, a tapestry of light and shadow, and I knew that whatever lurked outside, watching and waiting, was merely a reflection of the choices we had yet to make.

As we retreated from the balcony, the lighthouse's walls felt like they were closing in, heavy with unspoken words and unshared fears. The dim glow of the old lantern cast elongated shadows, flickering like the doubts swirling in my mind. I caught a glimpse of Hunter as he turned, his profile illuminated against the soft light. His brow furrowed in contemplation, a mix of intrigue and apprehension playing across his features. It struck me how utterly captivating he was, even in moments of uncertainty.

"I think it's haunted," I said, forcing a lightness into my voice that felt brittle at best. "Or at least, I'm haunted by the possibility of ghosts. Not exactly what I signed up for on this little adventure."

He chuckled softly, the sound a warm balm against the chilling atmosphere. "Or maybe it's just the lighthouse trying to keep its secrets. They say it's a guardian of sorts, protecting the coast from... well, everything."

"Like bad decisions?" I quipped, nudging him lightly. "I could use a guardian for that."

Our laughter echoed through the narrow space, a brief respite from the tension that had settled like dust. But as we moved deeper into the lighthouse, I felt the shadows loom larger around us. They whispered of past choices, regrets that threatened to resurface. I glanced back toward the stairs, half-expecting to see a figure lingering just out of sight, a specter from the stories I had heard growing up.

Hunter followed my gaze, sensing the shift in my mood. "You're not still thinking about that shadow, are you?"

"Not at all," I lied, forcing a casual smile. "Just considering the charm of your average haunted lighthouse. Who doesn't love a little ambiance?"

"Ambiance that could potentially kill us? Sounds delightful." He raised an eyebrow, the corner of his mouth twitching with amusement.

"Now you're just trying to freak me out," I said, the lighthearted banter easing some of the heaviness. "But it's working."

He leaned in slightly, a conspiratorial gleam in his eye. "Fine, I'll take that as a compliment. But let's at least keep an eye out for any ghostly apparitions, shall we? I'd hate to think I had to rescue you from a vengeful spirit."

"Are you sure it wouldn't be the other way around?" I challenged, stepping closer to him, heart racing with an adrenaline that felt more electric than fearful.

He took a moment, studying me, and then laughed, a rich sound that resonated deeply within the stone walls. "You might be right. There's definitely a fire in you. Just promise you won't turn into a wraith if I get too close."

Our banter felt like a dance, a delicate step through the uncertainty swirling around us. I could sense the weight of the journal in my pocket, a physical reminder of the emotional labyrinth we were traversing. The words I had read earlier haunted me, echoing with tales of betrayal and love lost, intertwining my own experiences with the ghosts of those who had come before.

"Why do you think they say the lighthouse is haunted?" I asked, shifting the conversation as we made our way down the stairs, the old wood creaking underfoot.

Hunter paused, glancing back at me, his expression turning serious. "Some say it's because of the shipwrecks. Lives lost to the waves. But others think it's just the memories trapped here, like echoes of their last moments. A lighthouse is supposed to guide, but what happens when it can't?"

"Maybe it's a metaphor for life," I mused, letting the words linger in the air. "Guiding us through darkness, only for us to face our own storms."

He nodded, contemplative. "You know, I've never thought of it that way. It's a bit poetic, really."

"Who knew I had a hidden talent for deep philosophical insights?" I smirked, enjoying the playful banter but feeling the weight of truth in my own words. The lighthouse was a reflection of our own struggles, a beacon that sometimes flickered uncertainly against the tides of our lives.

As we reached the ground floor, the darkness outside had deepened, the horizon now a shadowy line against the turbulent sea. I shivered, not entirely from the chill that settled around us. "We should head back. It's getting late, and I'd rather not turn into a lighthouse ghost myself."

"Agreed. I'm not ready to face any supernatural drama tonight." Hunter held the door open for me, and I stepped outside, the cool breeze brushing against my skin.

But as we emerged into the evening air, the hair on the back of my neck stood on end. The sensation of being watched returned, sharper now, as if the shadows themselves were alive with intent. I turned, scanning the horizon, the salty wind whipping my hair around my face.

"Did you see that?" I blurted, heart pounding as I pointed into the distance.

Hunter squinted against the darkness, a frown creasing his brow. "See what?"

"There—by the cliff! A figure. I swear I saw someone."

His expression hardened, and he took a step closer to me, protective instincts igniting. "Are you sure? It could just be the shadows playing tricks on us."

"Maybe, but I don't think so. We should—"

Before I could finish, a low rumble echoed from the cliffs, reverberating in my chest. It was the sound of thunder, but it was followed by something else—a soft, almost melodic whispering, threading through the wind. The sensation of being observed intensified, an invisible gaze locking onto us with palpable intensity.

Hunter grasped my wrist, a grounding force. "Let's move. Now."
As we hurried down the path leading away from the lighthouse, the whispering grew louder, swirling around us like the tide. With each step, my heart raced, the sensation of danger mingling with the thrill of the unknown. Whatever had been lurking in the shadows was no longer just a figment of my imagination—it was real, and it was here.

We stumbled away from the lighthouse, the wind howling as if in protest against our reckless curiosity. I could still feel the lingering gaze of whatever—or whoever—had been lurking at the edge of our perception. Each gust of wind seemed to carry the whispers of secrets long buried, secrets that were not meant to be unearthed. Hunter's grip on my wrist tightened, a reassuring presence in the chaos of the evening. I could sense the tension rippling off him as we walked, the sense of urgency quickening our pace down the winding path.

"Do you think it was just a trick of the light?" I ventured, though I didn't believe my own words. The shiver running through me felt too real, too urgent to be dismissed as mere imagination.

"Honestly? I don't know," he replied, glancing over his shoulder as if expecting to see something—or someone—emerge from the shadows. "But I'd rather not stick around to find out."

His practicality was refreshing, but it only added to my sense of foreboding. The night closed in around us, the darkness settling like a heavy blanket, muffling our footsteps as we hurried toward the car parked on the gravel road. Each step echoed the rhythm of my racing heart, a percussion that harmonized with the distant roar of the ocean.

When we reached the car, I fumbled with the keys, my fingers trembling as I struggled to find the right one. The sudden thought of being alone in the vehicle, surrounded by the encroaching darkness, felt claustrophobic. "Do you ever wonder if we're just playing with forces we don't understand?" I asked, trying to mask my unease with humor. "You know, like kids poking a sleeping bear?"

Hunter's eyes danced with a mix of amusement and concern. "More like poking a grumpy old lighthouse spirit. But then again, I've never been one to shy away from an adventure, even a foolish one."

"Good to know. I'll make sure to list your courage as a plus when they come looking for you on a milk carton," I shot back, managing a smile despite the knot of anxiety in my stomach.

Once inside the car, I locked the doors instinctively, the click sounding louder than it should have. I turned the ignition, and the engine roared to life, drowning out the sound of the wind outside. As I navigated the road away from the lighthouse, I felt Hunter's gaze fixed on me, a silent question in the air.

"Are you okay?" he asked, his voice softening. "You seem... distant."

"Just processing," I replied, keeping my eyes on the winding road ahead. "This evening was... intense, to say the least."

"Intense is one word for it," he agreed, his tone lightening as he leaned back in his seat. "But I think we can handle a few ghost stories. What's the worst that could happen? A haunting or two?"

"Famous last words," I countered, unable to hide my smile. The banter was a welcome distraction, and I could feel the tension slowly ebbing. But just as I was beginning to relax, my headlights illuminated a figure standing by the side of the road, silhouetted against the deepening twilight.

I slammed on the brakes, the tires screeching as we came to a sudden halt. "What the—"

"Is that...?" Hunter leaned closer, squinting into the darkness.

As the headlights caught the figure, I realized it was a woman, standing motionless, her long hair cascading down her back like a dark waterfall. Her dress fluttered in the wind, ethereal and out of place, like a specter drawn to the edge of reality. My heart raced, and a chill crept up my spine.

"Should we help her?" Hunter asked, a mix of concern and curiosity in his voice.

"Are you out of your mind?" I exclaimed, my instincts screaming at me to drive away. "This isn't some romantic novel where we save the day. It could be dangerous!"

"But what if she needs help?" he argued, and there was a fervor in his gaze that sent my pulse racing. "What if she's lost?"

Reluctantly, I glanced back at the figure. There was something hauntingly familiar about her, a sense of recognition that tugged at the edges of my memory. I couldn't explain it, but I felt drawn to her like a moth to a flame. "Okay, but we need to be careful."

Hunter nodded, his expression resolute. I shifted the car into park, and with a deep breath, we both stepped outside, the cool night air wrapping around us. The figure remained still, her gaze fixed on the horizon, as if waiting for something—or someone.

"Excuse me!" I called out, trying to keep my voice steady despite the way my heart hammered in my chest. "Are you alright?"

At the sound of my voice, she turned slowly, her eyes glinting in the headlights like two shards of ice. "I've been waiting," she said, her voice soft yet carrying an echo that resonated with the night. "For you."

"For me?" I repeated, confusion curling in my stomach. "Why?"

"It's time to remember," she said, her gaze piercing through me, as if she could see the very depths of my soul. "You have questions that only I can answer."

The air crackled with tension, and I exchanged a wary glance with Hunter. He took a cautious step closer, his protective instincts kicking in. "What do you mean? Who are you?"

She tilted her head, an enigmatic smile playing on her lips. "A keeper of secrets, a guide for those who seek the truth. You both have ventured into shadows that were never meant for you."

"What shadows?" I asked, my voice barely above a whisper, dread curling within me like smoke.

Before she could respond, a sudden rustling from the nearby bushes broke the moment, and I instinctively took a step back, the sense of being watched flooding back. "Did you hear that?" I asked, panic rising.

Hunter nodded, tension radiating off him. "Yeah, we should—"

But before he could finish, the woman took a step forward, her expression shifting from serene to urgent. "Run!" she shouted.

In an instant, everything changed. The world around us blurred as the shadows lengthened and twisted, the air thickening with an oppressive force. I grabbed Hunter's hand, and together we dashed back toward the car, the chilling realization settling over us like a cloak. Whatever had been lurking in the darkness wasn't just a figment of our imagination. It was real, and it was coming for us.

Chapter 11: Unwelcome Guests

The sun hung low in the sky, casting a golden hue over the weathered rooftops of Silverbrook as Hunter and I stepped out of the car. The warm breeze carried a hint of salt and adventure, but as we approached the familiar curve of my street, an icy dread curled around my stomach. It was the unmistakable scent of chaos; the kind that wrapped itself around your heart and squeezed.

"Something feels off," Hunter said, his voice low, almost drowned out by the rustling leaves. His eyes darted toward the shadows creeping in from the corners of the street, a darkness I had not noticed until he pointed it out. I nodded, clutching the strap of my bag tighter, wishing it could somehow shield me from the impending storm.

Our front door stood ajar, swinging slightly in the breeze like an eerie invitation into the unknown. I felt my breath hitch in my throat. "This isn't right," I whispered, almost to myself. Panic pooled in my chest, thickening my blood. Hunter moved closer, his protective presence wrapping around me like a warm coat in winter. It was comforting yet unsettling, a reminder of how our lives had intertwined in this chaos.

As we stepped inside, the world I had known crumbled before my eyes. The living room was a disaster zone—cushions overturned, drawers yanked open, and photographs scattered like fallen leaves on the hardwood floor. My heart sank at the sight of my mother's prized vase, shattered into a mosaic of porcelain shards. "No..." I breathed, feeling an ache in my chest that echoed the loss. "Who would do this?"

Hunter's hand found mine, squeezing tightly as if to ground me. "We need to figure this out. Whoever did this is sending a message." His voice was steady, and I envied his calm in the face of chaos. But as I looked into his eyes, I noticed a flicker of something deeper, something that went beyond just concern for my safety. The moment lingered between us, charged with unspoken words and unacknowledged feelings, before reality snapped us back into focus.

"We should check the rest of the house," I said, tearing my gaze away from his. Each room we passed revealed more devastation, the disarray a cruel reflection of our lives turned upside down. The kitchen was the worst—cabinets flung open, the contents strewn across the floor, a jumbled mess of what was once familiar. A chilling thought raced through my mind: whoever had done this was looking for something specific.

"Did you leave anything out?" Hunter asked, stepping carefully around a broken dish.

"Just some notes," I replied, my voice barely above a whisper. The notes contained my research about the lighthouse, the secrets I had unearthed, the truth that had felt so precarious until this moment. "But I didn't think they were important."

Hunter's brow furrowed, his mind clearly racing. "Clearly, someone thinks they are."

We made our way to the basement, my heart pounding louder with each step. The dim light flickered overhead, casting erratic shadows that danced across the walls. It felt as if the very air was thick with secrets, hiding from us just out of reach. When we reached the bottom, I hesitated, the darkness swallowing us whole.

"Are you sure we should..." I started, but Hunter cut me off, his determination unwavering.

"If they're looking for something, it's probably down here." He stepped forward, his body a shield against the encroaching darkness. With him leading the way, I felt a surge of courage, a shared resolve that made the chill of fear recede, if only for a moment.

The basement held remnants of the past—old boxes filled with dusty memories and the scent of mildew that whispered stories long forgotten. Hunter began sifting through a pile of cardboard, tossing aside old toys and clothes. "Nothing here," he muttered, frustration lacing his tone.

I knelt beside him, my fingers brushing against a box labeled "Summer Projects." Inside, I found a collection of my childhood art supplies. "I used to think I could be an artist," I said with a wry smile, attempting to lighten the mood. "Turns out, I'm better at unraveling mysteries than painting sunsets."

Hunter chuckled, the sound a balm against the tension. "You've always had a knack for finding trouble."

"More like trouble finds me," I countered, meeting his gaze. There was a warmth in his eyes, a flicker of admiration that sent my heart racing. But before I could dwell on it, my fingers brushed against something sharp. I pulled back, revealing a small, crumpled note that seemed out of place among the art supplies.

"Wait, what's this?" I whispered, unfolding the note with trembling hands. The message was scrawled hastily in black ink, each letter jagged and angry.

You should have left well enough alone. The truth isn't for you to find.

A shiver crept down my spine. Hunter leaned closer, his breath warm against my ear as he read the words. "They're watching us," he said, the gravity of the situation sinking in.

I crumpled the note, a wave of anger flooding my veins. "Whoever did this won't stop until they silence us," I said, my voice firm, although uncertainty gnawed at the edges of my resolve. "But we can't let them win."

Hunter nodded, determination sparking in his eyes. "Together," he said simply, his voice steadying me as I processed the enormity of our situation. We were no longer just a girl and a boy caught in a web of secrets; we were allies, bound by the need to uncover the truth that threatened to consume us.

The intimacy of our shared resolve was palpable, and as we stood there, I felt the weight of our growing connection. In the midst of chaos, we found solace in each other, an unspoken promise to stand firm against the looming shadows that threatened to engulf us. Little did I know, the real test of our bond was just beginning.

The shattered remnants of my home echoed the disarray swirling in my mind, and as we stood in the basement, I could feel the weight of the note still crumpled in my hand. "What do we do now?" I asked, my voice a mere whisper in the vast, echoing emptiness. The air felt thick, almost charged, as if the very walls held their breath, waiting for our next move.

Hunter glanced around, his brow furrowed in thought. "We need to regroup, maybe reach out to someone we trust. There's too much at stake here." He ran a hand through his hair, a gesture that seemed to send a jolt of electricity through me, igniting the tension that had begun to simmer between us. It was a subtle dance of fear and familiarity, the danger heightening the thrill of being near him.

"Like who?" I countered, the flickering overhead light casting shadows that danced around us. "The last time we involved anyone else, it led to this." I gestured to the chaos that surrounded us, the evidence of someone's invasion feeling like a personal affront. My heart raced as I imagined the faces of friends and family who might become targets if we pulled them into our spiraling chaos.

He met my gaze, a determination flickering in his deep-set eyes. "What if we call Jamie? He's been digging around in town politics. Maybe he's heard something about this?"

"Jamie? Our resident conspiracy theorist?" I couldn't help but smile despite the tension, remembering the wild tales he spun that danced dangerously close to truth. "What's the worst he could do? Suggest we join a cult?"

Hunter chuckled, the sound rich and warm, a welcome respite from the unease. "You never know. He might have some leads. Plus, he can keep a secret—at least, most of the time."

As the laughter faded, reality crashed back in, heavy and cold. "Fine. Let's call him." I took a deep breath, steeling myself for whatever was coming next. I pulled out my phone, the familiar screen lighting up with a comfort that felt out of place amidst the chaos. Dialing Jamie's number, I felt Hunter's presence beside me, a steadfast anchor amidst the storm.

"Hey, what's up?" Jamie's voice crackled through the speaker, upbeat and wholly unaware of the whirlwind we had just stepped out of.

"We've got a situation," I said, my heart pounding as I glanced at Hunter. "Can you meet us? It's...urgent."

"Like 'the world is ending' urgent, or 'my cat is stuck in a tree' urgent?" He quipped, but the underlying concern in his voice made it clear he sensed my seriousness.

"More like 'our homes have been ransacked, and we think someone is after us' urgent," I replied, my voice steady even as I felt the weight of dread settle in my stomach.

"Whoa. Yeah, I'll be there in ten." The line clicked dead, leaving us in an echoing silence filled with unspoken fears.

"Ten minutes," Hunter said, glancing at his watch. "We should clean up a bit before he arrives."

"Clean up? You mean, we're not going to just call the authorities and have them deal with this?" I raised an eyebrow, incredulity lacing my tone.

"Not if we want to keep this under wraps. Remember, we're dealing with something bigger than just a simple burglary." He motioned toward the scattered items on the floor. "Let's make it look less chaotic, at least until we know what we're dealing with."

Reluctantly, I nodded, and we began to gather the pieces of our lives, shoving them haphazardly back into place. Each item felt like a memory being shoved aside, an attempt to reclaim some semblance of normalcy. With each movement, my thoughts darted back to the note, the ominous warning that had become an unwelcome guest in my mind. The truth isn't for you to find. Who was I up against?

"What if we're in over our heads?" I murmured as I tossed a tattered magazine back into a drawer. "What if whoever did this finds out we're still digging?"

"Then we keep digging deeper," Hunter said, his voice resolute as he straightened up, a newfound energy pulsing through him. "We don't let fear dictate our next move. We have to find out what's really going on."

His words struck a chord within me, igniting a spark of defiance that I hadn't known I possessed. "You're right," I said, surprising myself with the conviction in my tone. "We can't just back down. Not now."

Hunter flashed me a quick smile, a glimmer of pride that sent a rush of warmth through me. The heat of the moment hung between us, thick with unacknowledged feelings, yet shadowed by the gravity of our situation. Before I could dwell on it, the sharp sound of the doorbell rang out, jolting us both back into the present.

"That's Jamie," I said, moving to open the door, eager to share the burden of our discovery.

He stood on the porch, a whirlwind of energy with tousled hair and an armload of what looked like snacks. "I brought backup!" he declared, grinning as he walked past me into the chaos. "What's a conspiracy without snacks?"

"Just what we need," I said, a mixture of relief and exasperation flooding me. "Because we're totally having a picnic in the middle of a crisis."

"Hey, food makes everything better." He spread the items across the counter, a variety of chips and energy bars spilling out like a feast fit for a... well, a group of amateur detectives.

"Jamie, focus," Hunter said, leaning against the counter, his demeanor serious. "We've been ransacked, and we think someone is after us. We need your help to figure this out."

"What?" Jamie's eyes widened as he processed the information, a mix of disbelief and excitement playing across his features. "You're serious?"

"Dead serious." I nodded, the weight of my fears spilling into the open air. "Someone is trying to keep us from uncovering the truth, and I don't think this is going to end well."

"Let's brainstorm," Jamie said, suddenly animated. "What do we know? What are the leads? Spill!"

As I began recounting the events, the shattered note and our discoveries at the lighthouse, the three of us formed a huddled circle of plans and possibilities, united against the unseen threat looming just beyond our doorstep. The tension crackled, an electric current of determination and urgency, as I caught Hunter's eye across the small table strewn with snacks and chaos. For the first time since everything had unraveled, I felt a glimmer of hope—a flicker that maybe, just maybe, together we could face whatever storm lay ahead.

The energy in the room crackled as we huddled around the scattered snacks, our fingers grazing over the assortment like we were uncovering hidden treasures instead of contemplating a very real threat. Jamie's eyes darted from me to Hunter, his excitement mixed with concern as we delved deeper into the tangled mess we had stumbled into.

"Okay, so we've been ransacked, and now we need a plan," Jamie said, leaning forward with the intensity of a detective on the brink of a breakthrough. "What do you think they were looking for? The lighthouse? Some kind of hidden treasure?"

"Let's hope it's not the treasure. I'm not sure I'm ready to be the star of an adventure movie where the treasure is actually a curse," I quipped, trying to ease the tension. Hunter smirked at my attempt at humor, but the shadow of seriousness lingered in the air.

"The lighthouse is definitely part of this," Hunter replied, his expression shifting from playful banter to grave contemplation. "Everything started there. Whoever is after us must think we found something important."

"Or that we know something they want to keep buried," I added, the weight of the note still heavy in my pocket, like an anchor dragging me down.

"Great, so we're not just the town's local misfits; we're now also targets in a conspiracy," Jamie said, a mixture of disbelief and fascination lighting up his face. "This is like something out of a movie."

Hunter rolled his eyes but smiled. "You're not helping, Jamie."

"I'm not trying to help; I'm just saying it sounds exciting. We could start a podcast! 'The Ransacked Chronicles' or something equally catchy." He paused, eyes sparkling with mischief. "I mean, who wouldn't listen to that?"

"Anyone with taste," I shot back, but the levity faded quickly. "This is serious, Jamie. People are involved, and not just us. We need to be cautious."

"Cautious, right." Jamie nodded, his expression growing somber. "So, what's our next move? We can't just sit here waiting for the next shoe to drop."

Hunter leaned back, his arms crossing over his chest as he pondered our options. "First, we need to secure this place. If someone wanted to find us, they probably wouldn't hesitate to come back. We should start by checking for any surveillance, and then maybe set up a few traps of our own."

"Traps?" Jamie's eyebrows shot up. "Like bear traps? I'm not sure that's a good idea."

"More like alerts," I clarified. "We can set up some kind of system—maybe a way to know if someone comes near."

"Perfect! I can rig something up with my old walkie-talkies and some string," Jamie said, enthusiasm rising again. "It'll be like an episode of 'Survivor' but with less starvation and more snacking."

"Let's just hope we don't have to go that far," Hunter replied, the corners of his mouth twitching upward. "But we need to get it done quickly."

The atmosphere shifted again, tension swirling around us like an electric current. I glanced around, my heart racing as I sensed that the danger wasn't just from outside forces but also from the secrets we were navigating. "What if we're not just being targeted because of the lighthouse?" I suggested, my voice barely above a whisper. "What if it's something about our pasts? Maybe they're trying to shut us up about something we didn't even know we knew."

"Like what?" Jamie asked, his playful demeanor faltering.

"I don't know," I said, frustration creeping into my tone. "But if they know we're digging into this, they might know more about us than we realize. It's not just a matter of keeping the truth buried; it could be about silencing us completely."

"Okay, that's unsettling," Hunter said, his brow furrowing. "But whatever it is, we can't back down. We need to find out who's behind this, and why."

As the gravity of our situation sank in, the sound of footsteps echoed outside, breaking our concentrated huddle. "Did you hear that?" I whispered, the hairs on the back of my neck standing on end.

"Yeah," Jamie replied, eyes wide. "Sounds like someone's outside."

We all exchanged glances, a silent understanding passing between us. The tension in the air thickened, and I felt the adrenaline surge through my veins. Hunter moved toward the window, peering out through the curtain. "I don't see anyone," he murmured, but I could sense the underlying fear that accompanied his words.

"Maybe it's just the wind?" I offered, though doubt crept into my thoughts. The feeling of being watched was overwhelming, a chill dancing across my skin.

"Or maybe it's our uninvited guests," Hunter said, his voice dropping lower as he turned back toward us. "Let's check the back."

The three of us crept through the house, the atmosphere thick with anticipation. As we made our way to the back door, I could feel the adrenaline coursing through me, mixing with a strange sense of camaraderie that had grown between us. There was a thrill in being part of something larger than ourselves, despite the dark clouds looming overhead.

We reached the back door, and with a swift motion, Hunter pulled it open. The night air hit us, cool and sharp, filled with the sounds of rustling leaves and distant waves crashing against the shore. The world outside felt like a different realm—a world that was filled with possibilities, both terrifying and thrilling.

But nothing prepared us for the sight that awaited us just beyond the threshold. Standing in the shadows, partially obscured by the towering pines, was a figure clad in dark clothing, their posture rigid and menacing. A shiver ran down my spine as recognition dawned.

"Who are you?" I shouted, my heart racing.

The figure stepped forward, revealing a face I had never expected to see again, the faint glimmer of moonlight catching the glint of a familiar gaze.

"Surprise," they said, a smirk playing at the corners of their lips, sending a jolt of confusion and dread through me. The air thickened with tension, and just like that, everything I thought I knew began to unravel.

Chapter 12: The Confrontation

The town hall stood like a sentinel against the sky, its once-white façade now dulled to a weary gray, as if it too had grown tired of holding secrets. I glanced at Hunter beside me, his jaw set and eyes ablaze with determination. We had reached a crossroads where curiosity met desperation, and I could feel the weight of our resolve pressing against the heavy wooden doors as we pushed them open. The interior was dimly lit, and the scent of old paper and varnished wood mixed with a subtle hint of mildew filled the air, a cocktail that seemed to echo the stale conversations of years past.

Inside, the elders loomed like statues carved from decades of bitter experience. Their faces were maps of hardship and defiance, etched with lines that told stories we had yet to hear. The heavy, oak furniture seemed to absorb the tension crackling between us as we stood before them, the sacred keepers of our town's history.

"What do you want?" barked Elder Grimshaw, a man with a voice like gravel, his gray brows knitted together in disapproval. He leaned forward, a living embodiment of skepticism. "This is no place for children to meddle."

I felt a rush of indignation. "We're not children. We deserve to know what's happening in our town. People are disappearing, and you have to know why!"

Hunter, always the tactician, stepped in beside me, his calm demeanor a sharp contrast to the rising heat of my anger. "We've heard the legends," he said, his voice steady. "You can't keep hiding the truth forever. There are connections to our families, and we demand to know what those are."

The room fell silent, a palpable shift that made the air feel electric. The other elders exchanged glances, their expressions revealing a mix of fear and reluctance, as if they were grappling with ghosts too stubborn to remain silent. I clenched my fists, the polished wood of the table cold against my skin.

Elder Grimshaw leaned back, folding his arms across his chest, a wall of resistance. "The past is a dangerous place to wander. Some truths are better left buried."

His words hung in the air, heavy with implication. I caught Hunter's eye, and a spark of defiance ignited between us. "But we can't ignore it anymore," I pressed, my voice tinged with a mix of fear and fury. "The legends, the disappearances—they're all connected. If you know something, you have to tell us."

With that, a firestorm erupted in the hall, accusations flying like arrows. Old grudges surfaced, a cacophony of voices raising in indignation, blame shifting from one family to another. My heart raced as I watched the elders turn on one another, revealing hidden wounds and bitter rivalries I had never suspected. It was like peeling back the layers of a rotting onion, revealing the stench of old betrayals.

"We warned them not to tamper with the relics," Elder Duvall exclaimed, his hands trembling as he gestured wildly. "They thought they could control the past, but the past never forgets!"

Hunter and I exchanged confused glances, caught between the chaos and the unsettling realization that we were standing on the precipice of something much larger than we had anticipated.

"What relics?" I shouted, my patience wearing thin. "What are you talking about?"

Their bickering quieted, and for a moment, the air became thick with something akin to dread. Elder Grimshaw finally turned to us, his expression softening slightly. "There are artifacts tied to our town's history—objects that were never meant to be disturbed."

"Objects like what?" I pressed, feeling the tension coiling tighter around us.

"Cursed objects," he muttered, as if the words themselves were a contagion. "Things that can unleash forces we cannot comprehend."

A chill ran down my spine. My mind raced with the implications. "What forces? What are you hiding?"

"We buried the past to protect the future," Elder Duvall interjected. "But some of us—" he shot a glance at Grimshaw "—believe that history is meant to be unearthed. That it's better to face our demons than let them fester in the dark."

Hunter stepped forward, his brows furrowed in concern. "What happened the last time someone tried to uncover the truth? Was it linked to the disappearances?"

Grimshaw's expression shifted, a flicker of something between fear and regret flashing across his features. "There were consequences," he replied quietly. "And blood was shed."

The words hung like a dark cloud over us. I felt my heart thudding against my ribs, each beat echoing the rising anxiety within. "Blood? What kind of blood?"

Suddenly, the room erupted into chaos again, the elders scrambling to silence one another, voices raised in a frenzy. It felt like the walls were closing in, and I could sense the history woven into the very fabric of this place—a tapestry of pain and denial that had been festering for generations.

Hunter gripped my arm, grounding me in the storm of voices. "We need to find out more. We can't let them brush this under the rug."

Just as I opened my mouth to agree, the door swung open with a creak that silenced the clamor, revealing a figure silhouetted against the harsh light of the hallway. It was Clara, her face pale and eyes wide with fear.

"You need to listen to them!" she gasped, her voice trembling as she stepped into the room. "You're in danger!"

The elders turned, a mixture of shock and indignation washing over their features. Clara's presence was a storm of urgency, pulling the focus from their squabbles to the very real threat that hung in the air.

"What do you mean?" I asked, the tension in my body shifting as I faced her.

"There are things you don't understand," she said, her voice shaking. "The legends are not just stories—they're warnings. And if you keep digging, you might unearth something that can't be put back."

My pulse quickened as I exchanged another glance with Hunter. The stakes had never felt higher, and now it was clear that the elders weren't just hiding their past; they were terrified of what we might discover. The lines between family loyalty and the quest for truth blurred, and I could sense that the heart of our community was rotting from within. As Clara's words hung heavily in the air, it became all too clear that the confrontation had only just begun.

Clara's sudden arrival sent a ripple of tension through the room, her wide eyes shimmering with a mix of fear and urgency. The elders, who had been so caught up in their own battles, shifted their focus to her, the air thickening with unspoken questions. I could feel Hunter's grip tightening around my arm, his body radiating a quiet intensity as we waited for Clara to gather her thoughts.

"You're in real danger," she repeated, her voice steadier now, yet still laced with urgency. "What you're searching for—it's not just buried memories. It's alive, and it doesn't want to be disturbed."

"Alive?" I echoed, incredulity blooming within me. "What are you talking about? You make it sound like we're hunting ghosts."

Clara shook her head, her expression turning grave. "No, it's worse. It's like an entity, a force that has been unleashed every time someone digs into the past. People have vanished before, and it's always when someone gets too close."

The elders seemed to shrink in their seats, a collective unease settling over them. Elder Grimshaw's gaze faltered, revealing a flicker of doubt beneath his stern exterior. "This is nonsense, Clara. You're letting your imagination run wild."

"No, I'm not," she insisted, stepping forward, the flickering fluorescent lights casting shadows on her determined face. "You think you can keep this town safe by ignoring the truth? It's time to stop pretending. The last time someone got too close to the relics, it nearly destroyed us all."

Hunter's eyes met mine, a shared understanding passing between us. "What relics? What happened?"

"I can't tell you everything," Clara replied, frustration and fear mingling in her tone. "But I can warn you. If you keep pushing for answers, you might end up like those who disappeared—lost to the town and its shadows."

"Clara, stop being so dramatic," Elder Duvall interjected, his voice tinged with irritation. "This isn't a fairy tale. We have responsibilities, and your meddling will only complicate things."

"Complicate things? Complicate? You mean make it harder for you to maintain your precious status quo!" Clara shot back, her words sharp as a knife. "You can't keep burying the past. It will come back to bite you, and the rest of us with it."

The room buzzed with energy, voices clashing and rising like a storm. I watched as the elders turned on one another, the air thickening with accusations and regrets they could no longer hide. Their faces flushed with years of concealed rage, and in that moment, I realized how deeply rooted their fears ran—how tightly woven their lives were with the fabric of the town's history.

"Stop it!" I exclaimed, my voice cutting through the chaos. "We're not here to pick sides. We need to understand what's happening, and you're all too busy arguing about whose fault it is to see the bigger picture."

Grimshaw's gaze settled on me, his eyes narrowing. "And what makes you think you're equipped to understand the dangers of this town? You're just a child with wild ideas."

"I might be a child," I shot back, "but I'm not afraid to confront the truth, no matter how ugly it is. This isn't just about us; it's about the entire town. People are missing, and you're more concerned about your pride."

The silence that followed was charged, a hesitant calm settling as everyone absorbed the weight of my words. Even Clara seemed taken aback by my sudden boldness.

"What do you propose we do?" Elder Duvall finally asked, the hostility in his voice muted but still present. "You want to dig up secrets? And then what? You think that just by knowing them, we can change what's already happened?"

I took a breath, my mind racing as I searched for the right words. "Knowledge is power. If we can understand what happened to those who vanished, maybe we can prevent it from happening again. We need to work together instead of hiding behind walls of pride and resentment."

Hunter nodded, his support lending me strength. "Let us help. We're willing to dig deeper, but we can't do it alone. You need to be honest about what you know, no matter how painful it might be."

Grimshaw's gaze hardened, but a flicker of respect shone through the stoic facade. "You're playing a dangerous game, young ones. If you want the truth, it comes at a cost."

"What kind of cost?" I asked, my heart pounding as dread curled in my stomach.

He leaned closer, his voice dropping to a conspiratorial whisper. "The past is filled with regrets, some of which are better left buried. Are you prepared to face the consequences of your curiosity?"

A silence enveloped the room, thick with unvoiced fears and buried memories. I hesitated, contemplating the implications. Did

I really want to dive headfirst into the murky depths of our town's secrets? The thought of uncovering long-hidden truths was both thrilling and terrifying, a paradox that made my head spin.

"I'll take that risk," I finally replied, my voice steady despite the turmoil within. "We need to know what happened. All of it."

Clara's eyes widened with concern, and I could feel Hunter's tension beside me, but there was no turning back now. I had stepped onto this precarious path, and I wasn't about to waver.

With a sigh, Grimshaw motioned for us to sit. "If we're going to do this, we'll need to be strategic. The last thing we want is to invite whatever force lies within the past back into our lives."

The elders reluctantly joined us in a circle, the atmosphere shifting from confrontation to reluctant collaboration. As we began to discuss the origins of the relics and the families connected to them, I couldn't shake the feeling that we were all entwined in a story much larger than ourselves, a narrative stitched together by secrets, betrayals, and an urgent need for redemption.

Yet, as the conversation unfolded, one question loomed above us, shadowing our every word: What would we awaken by unearthing the past? Would we find the answers we sought, or would we open the floodgates to a darkness that had long lain dormant, waiting for the right moment to strike? The answer felt as elusive as the shadows that danced around us, whispering promises of revelations yet to come, and I wondered if we were truly prepared for the storm we were about to unleash.

As the elders began to unfold their tangled web of stories, the atmosphere thickened with an unspoken dread. Shadows flickered in the corners of the dimly lit hall, seeming to listen in on our conversation. My heart raced as Elder Grimshaw recounted tales of a family curse—one that had been passed down through generations, cloaked in layers of myth and regret.

"It started long ago," he said, his voice gravelly yet laced with a hint of sorrow. "There was a time when our ancestors wielded power that was both revered and feared. They thought they could harness forces beyond their understanding."

"What kind of power?" I pressed, my curiosity igniting the already simmering tension.

Grimshaw exchanged glances with the others, their eyes reflecting a mixture of wariness and reluctance. "The kind that binds and breaks," he murmured, his gaze drifting to the window where the night deepened, wrapping the town in a cloak of darkness. "A dark ritual was performed to protect the town from an ancient evil, but it came at a great cost."

Elder Duvall interjected, his face flushed with anger. "We were never meant to meddle with those forces! But some in this town couldn't resist, believing they could change their fate. And that arrogance—" He paused, his voice thick with emotion. "That arrogance led to the first disappearance."

"What does that have to do with the relics?" Hunter asked, his tone firm yet tinged with apprehension.

"Each relic is tied to a story—a memory of betrayal," Grimshaw replied, his eyes narrowing. "They were hidden away, locked in the very walls of this hall, to prevent anyone from unwittingly awakening what was buried. But now? Now, you're asking questions that threaten to reopen old wounds."

As I listened, the pieces began to fit together in my mind, each revelation more startling than the last. "So, the disappearances were a consequence of trying to reclaim that power? And now, it's happening again?"

"Exactly," Clara said, her voice low and urgent. "Each time someone tries to uncover the truth, someone pays the price. This is more than just history; it's a warning."

The elders shifted uncomfortably in their seats, their expressions a blend of fear and resignation. It felt as though they were all acutely aware of the fragile balance we were treading, teetering on the brink of something monumental.

"What about our families?" I pressed, feeling the intensity of the moment. "Are we connected to these events? Is that why people are disappearing?"

Duvall scoffed, crossing his arms defiantly. "Your families have their own burdens to bear. Each generation bears the weight of its predecessors' sins. But that doesn't mean you are directly implicated."

Hunter leaned forward, his voice steady. "But we deserve to know how we fit into this puzzle. If our families are involved, we have to understand what that means. This isn't just about history; it's about our future."

There was a moment of silence as the elders contemplated his words, the tension coiling tighter around us. Finally, Grimshaw sighed deeply, the fight seemingly draining from him. "You're right. But knowing the truth doesn't come without consequences. Are you truly prepared to face what you might uncover?"

I felt my pulse quicken, a mixture of fear and resolve swirling within me. "We're prepared. We have to be."

Suddenly, Clara gasped, her face paling as if she had seen a ghost. "There's something else. If the relics are disturbed, if they're brought back to the light..." Her voice trailed off, the implications hanging heavy in the air.

"Then what?" I urged, leaning closer. "What will happen?"

"It's said that they awaken something—something that should remain hidden. Something that can't be controlled," she whispered, her voice shaking. "And if it awakens, it will not only come for the ones who disturb it. It will come for everyone."

A chill washed over me, and I exchanged a glance with Hunter. The weight of her words settled heavily, pulling us further into the depths of uncertainty. I sensed that we were being pulled into a dark narrative that transcended our lives, a story written long before we ever existed.

"Enough of this," Elder Grimshaw snapped, shaking off the dread that had settled like fog. "You're playing with fire. If you want to pursue this path, you'll have to do so on your own."

I felt a mix of frustration and determination boiling inside me. "We can't just walk away from this. People are counting on us—people who are missing. We owe it to them to find the truth."

"Then go," Grimshaw replied coldly, gesturing toward the door. "But know this: every action has a consequence, and the past is never far behind."

As we left the town hall, the weight of our decisions pressed heavily upon us, our minds swirling with the revelations and the unshakeable feeling that we had crossed an invisible line. The cool night air hit us like a wave, refreshing yet foreboding.

"What do we do now?" Hunter asked, his brow furrowed with concern.

"We find the relics," I replied, my voice unwavering despite the unease creeping into my heart. "They might be the key to everything."

"Just like that? We'll waltz into the lion's den?"

"Why not?" I said with a forced chuckle, trying to lighten the mood. "If we're going to deal with whatever is lurking in the shadows, we might as well do it with a little flair."

Hunter smiled faintly, but his eyes held a depth of worry that made my stomach twist. "And if we find what we're looking for?"

"Then we face it together," I said, feeling a surge of courage. "Whatever it takes."

With a shared look of determination, we set off into the darkened streets, guided by the faint glow of the streetlights, our path uncertain yet driven by an unyielding purpose. The night felt alive, charged with an energy that mirrored our own apprehension and resolve.

As we reached the edge of the town square, a low rumble echoed from the forest beyond, sending a shiver down my spine. "Did you hear that?" I asked, stopping in my tracks.

Hunter nodded, his expression turning serious. "It came from the woods. Something's out there."

Before I could respond, a flicker of movement caught my eye. A shadow darted between the trees, followed by a piercing howl that shattered the night's fragile calm. My heart raced as I glanced back at Hunter, his face taut with concern.

"Should we—" he began, but before he could finish, the howl echoed again, closer this time, a sound that reverberated through my bones.

"Let's get out of here," I said, my voice trembling with urgency.

But as we turned to leave, an unsettling sensation swept over me. It felt as though the shadows themselves were reaching out, drawing us back toward the secrets that lay hidden in the depths of the forest. I hesitated, caught between the instinct to flee and the pull of the unknown, knowing all too well that the answers we sought might just be lurking in the dark.

And in that moment of hesitation, the howl echoed once more, not just a warning, but an invitation—one that promised danger and discovery in equal measure.

Chapter 13: The Fractured Alliance

The town hall meeting had spiraled into chaos faster than I could have imagined. The echo of my voice had barely faded before angry shouts filled the room, a cacophony of fear and mistrust ricocheting off the walls. Hunter's hand had tightened around mine as we stood side by side, and I could feel the tension in his grip—a mixture of solidarity and the silent acknowledgment that we were on precarious ground. I had tried to voice our plan, to bridge the gap between us and the townspeople who felt wronged by the shadow that loomed over our lives, but my words had landed like stones thrown into a tempest, creating ripples that only deepened the divide.

Now, as we retreated to Hunter's home, the air thickened with unspoken words. The moment we stepped inside, I felt the familiar warmth of his place wrap around me, but it felt different tonight, like a woolen blanket pulled too tightly around my shoulders. The walls seemed to close in, the shadows stretching like accusing fingers toward us. Hunter's home, once a refuge, now felt like a prison of our own making, filled with the weight of everything left unsaid.

We stood in the dim light of the living room, where the flickering glow from a lamp cast long shadows across the floor. The soft hum of the refrigerator was the only sound breaking the suffocating silence. I could see Hunter's jaw clenching, his normally easy smile replaced by a brooding frown. He paced back and forth, his hands shoved deep into his pockets, as if they were the only anchors he had in this swirling sea of confusion.

"Why didn't you just let me handle it?" he said suddenly, his voice low but edged with frustration. "You had no right to speak up like that. You don't understand what's at stake here."

I felt a rush of indignation push its way to the surface, the remnants of the meeting mixing with the tension crackling between us. "And you think isolating ourselves from the townspeople is the answer? They need to see that we're on their side!"

His gaze flickered to mine, and for a moment, I thought I saw something softer there—an understanding, perhaps. But it vanished, replaced by that familiar stubbornness. "They don't want our help, Isla. They want blood. They want someone to blame, and right now, that's us."

"Is that how you truly see them?" I asked, feeling the sting of disappointment wash over me. "We're not the enemy here, Hunter. We're trying to—"

"To what?" he interrupted, his voice rising. "To save them? To save us? Or are you just trying to prove a point?"

The accusation hung between us like a fog, thick and suffocating. I opened my mouth to respond, but the words caught in my throat. Instead, I turned my gaze to the window, watching the trees sway in the darkness, their branches clawing at the night sky. Outside, the world felt distant, a reality I couldn't quite grasp.

"This isn't just about the townspeople, is it?" I said, my voice steadier than I felt. "It's about you and me. You're scared. And I am too. But that doesn't mean we should fight against each other."

He paused, the air heavy with a different kind of silence. I could see his shoulders relax slightly, as if I had spoken a truth that lingered just beneath the surface. "I don't want to lose you, Isla," he finally admitted, his voice barely above a whisper.

The vulnerability in his tone disarmed me, stripping away the anger I had clung to. I stepped closer, my heart racing as I processed the weight of his admission. "You won't lose me," I promised, searching his eyes for that familiar spark. "But we need to figure this out together."

Just then, a loud crash shattered the fragile moment we had built. The sound reverberated through the house, pulling us both back into the chaotic reality we were desperately trying to escape.

I jumped, my heart racing anew as adrenaline coursed through me. Hunter's expression shifted from introspective to alarmed, and he moved toward the sound instinctively.

"Stay here," he ordered, his tone leaving no room for argument. But my feet wouldn't let me linger in place.

I followed him into the kitchen, where we found the source of the disturbance: a window had been thrown open, the glass shattered around the frame like jagged teeth. The wind howled through the gap, and with it came a gust of cold air that sent chills racing down my spine. I felt the weight of the night pressing in on us, a stark reminder that whatever had once felt like safety was now a fragile facade.

"Who could have done this?" I asked, my voice trembling slightly. I scanned the darkened yard, my instincts on high alert.

"I don't know, but we need to be careful," Hunter replied, his tone serious. "This isn't just about us anymore. If someone's willing to come after us in our own home, then everything has changed."

I felt a shiver run down my spine, a sense of dread pooling in my stomach. It was no longer just a confrontation with the townspeople; this was a direct threat, an escalation that promised further chaos. As Hunter's fingers brushed against mine, I could feel the tension between us morphing again—into something deeper, yes, but also something darker. We were standing at the precipice of a storm that threatened to pull us both under, and I couldn't shake the feeling that the real battle was only just beginning.

The broken window stood as a stark reminder of the chaos swirling outside, its jagged edges gleaming like teeth against the dark. Hunter's hands clenched into fists at his sides as he stepped closer to the gaping hole, his silhouette outlined against the pale moonlight streaming in. I could sense the tension crackling between us, an electric current of unresolved feelings and new fears that made it hard to breathe.

"What do we do now?" I asked, my voice steady but laced with urgency. The thrill of danger wrapped around us, twisting our emotions into a knot. "Should we call the police?"

Hunter shook his head, his brow furrowing in thought. "They'll only add to the noise. We need to figure out who did this without drawing more attention. Whoever it was, they want us to feel scared."

"I already feel scared," I muttered under my breath. "So, great job there."

His lips twitched into the hint of a smile, despite the situation. "Can't say I'm surprised. The night is young, and we're on the menu."

As much as I wanted to laugh, the seriousness of the moment anchored me. I stepped toward the window, peering into the night. The yard stretched out before us, shadowy and ominous. There was something unnervingly quiet about the world outside; even the crickets had stilled, as if holding their breath, waiting for the next act in this strange play.

"Stay back," Hunter said, his voice firm, grounding. "We don't know if whoever did this is still around."

"But we can't just stand here like sitting ducks," I protested. The idea of being trapped in this house, waiting for someone to make their next move, was worse than facing whatever was out there. "We should check the perimeter. If someone came in, they might not be far."

He hesitated, weighing the risk. "You're really not going to take no for an answer, are you?"

"Nope," I said, my determination firm. "I'll grab a flashlight. If we're going to do this, let's at least be prepared."

As I dashed into the kitchen to retrieve a flashlight, I felt the adrenaline pumping through my veins, a familiar companion in moments of tension. I flipped it on, the beam cutting through the darkness like a sword, illuminating the corners of the room and spilling out into the hallway. Hunter stood beside me, his eyes dark and serious, the easy charm he usually wore replaced with a focus I hadn't seen before.

"Let's stick together," he said, his voice low. "No splitting up."

"Agreed. I'm not keen on playing horror movie heroine tonight," I replied, attempting a playful tone to ease the tension.

We crept out into the hallway, the wooden floors creaking beneath our feet, sounding far too loud for the stealth we hoped to maintain. Hunter led the way, his presence both comforting and intimidating. He moved with a quiet grace, alert to every sound, every shift in the shadows. The house felt alive around us, the walls breathing in rhythm with our hearts.

Outside, the night was thick with humidity, the air heavy and warm against my skin. I shone the flashlight across the yard, catching glimmers of movement—a rustle in the bushes, a fluttering of leaves. The neighborhood, once filled with familiar laughter and the scent of barbecues, now felt foreign, transformed into a landscape of lurking dangers.

"Do you think it was someone from the town?" I asked, keeping my voice low as we moved toward the edge of the property.

"Hard to say," Hunter replied, scanning the trees that bordered the yard. "People are scared and desperate. That can make anyone act irrationally."

"Like breaking windows?" I muttered, the sarcasm slipping out before I could stop it.

He shot me a sidelong glance. "Yeah, like breaking windows. You've got a real way of putting a positive spin on things, Isla."

"I aim to please," I replied, my voice teasing but my heart racing. Just as I finished speaking, a loud thud echoed from the back of the house, making us both freeze.

"What was that?" Hunter whispered, eyes wide.

"I don't know," I said, my pulse quickening. "It came from inside."

With quick, silent movements, we retreated back into the house, moving like shadows, avoiding the squeaky spots in the floor. As we reached the living room, the source of the noise revealed itself—a fallen book, its spine cracked, pages fluttering as if recently disturbed. The book lay open on the floor, an innocent artifact now dripping with a sense of foreboding.

"That's... odd," I said, eyeing the mess it made. "Did we leave that out?"

Hunter's brow furrowed as he picked it up, glancing at the title before flipping through the pages. "It's a journal. Someone's been reading it."

My stomach twisted at the thought. "That's not creepy at all. Who would break in just to read a journal?"

He grimaced, continuing to flip through the pages. "Looks like they were looking for something."

A chill raced down my spine, the implications sinking in. "Do you think it's connected to the town hall meeting? Maybe they want to know what we know?"

"Or they think we're hiding something." Hunter's expression turned serious again, the tension building around us like an invisible wall.

I stepped closer, peering over his shoulder at the entries, hoping to glean some insight. The handwriting was hurried, scrawled in a way that suggested fear and urgency. "What does it say?"

"It's a mix of notes and sketches," he said, tracing a finger over the pages. "Some about the town's history... and some about us."

I felt a prick of unease. "Us?"

"Yeah, like they're keeping track of our movements, what we do, who we talk to." He turned a page, revealing a crude sketch of the two of us, surrounded by notes scribbled in the margins. "This isn't just a journal; it's a profile."

A wave of panic surged through me. "Someone's been watching us."

Before we could process the implications, the front door creaked open slowly, its hinges protesting like a wounded animal. We both whipped around, our bodies tensed for flight or fight, the weight of the unknown pressing in on us like a vice. The door swung wide, revealing a figure silhouetted against the dim porch light.

"Hunter! Isla!" A voice, frantic and familiar, broke through the heavy air. It was Jenna, my best friend, her eyes wide with fear, the usual spark of mischief replaced by desperation. "You need to come with me, now."

Her urgency was palpable, and my heart raced as I exchanged a glance with Hunter, silently questioning what danger had driven her to us. The night was unraveling faster than I could grasp, and suddenly, it felt like the stakes were higher than I'd ever imagined.

Jenna burst through the door, her wild eyes wide with urgency, sending my heart racing. I could see the urgency in her stance, her breath coming in quick bursts, as though she had sprinted here through the night. "You need to come with me, now," she insisted, glancing over her shoulder, as if she expected something—or someone—to follow her inside.

"What's going on?" I asked, stepping closer. "What happened?"

Hunter exchanged a wary glance with me before taking a step forward. "Is it the townspeople? Did they come after you?"

"No," Jenna shook her head, her fingers twitching with anxiety. "It's worse. There's a group gathering in the old church. They're talking about you two—about us. They're blaming you for everything. They think you're behind all the strange happenings."

The weight of her words settled heavily in the room. I felt a mixture of disbelief and dread knotting in my stomach. "But we're not behind any of it! We're trying to help!" I exclaimed, my frustration bubbling over.

"It doesn't matter what we're trying to do," Hunter replied, his voice low and tense. "What matters is what they believe. And right now, it sounds like they're ready to take matters into their own hands."

Jenna stepped closer, her eyes scanning the dimly lit living room. "I overheard them talking about a meeting. They want to take a vote, decide if you two should be forced out of town. Or worse."

My breath hitched in my throat, the reality of the situation crashing down like a tidal wave. "Forced out? How can they do that? We haven't done anything wrong!"

"Tell that to them," Hunter said grimly, running a hand through his hair. "It's a mob mentality. Once they get it in their heads that you're the enemy, there's no reasoning with them."

Jenna stepped back, clearly agitated. "We need to leave—now. If they're gathering, it means they're ready to act. And we can't let them catch us here. Not like this."

"Where do we go?" I asked, feeling the panic clawing at my insides. The warmth of Hunter's presence beside me did little to ease my anxiety. "We can't just run into the night without a plan. They'll track us down."

Hunter took a deep breath, grounding himself before responding. "We need to get to the woods. If we stick to the shadows, we can avoid them until we figure out what to do next."

"Right," I said, steeling my resolve. "Let's go. We can't stay here."

As we moved toward the door, the night outside felt charged, almost electric. The moon hung low in the sky, casting a pale glow over the world, illuminating the path that lay ahead but leaving the woods shrouded in darkness. I took a deep breath, the air heavy with the scent of pine and damp earth, and pushed the door open.

The moment we stepped outside, I felt a rush of adrenaline. Jenna led the way, darting across the yard with the stealth of a deer, her movements swift and sure. Hunter and I followed closely, the shadows of the trees swallowing us whole as we moved deeper into the woods. Each crack of a branch beneath our feet felt like a shout in the silence, an invitation for danger to catch up with us.

"Stay close," Hunter urged, his voice barely above a whisper. "We need to keep our voices down."

"Do you think they'll follow us?" Jenna asked, glancing back nervously.

"Probably," I said, my heart thudding in my chest. "But they won't find us if we stick to the paths and avoid the open areas."

The darkness enveloped us, but the moonlight filtered through the leaves, creating a patchwork of silver and shadows. I focused on the sound of our footsteps and the rustling of leaves, trying to drown out the echoes of doubt creeping into my mind.

After what felt like an eternity of careful navigation, we found a small clearing surrounded by thick trees. "Let's rest here for a moment," I suggested, my breath coming in gasps. "We can regroup and figure out our next move."

Hunter nodded, his gaze scanning the perimeter as we settled into the safety of the clearing. "We need to come up with a plan. We can't let them force us out without a fight."

Jenna nodded, her expression grave. "But how do we convince them we're on their side? They've made up their minds."

I bit my lip, frustration bubbling to the surface. "What if we turn the tables? We could gather evidence—show them that something else is going on. Something bigger than us."

Hunter looked at me, a glimmer of respect in his eyes. "That might actually work. If we can get them to see the truth, we might be able to change their minds."

"Okay, so we gather evidence," Jenna said, her voice stronger now. "But where do we start? We don't even know what we're looking for."

"Remember the old church?" I suggested, suddenly feeling the weight of an idea take shape. "If they're meeting there, they might have information. We could sneak inside and see what they're up to."

"Are you insane?" Hunter said, incredulous. "You want to walk straight into the lion's den?"

"If we're going to convince them we're not the enemy, we need to know what they're planning," I replied, my determination solidifying. "Besides, it's the only lead we have."

Silence fell over us as we contemplated the plan. I could feel the tension hanging thick in the air, a shared understanding settling among us. This was more than just a fight for our safety; it was a fight for our home. The stakes were higher than ever.

"Alright," Hunter said finally, his voice steady. "Let's do it. We'll head to the church, but we need to move quickly. If we linger too long, we could find ourselves in a world of trouble."

As we stood in the clearing, our resolve strengthened, a low growl broke through the stillness of the night, reverberating through the trees. My heart sank as I exchanged worried glances with Jenna and Hunter.

"Did you hear that?" Jenna whispered, her eyes wide with fear.

Before I could respond, the shadows around us shifted, and the growl intensified, vibrating through the ground beneath us. I turned, the flashlight beam trembling in my hand, illuminating a massive figure emerging from the trees—a dark silhouette with glinting eyes and bared teeth.

Panic surged through me as I realized the danger had found us, and in that moment, I understood the night had only just begun to unfold its horrors.

Chapter 14: The Haunting

The chill of the night air was a cruel reminder that Firestone Bay had secrets hidden deeper than the ocean could fathom. As I stepped out into the gloom, my breath visible in puffs of white, it felt as if the very shadows were alive, twisting and writhing in anticipation. A low crash echoed from the direction of the old lighthouse, a structure long abandoned yet eternally haunted in our town's folklore. With every hesitant step toward the sound, a primal instinct clawed at my gut, urging me to turn back, to retreat into the warm glow of home and forget the darkness waiting just beyond the safety of the streetlamp's halo.

"Are you sure this is a good idea?" Jess's voice quivered beside me, slicing through the silence. She stood clutching her phone like a lifeline, the light from the screen flickering as if it too was unsure about our destination. I caught the flicker of fear in her eyes, mirroring my own dread. The stories we had heard growing up—ghosts, lost sailors, a tragic love that echoed in the salt-laden air—whirled in my mind like a tempest, stirring memories I had buried deep.

"Look, if we don't investigate, who knows what we'll miss?" I offered, though even I struggled to believe the bravado in my tone. "What if it's just some kids messing around? They might need our help." The thought of confronting the unknown thrilled me, even as a chill skated down my spine. We both knew it was more than just kids playing pranks; the ominous feeling in the air wrapped around me like a heavy cloak, pulling me into its depths.

We edged closer to the lighthouse, its silhouette looming against the star-studded sky, a jagged line of stone and forgotten history. The wind whistled mournfully through the cracked windows, creating a symphony of eerie echoes that seemed to call our names. I couldn't help but think of all the things I'd pushed aside—the failures, the regrets, the shadow of my father's disapproval that had always loomed over my choices like the lighthouse itself. I felt Jess's hand slip into mine, grounding me against the tumult of thoughts swirling in my head.

"What if we see something... unexplainable?" she whispered, her voice trembling like the leaves rustling in the trees surrounding us. I could feel the weight of her uncertainty pressing down, yet the thought of unearthing the lighthouse's mysteries pushed me forward.

"Then we'll figure it out together," I promised, squeezing her hand. "It's not like we've never faced a little danger before, right?" I attempted a smile, one that felt more fragile than I intended. But as I led Jess toward the entrance, a sense of determination ignited within me—a flicker of defiance against the chains of fear.

The door creaked open with a reluctant groan, revealing a cavernous space shrouded in darkness. I flipped my phone to illuminate the interior, casting a harsh glow on the dusty floor and peeling walls, the remnants of a past long abandoned. The scent of damp wood and rusted metal mingled in the air, a tang of decay that spoke of years gone by. Shadows danced around us as we stepped inside, each movement drawing us deeper into the heart of the lighthouse.

"Do you hear that?" Jess asked, her voice barely above a whisper, eyes wide as she scanned the darkness. I paused, straining to listen, and felt it—a soft melody, haunting yet familiar, echoing through the air like a lullaby lost to time. It tugged at my memory, bringing forth images of my childhood, nights spent huddled under blankets, listening to my mother's soothing voice as she spun tales of love and loss, of ghosts waiting for redemption.

"That's... it's beautiful," I breathed, the melody wrapping around my heart. I stepped further in, almost entranced, pulling Jess along as we followed the sound, the music rising and falling like waves crashing against the shore. It seemed to guide us, beckoning us toward the spiral staircase that wound upward into the darkness.

"Wait!" Jess exclaimed, but the allure of the melody was irresistible, weaving its spell around me. I ascended the stairs, each step creaking underfoot, the light from my phone barely illuminating the walls. Shadows leapt and twisted, seeming to reach for us, as if the very walls were alive, breathing in time with the haunting tune.

Reaching the top, we emerged onto the lantern room, the panoramic view of Firestone Bay sprawling beneath us. But the melody shifted—no longer a gentle lull, it became urgent, filled with longing and despair. In the center of the room stood a figure cloaked in shadow, their back turned toward us, framed by the glimmering glass of the lantern that had once guided ships safely home.

"Who's there?" I called out, my voice shaky yet defiant. The figure turned slowly, revealing a familiar face marred by sorrow—my mother. The ghostly image bore the same soft smile, but her eyes, once bright with love, now held a depth of pain that twisted my heart.

"Why are you here?" she whispered, her voice echoing like the fading notes of the melody, mingling with the wind outside. I felt the air thicken around us, each word weighed down with an emotion I could scarcely comprehend.

"Mom?" The word escaped my lips, filled with disbelief and longing, as my heart raced in tandem with the tempest of emotions that swirled within me. This was no mere vision; this was a confrontation with the past I had long since tried to escape.

"I'm here to remind you," she said, her voice a soft caress that belied the tumult around us. "To confront what you've buried. You can't run from the truth, my love." Each word pulled at the fabric of my resolve, unraveling the tight hold I had on my fears.

The weight of her presence anchored me, and in that moment, surrounded by shadows and echoes of the past, I felt both terrified and liberated. I had to confront the truth, no matter how deeply it lurked within the recesses of my heart.

My mother's ethereal form flickered like a candle in the wind, her gaze steady yet filled with an inscrutable sadness that left me teetering on the brink of despair. I could hardly breathe as I searched for words, my throat tight with a mixture of disbelief and longing. "What do you mean?" The question felt feeble, like a paper boat set adrift on a stormy sea.

She stepped closer, the shadows seemingly parting around her, revealing a face that was both familiar and foreign. "You've run away from so much, from me, from your fears. But they're still here, lurking beneath the surface." Her voice was soft but carried an authority that made my heart pound with recognition. "It's time to face them."

A wave of emotion surged through me, crashing against the walls I had built to keep my feelings at bay. "I've tried! You don't know how hard it's been." Each syllable trembled with the weight of unspoken truths, the kind I'd pushed away for far too long.

"Then let's break those walls," she urged, her eyes shimmering like the sea at dawn. "Together."

Jess stood beside me, her expression shifting from fear to compassion, her fingers tightening around my arm. "You can do this, Emily. You've always been stronger than you think." Her voice was a lifeline, reminding me that even in this tempest of emotions, I wasn't alone.

With a deep breath, I turned back to my mother, feeling the tremors of my past seep into the present. "What do I need to confront? What am I hiding from?" The question felt like an invitation to dive into the depths of my soul, where I had tucked away pain and regrets I thought I had long buried.

"Your fear of losing those you love. The weight of expectations you've placed on yourself," she replied, her voice growing stronger. "It's time to let go of the past that haunts you."

As her words hung in the air, I was flooded with memories—the frantic nights spent pacing the floors after my father's scornful remarks, the stinging rejections from friends who had drifted away as I struggled to fit into a mold I never wanted to be in. But most haunting of all was the night my mother had passed, leaving me stranded in a sea of grief that felt insurmountable.

"I can't just forget," I whispered, feeling a tear slip down my cheek. "How can I move on when the pain is so raw?"

My mother stepped closer, and the air around us shifted, becoming warmer, infused with a sense of understanding. "You don't have to forget, but you must forgive. Yourself, and those who have hurt you. It's a burden you don't need to carry any longer."

The truth of her words resonated within me, rippling through the cracks of my carefully constructed barriers. But a small voice, tinged with skepticism, nagged at my mind. "What if I can't?"

"You can. And I will help you." The assurance in her tone sparked a flicker of hope deep within my chest.

As I looked into her eyes, I was reminded of the love she had always shown me, the warmth that enveloped me like a cozy blanket on a cold winter's night. It was a gentle push, coaxing me to face the storm instead of retreating into its eye.

With a newfound determination, I straightened my shoulders, ready to embrace the confrontation that awaited me. "What do I need to do?" I asked, my voice steadier than I felt.

"Face the shadows of your past. Confront the moments that have defined you, the choices that have bound you." She gestured toward the stairs we had just ascended, her expression a mixture of pride and sorrow. "The answers lie within. You need to go back, to the beginning."

"What does that even mean?" Jess interjected, her brow furrowing. "How do we go back to something that's already happened?"

I turned to her, the gears in my mind whirring to life. "Maybe it's about revisiting the places where everything changed." A realization hit me like a wave crashing against the shore. "The beach... the day she..." I faltered, the words tasting bitter on my tongue. "The day she died."

My mother's eyes softened, a glimmer of understanding passing between us. "That day is where you must begin. It holds the key to unlocking your heart."

I swallowed hard, the memory flooding back—sunlight filtering through the trees, the sound of laughter mingling with the crash of waves, and then the sudden shift into chaos that forever altered my life.

"Let's go," I said, my voice laced with resolve. "Let's go to the beach."

With Jess at my side, we descended the stairs, the path ahead illuminated by the light of my phone and the steady beat of my heart. Each step felt significant, a reclaiming of my agency as I prepared to face the ghosts that lingered in the corners of my memory.

Outside, the wind howled like a restless spirit, wrapping around us as we made our way to the beach. The moon hung low, casting a silvery glow across the water, each wave a reminder of the ebb and flow of life. I took a deep breath, letting the salty air fill my lungs, steeling myself for the confrontation ahead.

The beach was nearly deserted, the only sounds the whisper of the waves and the soft rustling of the sand beneath our feet. As we reached the spot where I had lost so much, the memories flooded over me—her laughter, her gentle touch, and the horror of seeing her slip away.

"Are you ready?" Jess asked, her voice barely above a whisper.

I nodded, though uncertainty gnawed at my insides. The past was a wild thing, clawing at my consciousness, and I knew that this moment would change everything.

As I stepped closer to the water, a figure materialized from the shadows, the silhouette of my mother appearing before me, not as a ghost, but as the vibrant woman I remembered. "You've come home," she said, her voice echoing across the water, resonating with the very essence of my being.

"Now it's time to remember," I whispered, tears pooling in my eyes, ready to embrace the truth that had been buried for too long.

The wind whipped around us as I stood at the water's edge, my heart pounding against my ribcage like a caged bird desperate for freedom. My mother's apparition shimmered in the moonlight, her eyes reflecting the waves that crashed rhythmically behind us, as if the ocean itself was listening, waiting for my next move. I could almost hear her laugh—a soft, melodic sound that once filled our home with warmth.

"Don't you dare look at me like that," I managed, anger flaring as the ache of her absence bubbled up. "You left! You left me to pick up the pieces!" The words felt raw and jagged, slicing through the silence.

Her expression shifted, eyes clouding with the depth of unspoken sorrow. "I know," she said, her voice trembling like the wind. "But I didn't choose to leave you. That day... it was a storm neither of us could control."

I swallowed hard, wrestling with the weight of that truth, the memories swirling around us like a tempest. It was true; life had unraveled in an instant, the fabric of our existence torn apart by fate. But to stand here, facing a ghost of my past, felt like an insurmountable challenge.

"You can't just appear and expect me to forgive everything," I spat, my voice tinged with bitterness. "You don't get to waltz back into my life and—"

"Emily, I'm not here to hurt you," she interrupted, stepping closer, the shadows around her flickering with every movement. "I'm here to help you understand."

"Understand what?" I shot back, frustration bubbling to the surface. "That I can't live without you? That I've been a mess ever since?"

She drew a shaky breath, the moonlight illuminating the contours of her face, revealing the wear of grief etched in her features. "You've been carrying the weight of my loss, and it's time you set it down."

"But how? How do I let go of something that feels like it defines me?" I glanced at Jess, who stood a few paces back, her face a mask of concern and empathy. "I don't even know who I am without it."

"Let me show you," my mother replied, extending her hand, a gesture that felt both inviting and terrifying.

Despite the hesitation gnawing at me, something deep within urged me to take a leap of faith. I stepped forward, clasping her hand, feeling an electric connection that sent chills down my spine. The world around us blurred, colors bleeding together as if we were suspended in time.

Suddenly, we were transported back to a day I thought I had buried—an afternoon at the beach, the sun glistening off the waves like shards of broken glass. My younger self raced across the sand, laughter ringing out as I chased after my mother, the wind tugging at my hair. I felt the warmth of the sun on my skin, a stark contrast to the cool night air we had just left behind.

"Mom!" I called out, running toward her, the joy of the moment infectious. "Look at me!"

"Slow down, Emily!" she laughed, her voice rich and full of life. "You'll trip!"

But I didn't care. I was untouchable, a wild child in a world of endless possibilities. The past wrapped around me like a comforting blanket, yet lurking beneath it was the inevitable storm that would change everything.

The scene shifted, and suddenly I was no longer the carefree child but a spectator of my own heartbreak. I watched as dark clouds rolled in, the once golden beach turning ominous and gray. The wind picked up, howling like a wounded animal, and I could sense the tension in the air.

"Mom, we need to go!" I shouted, but my voice was lost in the cacophony. I saw her look around, confusion flickering in her eyes, and my heart dropped as I felt the storm approaching.

"Emily, come back!" she cried, but I couldn't move, rooted in place as the shadows swallowed us.

In that moment of sheer terror, I realized I was watching my own failure unfold. I was the reason she had turned back to try to find me, the reason she had been swept away by the waves. Guilt wrapped around me like a vice, squeezing until I could barely breathe.

"I never wanted to be the cause of your pain," my mother's voice broke through the chaos, pulling me from the depths of despair. "But you must forgive yourself. The past does not define who you are. It's how you choose to move forward that matters."

Tears streamed down my cheeks as I struggled against the weight of her words, fighting against the suffocating guilt. "How can I forgive myself when I couldn't save you?"

"You didn't fail me," she insisted, her voice unwavering. "You loved me fiercely, and that is what truly matters."

The scene shifted again, pulling me back to the present, where Jess was still standing beside me, her eyes wide with understanding.

"What just happened?" she whispered, glancing between me and the spot where my mother had stood.

"I saw it," I stammered, breathless. "I saw what happened that day."

Jess took a step closer, her expression gentle yet probing. "And?"

"I need to forgive myself," I replied, my voice steadier now, as if the realization had anchored me amidst the chaos. "I need to let go of the past."

But just as a sense of clarity washed over me, the wind shifted, howling louder than before. The ocean roared, and dark clouds gathered on the horizon, swirling ominously above the water.

"Emily, look out!" Jess shouted, pointing toward the sea.

I turned just in time to see a massive wave rising, impossibly high, its crest frothing with fury. A sense of dread washed over me, and instinct kicked in. "Run!" I yelled, grabbing Jess's hand and sprinting toward the beach house, adrenaline propelling us forward.

As we raced, the ground shook beneath us, each step echoing like thunder. I glanced back, fear clawing at my throat as the wave surged closer, a wall of water that threatened to engulf everything in its path.

"Keep going!" Jess urged, her voice barely audible over the roaring winds.

I could feel the chill creeping in, a reminder of the darkness that had haunted me for so long, but this time, I was ready to face it. Just as we reached the entrance of the beach house, the wave crashed down behind us with a deafening roar, the force sending a spray of water cascading over our heads.

"Emily!" Jess screamed, pulling me through the door just as the wave struck, flooding the porch with a torrent of icy water. The impact reverberated through the house, and I could barely keep my balance, fear igniting my instincts.

But as I stumbled inside, my heart raced not just from terror, but with a newfound resolve. I would confront my past, no matter how tumultuous it may be, because in the heart of Firestone Bay, I was ready to uncover the truths that had been buried beneath layers of grief and guilt.

And as the wave receded, leaving behind an eerie silence, a chilling whisper echoed through the empty halls—a reminder that the shadows of the past were far from gone.

Chapter 15: Revelations in the Dark

The woods were alive with whispers, a symphony of rustling leaves and the distant calls of birds retreating to their nests. As Hunter and I stepped beneath the canopy, the daylight waned, replaced by a soft twilight that clung to the branches like a shroud. The air was thick with the scent of damp earth and decaying foliage, a heady aroma that filled my lungs with the weight of history. I could feel a peculiar tension in the atmosphere, like a current just beneath the surface, waiting to be disturbed.

Hunter walked beside me, his tall frame cutting an imposing silhouette against the waning light. I stole glances at him, my heart fluttering in an erratic rhythm, unsure whether it was the thrill of adventure or the proximity of his warmth that made me feel this way. We had shared secrets and fears, our laughter blending with the eerie chorus of the woods, and it felt as though we were bound together by something inexplicable, something that went beyond mere friendship.

"Do you think we'll actually find anything out here?" he asked, his voice low and tinged with a mix of skepticism and excitement.

"Only one way to find out," I replied, trying to sound braver than I felt. It was strange how easily our banter flowed, like water from a stream, yet there was an undercurrent of gravity that made every word seem loaded with meaning.

We ventured deeper, the underbrush crunching beneath our feet, each step echoing in the quiet that enveloped us. It wasn't long before we stumbled upon the cabin, half-hidden by a tangle of wildflowers and creeping vines that clung to the wooden frame as if trying to reclaim it. The sight sent a thrill through me—this was not just an old structure; it was a portal to another time, a keeper of secrets long buried.

The door creaked open with a reluctant groan, revealing a dim interior filled with shadows and dust motes dancing in the air. I stepped inside first, Hunter close behind, and immediately felt the chill of the place seep into my bones. It was as if the cabin had been waiting for us, preserving the echoes of lives once lived within its walls.

A flickering beam of light from my phone illuminated the room, casting ghostly shapes across the faded wallpaper that peeled like forgotten memories. Old furniture lay strewn about, draped in a layer of dust, each piece telling a silent story. I noticed a rocking chair that swayed slightly, as if still haunted by the gentle motion of someone long gone. The air was heavy with the weight of time, pressing down on my shoulders as I stepped further inside.

"Look at this," Hunter called, kneeling near the hearth, his fingers brushing against something partially hidden beneath a fallen beam. I rushed to his side, curiosity piquing my interest.

He pulled out a leather-bound diary, its edges worn and frayed, and the moment our eyes met, an electric jolt of anticipation surged between us. "This could be important," he said, flipping it open with care, revealing pages filled with elegant, swirling script.

I leaned closer, the faint scent of aged paper enveloping me as if inviting me into its world. The words seemed to leap from the pages, weaving a narrative of heartache and resilience, of a family torn apart by secrets and tragedy. It was there, amid the ink-stained revelations, that I found a connection to my own lineage, a tale that intertwined with the very roots of this cabin and its former inhabitants.

As we read, the night deepened around us, and the shadows stretched longer, encroaching upon our little sanctuary. The diary spoke of dreams unfulfilled and love lost, of promises made in the dark only to be shattered by the harsh light of reality. Each entry seemed to pull at the threads of my own life, exposing fears I had buried deep within.

"It's all so tragic," I murmured, feeling a pang of sorrow for those who had come before us. "They suffered so much."

Hunter glanced up, his expression serious. "It's not just about them, is it? There's something here that ties us to this place. To them."

The realization hung in the air, palpable and heavy. I nodded, suddenly aware of the enormity of our discovery. The diary was more than a mere artifact; it was a testament to the struggles of those who had lived in this cabin, a reflection of the shadows that had always loomed over my family.

We continued to explore the cabin, uncovering fragments of lives once vibrant. A rusted locket lay hidden beneath a loose floorboard, and I felt compelled to lift it gently from its resting place. Inside was a faded photograph of a woman with a kind smile, her eyes sparkling with life. Who was she? A long-lost ancestor?

"Everything here tells a story," Hunter said, his voice barely above a whisper. "It's like we've walked into a time capsule."

"Or a graveyard," I replied, unable to shake the sense of foreboding that crept over me.

"Let's not think about it that way." Hunter's tone was light, attempting to banish the chill that clung to my spine. "It's more of a...rediscovery. Like unearthing hidden treasures."

"Treasure doesn't usually come with a warning label," I countered, but I couldn't help the smile that tugged at my lips. The tension that had sparked between us morphed into something warm and real, a shared understanding forged in the face of our fears.

As we continued our exploration, I felt the weight of the diary in my hands, its words resonating deeply within me. It was as if the stories had merged with my own, intertwining our fates in a way I had never anticipated. The darkness outside seemed to whisper secrets, urging us to dig deeper, to uncover the truth that had been buried alongside the cabin.

With each turn of the page, I felt a flicker of hope igniting within the shadows, a promise that perhaps, just perhaps, we could untangle the threads of our shared past and weave a new future. And in that moment, standing beside Hunter in the dim light of the cabin, I knew I was ready to face whatever came next.

The diary lay open between us, its fragile pages a bridge between the past and the present. I traced the delicate script with my fingertips, each letter a heartbeat echoing through time. Hunter leaned closer, his shoulder brushing against mine, sending a ripple of warmth through me that contrasted sharply with the chill of the cabin.

"Did you see this?" he murmured, his voice barely above a whisper, as if speaking too loudly might shatter the fragile connection we were forging. "This entry talks about a family feud, something about a hidden treasure."

I raised an eyebrow, intrigued. "Hidden treasure? Now that sounds like something worth uncovering. Unless it's a family heirloom that's cursed or something equally dramatic."

He chuckled softly, his laughter a soothing balm against the tension. "Well, what's a little family drama without a few curses thrown in for good measure?"

As we delved deeper into the diary, the story unfolded like a well-worn map, guiding us through heartbreak and betrayal. The previous owners of the cabin had faced their own demons, battling against the tides of misfortune that threatened to engulf them. I could feel a strange kinship with them, an unsettling recognition of the pain and longing that seeped from the pages.

"Look at this," I said, pointing to a passage that described a fire that had consumed the cabin in a blaze of chaos. "They lost everything. Their memories, their history—all gone in an instant."

Hunter's expression shifted to one of empathy. "It's a reminder of how fragile our lives can be, isn't it? One moment you think you're safe, and the next, everything you know is gone."

The atmosphere in the cabin thickened, a tangible heaviness settling over us as the realization of our shared fears sank in. I couldn't shake the feeling that we were not just uncovering the past; we were also unearthing our own vulnerabilities. The weight of unspoken fears hung between us, a silent acknowledgment of the uncertainties that lay ahead.

"Hey," Hunter said, breaking the silence, his voice laced with determination. "We can't let this place get to us. It's just a cabin, and those stories are just echoes of the past. We're not bound by their mistakes."

"Easier said than done," I replied, unable to suppress a wry smile. "But I appreciate the pep talk. Should I prepare a motivational poster with a kitten hanging from a branch next?"

He laughed again, the sound warm and genuine, and for a moment, the darkness around us felt less daunting. But as I glanced back at the diary, the weight of the revelations loomed large. It wasn't just the past we were facing; it was the intertwining threads of our lives that seemed destined to clash.

I turned another page, and my heart sank at what I found. A faded photograph slipped out, landing softly on the floor. It depicted a group of solemn faces—men and women standing in front of the very cabin we inhabited. Among them was a woman who bore an uncanny resemblance to me, her eyes a mirror to my own.

"Wow," Hunter said, picking it up and holding it to the light. "Is that...?"

"I think it is," I whispered, my voice shaky. "That's my great-grandmother."

He studied the image closely, the realization dawning on him. "So, you're saying this cabin is part of your family history?"

I nodded, a chill running down my spine. "It seems so. But the entries talk about so much pain and resentment. I had no idea this was connected to my family."

"Then it's our job to turn this story around," he said firmly. "You don't have to shoulder this burden alone. We'll figure it out together."

His words wrapped around me like a comforting blanket, and I felt a surge of gratitude. The prospect of facing my family's tumultuous legacy alongside him made the journey seem less daunting.

We returned to the diary, flipping through the brittle pages with renewed purpose. The entries grew darker, detailing a hidden family secret—something that had sparked the feud and ultimately led to the cabin's destruction. As we pieced together the clues, it became clear that the treasure spoken of earlier was not material wealth but something far more valuable: the truth itself.

Suddenly, a loud crack echoed outside, shattering our reverie. We both jumped, hearts racing, as the sound of snapping branches reached our ears. "What was that?" I asked, my voice barely above a whisper.

"I have no idea," Hunter replied, his expression shifting to one of concern. "Maybe we should check it out?"

I glanced at the door, shadows pooling in the corners of the room. "Or we could just stay here and pretend we didn't hear anything?"

He grinned, that infectious smile that made my heart flutter. "C'mon, where's your sense of adventure?"

"Last seen fleeing into the woods, screaming," I shot back, but I couldn't help the spark of excitement igniting within me.

With a shared look of resolve, we stepped cautiously outside, the dim light of the cabin behind us a beacon of safety. The woods loomed, dark and enigmatic, the rustling leaves a reminder of the secrets they concealed.

"Alright, let's investigate," I said, my pulse quickening as we moved deeper into the underbrush.

The world around us transformed as we ventured further from the cabin, each step taking us into the heart of the unknown. The branches above wove a thick tapestry, allowing only slivers of moonlight to pierce the darkness. Every rustle, every whisper of wind seemed magnified, an orchestra of nature conspiring to heighten the tension.

"Over there," Hunter pointed, and I followed his gaze. A flicker of movement caught my eye—something darting between the trees. "What do you think that was?"

"I don't know, but it looks like it's trying to avoid us," I said, a mixture of curiosity and trepidation bubbling within me.

Hunter hesitated, his eyes narrowing as he tried to discern the shape lurking just beyond the reach of the light. "Maybe we should split up? I'll go this way, and you can circle around."

"Split up? In a horror movie, that's the absolute worst plan," I protested.

"Exactly! We're not in a movie, so it can't end badly," he teased, but there was a glint of seriousness in his eyes.

"Fine," I relented, rolling my eyes but unable to suppress a smile. "But if you don't come back in five minutes, I'm sending in a rescue party."

"Deal."

We moved cautiously, my heart pounding in sync with the rhythm of my footsteps. As I ventured deeper into the underbrush, the air felt charged, alive with anticipation. The night was thick with the scent of damp earth and decaying leaves, the shadows shifting like phantoms. I strained my ears, listening for any sound that might give away what lurked nearby.

And then I heard it—a soft whimper, almost too quiet to catch. It sent a jolt through me, my instincts screaming that something was wrong. I darted toward the sound, adrenaline coursing through my veins as I pushed through the underbrush, desperate to uncover the source of the cry.

As I rounded a tree, the scene that unfolded before me was both shocking and surreal. A small creature, tangled in a net of twigs and branches, looked up at me with wide, frightened eyes. It was a fawn, its delicate frame trembling as it struggled against its bonds.

"Oh no, you poor thing!" I exclaimed, dropping to my knees beside it. The fawn's coat shimmered under the pale moonlight, a tapestry of browns and whites that spoke of innocence and vulnerability.

"Hey there, it's okay," I whispered, extending my hand cautiously. "I'm here to help you."

As I worked to free the fawn, I felt a presence behind me. I glanced over my shoulder to see Hunter approaching, concern etched across his features.

"What happened?" he asked, kneeling beside me.

"It's stuck," I said, my voice barely above a whisper. "We have to help it."

Together, we worked to untangle the fawn, carefully prying the twigs from its legs. As we freed it, a sense of triumph washed over me. The fawn took a hesitant step back, then paused, looking up at us with its big, grateful eyes.

"You did it," Hunter said, his pride evident as he watched the creature regain its footing.

I felt a swell of joy in my chest. "We did it," I corrected, sharing a triumphant grin with him.

With one last glance back at us, the fawn bounded into the darkness, disappearing into the thicket. I took a deep breath, the weight of the night pressing down on me, but this time it felt different. We had turned a moment of uncertainty into something beautiful—a connection forged not just in fear, but in kindness.

Hunter looked at me, and in that moment, everything shifted. The darkness around us felt less foreboding, filled instead with a sense of purpose and adventure. Whatever lay ahead—be it treasure or tragedy—we were in it together, ready to face the shadows that danced just beyond our reach.

The woods wrapped around us like an old cloak, heavy with secrets and whispers. Each step deeper into the forest felt like an incantation, summoning shadows that danced among the trees. Sunlight barely penetrated the thick canopy above, leaving patches of light that flickered like fireflies, illuminating the way to our destination: a decrepit cabin that stood in silent defiance of time and nature.

Hunter led the way, his silhouette a steady beacon against the encroaching twilight. "You know, this place looks like it could tell a story or two," he remarked, kicking at a cluster of weeds that had claimed dominion over the cabin's threshold. His casual bravado was a thin veil over the uncertainty we both felt.

"More like a horror story," I retorted, peering into the gloom that seemed to exhale a breath of musty air. "Should we really be here? What if we disturb something that should remain undisturbed?"

"Like ghosts? Or maybe just a raccoon with an attitude problem?" Hunter grinned, his eyes twinkling with mischief. I couldn't help but smile back, even as a chill crept down my spine.

As we stepped inside, the door creaked ominously, echoing our presence into the darkness. Dust motes floated lazily in the few beams of light that dared to enter, creating an almost ethereal atmosphere. The interior was a mausoleum of forgotten lives; old furniture sagged under the weight of dust, and cobwebs draped like veils over cracked mirrors. Yet, it was the diary on a weathered table that caught my eye—a forlorn relic yearning to share its story.

"Look at this," I whispered, brushing off the dust to reveal the leather-bound cover. Hunter approached, his curiosity piqued.

"Are you thinking what I'm thinking?" he asked, leaning closer. The air between us crackled with the thrill of discovery.

"Only one way to find out," I replied, opening the diary with a reluctant reverence. The pages were yellowed, the ink faded yet legible, revealing a woman's elegant script that spoke of heartache, fear, and an all-consuming darkness.

"I, Eleanor Prescott, take up this pen in the hopes of exorcising the shadows that plague my family..." the first entry read. As I continued to read aloud, the words unfurled like a dark tapestry, weaving tales of despair interlaced with vivid dreams that had twisted into nightmares.

Hunter listened intently, his eyes narrowing as I recounted Eleanor's encounters with a presence that seemed to haunt her lineage—a relentless pursuit of the Prescott bloodline, wrapped in the enigma of our shared fears. Each entry detailed a descent into madness, chronicling Eleanor's attempts to shield her loved ones from an unknown terror, but it was the last passage that struck a chord deep within me.

"If this diary falls into the wrong hands, the legacy of despair shall claim yet another," it warned, the ink almost smeared with the weight of urgency. "I fear for my child, for they carry the mark of our family's curse. We are bound, entwined with fate, and I can no longer protect them..."

As I closed the diary, the weight of Eleanor's words pressed heavily upon us. "What do you think she meant by 'the mark of our family's curse'?" I asked, my voice barely above a whisper, as if speaking too loudly might awaken the very darkness she had feared.

Hunter's brow furrowed in thought. "Could it be that whatever haunted her is still lurking? Maybe it's what's drawn us here in the first place."

The connection between us felt almost palpable, a thread woven tighter with each revelation. "But why us? What do we have to do with her?"

"I think," he began slowly, "that we are more connected to this than we realize. Maybe we're part of a cycle that needs to be broken." His eyes searched mine, earnest and bright amidst the encroaching darkness.

Just then, a distant rustling sound echoed from outside, followed by a soft thump that made my heart race. We exchanged a glance, a silent agreement passing between us—fear and determination coiling together like the vines outside.

"Did you hear that?" I asked, my voice barely steady.

"Yeah," Hunter replied, his gaze shifting to the door. "Stay close." He stepped forward, his protective instinct igniting like a flame in the dark.

As we approached the door, a shadow darted past the cabin, vanishing into the underbrush. Hunter hesitated, uncertainty flickering across his features. "Should we investigate?"

"Do we have a choice?" I replied, the thrill of adrenaline coursing through my veins.

We crept outside, the fading light casting eerie shapes across the ground. The rustling had ceased, leaving an unsettling silence that clung to us like a shroud. Suddenly, a figure emerged from behind a tree—a boy, no older than us, with wild hair and wide, fearful eyes.

"Help! Please!" he gasped, stumbling toward us, breathless and trembling. "It's coming! You have to run!"

The urgency in his voice sent a jolt of fear coursing through my veins. "What's coming? Who are you?" I demanded, trying to keep my voice steady despite the rising panic.

"The darkness! It's been searching for you!" His eyes darted around, as if expecting something sinister to emerge from the shadows. "You have to hide—now!"

Before we could respond, a low growl echoed from the depths of the woods, sending a wave of dread crashing over us. Hunter stepped in front of me instinctively, shielding me from whatever lurked just beyond the tree line. The boy's gaze hardened, his expression shifting from fear to desperation.

"There's no time! It'll be here any second! You don't understand!" he shouted, but his warning was drowned out by the growing roar of something unseen.

Just as the underbrush exploded in motion, I felt the world tilt on its axis—a flash of fur and claws as a massive figure barreled toward us, eyes glinting like shards of ice. We were rooted in place, caught between the urge to flee and the instinct to stand our ground.

In that heartbeat, I realized that whatever dark legacy Eleanor had written of was not just a story from the past. It was our reality now, and the shadows were no longer content to remain hidden. The weight of our fates pressed down on us, intertwining our destinies in a way that neither of us could have anticipated.

Then, without warning, the ground trembled beneath us, and the world plunged into chaos.

Chapter 16: Love's Reckoning

The moon hung low over Firestone Bay, casting silvery threads across the dark waters, shimmering like secrets begging to be uncovered. I stood on the creaking wooden dock, the scent of salt and seaweed mingling with the faint hint of rain lingering in the air. My heart was a frantic drum in my chest, each beat echoing the tumult of emotions that surged within me. Hunter's presence beside me was both a balm and a blaze, igniting a passion that threatened to consume us both. The night had transformed; the air buzzed with anticipation, and the shadows whispered of the danger lurking just beyond the reach of the moonlight.

"I can't believe it's come to this," Hunter said, his voice low but steady, his eyes scanning the inky horizon where the water kissed the sky. "I thought we'd have more time before—"

"Before what?" I interrupted, unable to hide the tremor in my voice. "Before we had to fight for our lives? Or before we had to confront whatever it is that's hunting us?"

He turned to face me, the moonlight catching the angles of his jaw and the determined glint in his deep-set eyes. "Before we had to confront this... truth between us," he said, stepping closer, the warmth radiating off him wrapping around me like a cherished blanket.

The pull of his body was magnetic, a force that demanded attention and ached for acknowledgment. I could feel the heat rising in my cheeks, but beneath that warmth was a pang of fear. Fear of the unknown and fear of losing what we had just begun to grasp. "This isn't just about us, Hunter. They know we're onto them," I replied, trying to tether my thoughts to the urgency of the moment. "And they're not going to let us walk away from this."

His brow furrowed, a shadow of concern flitting across his face. "I can handle danger," he said firmly, but the tremor in his voice betrayed him. "What I can't handle is losing you. Not now."

Those words ignited a firestorm within me. Love was supposed to be a refuge, but this love was a tempest, wild and untamed, battering against the walls I had erected. "And what if it means putting you in danger?" I challenged, taking a step back, the reality of our situation crashing over me like a wave. "What if loving you means drawing the storm even closer?"

Hunter's expression softened, and he reached for my hand, his grip warm and reassuring. "Then let's face the storm together. I'd rather fight beside you than stand alone in the light of day, pretending everything is fine."

For a heartbeat, I lost myself in the depths of his gaze, the promise of connection and safety swaying my resolve. But the reality was unyielding, a bitter truth that clawed at my insides. I was more than just an unsuspecting girl caught in a love story; I was a pawn in a larger game of shadows and secrets, one that had already taken too much from me.

A rustle broke the silence, sharp and unwelcome. My heart leapt, instinct urging me to prepare for the worst. "Did you hear that?" I whispered, my pulse quickening.

Hunter nodded, eyes narrowing as he scanned the treeline flanking the dock. "Stay close," he instructed, his voice now a low growl. The protective instinct in him was undeniable, the urge to shield me evident in the way he positioned himself between me and the darkness beyond.

The rustling grew louder, the sounds of leaves crunching underfoot invading the fragile calm of our moment. I felt a cold prickle of fear crawl up my spine. "What if it's them?" I breathed, the dread pooling in my stomach.

"Then we'll be ready." His certainty ignited something deep within me, a blend of courage and trepidation.

Before I could respond, a figure emerged from the shadows, moving with fluid grace. It was a girl—no, a woman—her long, dark hair flowing like a river of night, eyes gleaming with an unnatural light. "You should not be here," she said, her voice a chilling whisper that cut through the stillness.

My breath hitched as I recognized her, the woman whose presence had haunted my dreams, a specter entwined with the secrets of Firestone Bay. "What do you want?" I asked, my voice steadier than I felt.

Her gaze flickered between Hunter and me, calculating, predatory. "You are delving too deeply into matters that do not concern you. Leave this place, or face the consequences."

Hunter stepped forward, his protective nature surging to the forefront. "You don't scare us," he challenged, but the uncertainty in his tone made my heart sink. "We'll uncover the truth, no matter what you say."

"Then you will be the ones who suffer," she hissed, a sinister smile playing on her lips. The air thickened with tension, each breath feeling heavier than the last, laden with the weight of our choices.

In that moment, I felt a shift, an unspoken understanding between us. This woman was not just a messenger; she was a herald of the storm we had invited into our lives. "Hunter, we need to leave," I urged, my instincts screaming at me to escape.

He hesitated, his jaw clenching, but the danger looming behind the woman was palpable. With a reluctant nod, he grabbed my hand, and together we turned to flee down the dock, the echoes of our footsteps merging with the crashing waves, a chaotic symphony of fear and determination.

The night had transformed into a battleground, and as we raced toward the safety of the shore, I realized we were not just running from a threat but toward something else entirely—an awakening, a reckoning that would change everything we thought we knew about love, loyalty, and the darkness that shadows our lives.

The wind whipped through the trees like a restless spirit, carrying with it the scent of impending rain and the distant murmur of the ocean. Hunter and I dashed across the dock, my heart pounding in rhythm with our hurried steps. The moon, now obscured by a creeping mass of clouds, cloaked the world in darkness, amplifying the sense of urgency that hung in the air like a thick fog.

"We need to get to the car," Hunter urged, his voice a low murmur as he shot a glance over his shoulder. "If we can reach the road, we can—"

"Are you sure that's a good idea?" I interrupted, the tightness in my chest constricting further. "What if she follows us? We can't just run without a plan."

"Better to run than stand here waiting to be caught," he countered, a stubborn spark igniting in his hazel eyes. "I won't let anything happen to you. You mean too much to me."

His words hung between us, warm and weighty, but the urgency of our situation made it hard to savor their sweetness. I understood the risks, and the idea of being exposed to whatever darkness lurked in the shadows sent shivers through my spine. Yet, with Hunter beside me, the fear morphed into a different kind of thrill, the adrenaline of our escape feeding the flame of our connection.

As we sprinted down the dock, the creaking wood beneath our feet echoed ominously, as if the very structure was warning us of the danger lying in wait. The night felt alive, electric, charged with the potential for both revelation and ruin. I could hear my heart thrumming in my ears, drowning out the sounds of the waves crashing against the shore. Each step felt like a leap into the unknown, propelled by a mixture of fear and determination.

Suddenly, a shadow darted across our path, a figure emerging from the thickened gloom. I halted, my breath catching as the world around me seemed to freeze. Hunter stepped in front of me instinctively, his posture tense, ready to confront whatever threat lay ahead.

"Who's there?" he demanded, his voice unwavering despite the pounding of his heart.

"Relax, it's just me." A familiar voice cut through the tension, and the figure stepped into the faint light cast by a nearby lantern. It was Jake, my best friend, his face twisted in concern.

"What are you doing here?" I exclaimed, a mixture of relief and irritation flooding my system. "This isn't safe!"

"I could say the same for you," he shot back, his brow furrowing as he looked between Hunter and me. "I heard something—some whispers in town. People are starting to talk, and they're looking for you."

"Great," I muttered, running a hand through my hair, my mind racing. "What did they say?"

"That you've gone missing, that you might be in danger," he replied, glancing over his shoulder nervously. "I didn't know what to think. When I saw your car parked near the cliffs, I figured I had to check."

Hunter's eyes narrowed as he processed this information. "You need to get out of here, Jake," he said, his tone urgent. "It's not just whispers anymore. They're real threats, and they're not going to let us go easily."

"Hold on," Jake interjected, raising his hands in a placating gesture. "You're telling me there are actual dangers lurking in the shadows? What happened?"

Before either of us could respond, the air around us shifted again. A chill crept down my spine, the unmistakable feeling of being watched prickling at the back of my neck. "We don't have time to explain," I urged, grabbing Hunter's arm. "We need to leave, now."

The three of us started to move quickly along the dock, the rhythmic sound of our footsteps mingling with the crashing waves. The tension was palpable, every rustle of leaves and creak of wood amplifying the sense of urgency. I glanced over my shoulder, half-expecting the woman to emerge again, her sinister smile etched into my memory.

As we reached the end of the dock, I fished the keys from my pocket, my hands shaking slightly. I fumbled them for a moment before finally finding the right one. "I've got it," I said, trying to sound more confident than I felt. "Let's get to the car."

In the darkness, the headlights of my old sedan flickered to life, illuminating the path ahead but also casting eerie shadows that danced around us. Hunter slid into the driver's seat, and Jake hopped in the back, the tension still thick in the air.

"Where to?" Hunter asked, gripping the steering wheel as if it were the only thing tethering him to reality.

"Anywhere but here," I replied, my voice steadier than my heart. "We need to regroup and figure out our next move."

As Hunter revved the engine and pulled away from the dock, I could see the shimmering water fading into the distance. I felt a strange mixture of relief and fear; the danger was still out there, and we had no real plan, but at least we were moving.

"Let's head toward the cliffs," Jake suggested, his voice steady, cutting through the silence that settled in the car. "There's an old lookout spot I know—should be quiet, and we can talk without being overheard."

"Fine by me," Hunter said, glancing at me, gauging my reaction. I nodded, grateful for Jake's initiative.

As we drove, the landscape rushed by in a blur of shadow and light. My mind raced, spiraling through everything that had happened—the revelations, the danger, and the undeniable connection I felt with Hunter. Each moment we spent together felt more profound, more weighty, as if we were unwittingly writing the story of our lives in ink that could never fade.

"I can't believe you guys are in this mess," Jake said, breaking the silence as we approached the winding road leading to the cliffs. "I mean, who knew Firestone Bay had this kind of drama? It's like a real-life thriller."

"Right? And I didn't even pack popcorn," I quipped, trying to lighten the mood as Hunter shot me an amused glance, his lips twitching into a half-smile.

"Just be glad you're not starring in it," Hunter replied dryly, his fingers tapping against the steering wheel in a rhythm that mirrored my racing heart. "I'd hate to see how that plot twist would end."

"Very funny," I shot back, the nervous energy in the car shifting as we turned onto the narrow road leading to the cliffs. But even as I tried to joke, a sense of dread lingered. Whatever awaited us at the lookout was as uncertain as the shadows chasing us through the night.

As we rounded the final bend, the rocky cliffs loomed ahead, their jagged edges silhouetted against the now star-studded sky. The ocean rumbled beneath, waves crashing against the rocks like nature's own heartbeat, fierce and untamed. It felt as though we were on the edge of something monumental, poised to dive into the depths of whatever lay beneath.

The cliffs towered above us like ancient sentinels, their rocky faces scarred by time and the relentless kiss of the sea. As Hunter parked the car, the engine's hum faded into the background, leaving us surrounded by the haunting sound of waves crashing against the rocks below. I could feel the energy shift in the air, a palpable tension that thrummed beneath the surface, drawing us toward the precipice where we would confront the truth we had unearthed.

"Are you ready for this?" Hunter asked, turning to face me, his expression a blend of determination and vulnerability. The soft glow from the dashboard illuminated the strong lines of his jaw, and I caught a glimpse of the turmoil swirling behind his eyes.

"Honestly? I'm terrified," I admitted, the confession spilling from my lips before I could second-guess myself. "But I'd rather face the fear than let it control me."

A flicker of admiration sparked in his gaze, and he nodded, his resolve solidifying. "That's the spirit. Whatever comes next, we face it together. No more running."

With that, we stepped out into the cool night air, the breeze carrying with it the brine of the ocean and the scent of earth after rain. I followed Hunter as he led us toward the lookout, the crunch of gravel beneath our feet punctuating the silence. Each step felt heavy with purpose, the gravity of the moment urging us onward.

As we reached the edge of the cliff, I took a moment to absorb the breathtaking view. The moonlight danced on the surface of the water, illuminating the crests of waves like silver jewels scattered across a dark expanse. But the beauty was overshadowed by the knowledge of the dangers that lurked in the shadows, threats waiting to pounce.

"Do you think she'll follow us?" I asked, trying to mask my apprehension with bravado.

"I don't know," Hunter replied, his eyes scanning the horizon. "But I'd rather be here than at the dock, where we'd be trapped. If she's coming, we'll be ready for her."

"Do you always have to be so logical?" I teased, nudging him playfully. "Sometimes a little chaos is fun."

"Chaos is only fun when you're not the one living it," he shot back with a smirk, though I could see the tension in his shoulders.

We stood in silence for a moment, the roar of the ocean below matching the pounding of my heart. Just as I began to feel the weight of the world pressing down on my chest, a flicker of movement caught my eye at the edge of the cliff. A shadow, darker than the night itself, crept closer, and I felt my breath hitch in my throat.

"Did you see that?" I whispered, my voice barely above the sound of the wind.

Hunter turned sharply, eyes narrowing as he focused on the spot. "Yeah. Stay close."

The shadow twisted and contorted, as if it were alive, morphing into something that defied reality. My pulse quickened, and I instinctively stepped closer to Hunter, the warmth of his body grounding me. We were in this together, but the fear gnawed at the edges of my courage.

Then, out of the darkness, she appeared—the woman from the dock, her expression a mask of fury and desperation. The moonlight glinted off her eyes, transforming them into pools of midnight. "You shouldn't have come here," she said, her voice a low hiss that sent shivers down my spine.

"Why are you doing this?" I asked, trying to sound braver than I felt. "What do you want from us?"

Her lips curled into a smile that held no warmth, a predatory glint flashing in her gaze. "What I want is inconsequential. What matters is what you've discovered. Knowledge is dangerous, especially in the wrong hands."

"What are you talking about?" Hunter challenged, stepping in front of me protectively. "You're the one who's in the wrong here. You're threatening us for asking questions."

"Questions that should remain unanswered," she replied, advancing slowly, her presence wrapping around us like a cold mist. "But now that you know, I can't let you leave. You're too close to the truth, and that cannot be allowed."

I felt a spark of defiance ignite within me, the urge to fight back against the fear gripping my heart. "You think you can intimidate us into silence? We won't back down, no matter what you threaten," I declared, my voice trembling but resolute.

She laughed, a chilling sound that echoed off the cliffs and mixed with the crashing waves. "You're brave, I'll give you that. But bravery alone won't save you."

Before I could respond, she lunged, the movement so swift that it blurred at the edges. Hunter reacted instantly, pushing me aside as he stepped forward, fists clenched and ready to defend. "Stay back!" he shouted, his voice a fierce roar that resonated through the night.

But the woman was relentless, her form shifting as she lunged toward him, a darkness that seemed to pulse with its own energy. I watched in horror, my heart racing as I desperately searched for a way to intervene. "Hunter!" I screamed, fear gripping me like a vice.

In an instant, everything spiraled out of control. Hunter sidestepped just in time, the woman narrowly missing him as she stumbled forward. The force of her movement caused a cascade of stones to tumble from the cliff's edge, sending them crashing down toward the rocks below.

"Run!" he shouted, his voice piercing through the chaos. "We need to get out of here!"

The urgency in his tone galvanized me into action. I sprinted toward the car, the adrenaline coursing through my veins as I glanced back to see Hunter grappling with the woman.

"Go!" he yelled again, but I couldn't leave him. Not now. I turned, ready to help, but the sight that met my eyes froze me in place.

The woman had twisted her body, her hands gripping Hunter's collar as she lifted him off the ground with an ease that belied her delicate frame. "You're not leaving," she hissed, her eyes darkening with malice.

"Hunter!" I shouted, panic flooding my voice as I rushed back, instinctively reaching for anything I could use as a weapon.

Just as I was about to throw a nearby rock, a piercing scream shattered the night air, echoing off the cliffs and reverberating in my chest. It wasn't just a sound; it was a cry filled with anguish, an otherworldly wail that sent chills racing down my spine.

The woman turned, her grip loosening on Hunter as her eyes widened with shock. "No!" she cried, stumbling back as if struck by an unseen force.

I seized the moment and dashed toward Hunter, pulling him down just as the darkness surged forward, enveloping the cliff in an ominous shadow. We hit the ground hard, my heart pounding in my ears as the world around us began to tremble.

The scream continued to echo, a haunting lament that reverberated through the very bones of the earth. I glanced up, eyes wide with fear, and saw the shadow swirl, its form shifting and expanding, growing monstrous in its fury.

"Get up!" Hunter urged, his voice a strained whisper as he scrambled to his feet.

As I rose, the shadow flickered, revealing the outline of figures emerging from the depths, a collective presence that felt both terrifying and strangely familiar. They loomed above us, their faces indistinct but their intent unmistakable.

"Run!" I shouted, but it was too late. The darkness surged forward, and as it engulfed us, I felt an unyielding grip seize my heart, pulling me into the depths of a nightmare from which I feared we might never escape.

Chapter 17: The Final Stand

The night air was thick with tension, a palpable force that settled over Firestone Bay like a fog, cloaking us in unease. As I stood before the gathering of townsfolk, the flickering lanterns cast ghostly shadows against the weathered clapboard walls of the old town hall. The air was redolent of salt and earth, but beneath it lay something more ominous, a whisper of fear that crept into the cracks of our resolve. Hunter stood beside me, his presence a steady anchor against the rising tide of uncertainty. The murmur of anxious voices surged like the waves outside, each person wrestling with their own memories of dread—the missing children, the flickering lights, the figure that haunted the edges of our consciousness.

"Listen, everyone," I began, my voice steadier than I felt. "We've faced shadows before, and we've always come out on the other side. But this time, we're not alone." The words rolled out, buoyed by the hope that had been building in the pit of my stomach. The townsfolk shifted uneasily, their expressions a tapestry of doubt and determination.

"I know it's been hard," I continued, pacing before the crowd, allowing the weight of my gaze to connect with each face. "But if we join together, we can confront the darkness. Hunter and I have uncovered the truth—about the figure, about our past. We must stand united against this fear."

A low rumble of discontent broke through the crowd, the voice of old Mrs. Hargrove rising above the rest. "And what makes you think this will work? We've tried before, and it only got us hurt."

Her eyes, sunken and weary, reflected years of unspoken pain. My heart ached for her, for every soul standing there, etched with memories of loss. "Because we can't let fear dictate our future anymore. We've lost too much already. It's time to reclaim our lives!" The words hung in the air, fragile yet fervent.

Hunter stepped forward, his deep voice resonating with authority. "This isn't just about the past. It's about our children, our families, and our future. We've let the darkness win for too long. If we face this together, we can break the cycle."

The energy in the room shifted, palpable as the sea breeze swirled outside, but doubt still lingered. I could see it in the furrowed brows and the skeptical glances exchanged. My heart raced as I surveyed the crowd, desperate to ignite a spark of courage. Just then, a low growl echoed from the entrance, slicing through the tension like a knife.

Everyone turned, eyes wide with fear. The figure that had haunted our lives appeared, emerging from the shadows like a nightmare given flesh. Cloaked in darkness, its form was barely discernible, but the aura of malice was unmistakable. It stepped forward, and my breath caught in my throat as I recognized the cold gleam of its eyes.

"Enough of this," it rasped, voice like gravel sliding over stone. "You think you can defy me? I have fed on your fear long enough." The words slithered through the hall, and the room trembled under their weight.

I felt Hunter's hand on my shoulder, grounding me. "We can't let it intimidate us!" he whispered fiercely, his eyes burning with defiance. "Together, we stand. Remember why we're here."

"Why don't you show us your true form, shadow?" I challenged, surprising myself with the strength of my voice. "Let everyone see what you truly are!"

The figure hesitated, and for a moment, the shadows flickered around it, revealing a glimpse of the true horror within—a twisted visage that seemed to shimmer and warp in the lantern light, each feature a grotesque mockery of the people we once knew. Gasps of horror erupted from the crowd, but instead of faltering, I felt a surge of strength. "You don't scare us anymore! We know your secret!"

With a sudden flick of its wrist, the figure conjured a tempest, gusting through the hall and sending lanterns crashing to the ground. Darkness enveloped us, but I could hear the sounds of movement as people scrambled to regain their footing. Hunter's voice rose above the chaos, urging everyone to gather closer.

"Focus! We are stronger together! Use the light!" His command pierced the darkness like a beacon.

As if guided by some unseen force, the townsfolk began to light the lanterns anew, a flicker of flame against the encroaching dark. The light danced and flickered, illuminating the faces of the brave souls who stood by us, determination kindling in their eyes.

The figure recoiled as the glow intensified, a hiss escaping its lips. "You think you can banish me? I have lived in the shadows far longer than you've drawn breath."

But our resolve only deepened. "We're not afraid of you!" I shouted, the words igniting a fire in my heart. "You've fed on our fear for too long. No more!"

With every shout, every flicker of light, I could feel the energy building, an electrifying pulse that flowed through us all. The townsfolk rallied, their voices rising, blending into a harmonious roar that pushed back against the darkness. I locked eyes with Hunter, and in that moment, we understood—we were not merely fighting a figure of shadows but a manifestation of our own fears.

"Push it back!" Hunter yelled, drawing strength from the crowd. "Together!"

And we did. The air shimmered with energy, a tapestry of bravery woven by our united front. The figure faltered, the darkness around it quaking as our light surged forward, a wave of incandescent fury.

"Enough!" it screeched, the cry reverberating through the hall.

But we pressed on, the fire within us refusing to be snuffed out. The shadows writhed, and with each flicker of our lanterns, we chipped away at the veil of terror that had held us captive for too long. In that moment, I realized we were more than just a town; we were a force of nature, a collective spirit that would not be broken.

The figure howled, its form dissolving like mist in the morning sun, and I felt a thrill course through me. Hope surged, a powerful current igniting the air. We were finally taking a stand against the fear that had kept us shackled. Together, we were lighting the way toward a new dawn, one where shadows could no longer dictate our lives.

The flickering light of the lanterns bathed the room in a warm glow, but the atmosphere was anything but comforting. The figure's retreat had felt like a victory, but a gnawing sensation in my gut warned me it was merely the calm before the storm. As the last vestiges of darkness faded away, the townsfolk began to regain their composure, their expressions shifting from fear to something resembling hope. I exchanged a glance with Hunter, who was scanning the crowd, his brow furrowed with concern.

"Now that we've faced it," he said, leaning closer, "what do we do next? I can't shake the feeling that it's not finished with us yet."

I could feel the weight of the town's collective gaze on us, a mixture of gratitude and expectation. "We need to fortify our defenses. It's not just about what it wants; it's about what we need to protect." The words felt heavy, but they ignited a spark of determination within me. We couldn't allow fear to take root again.

A murmur of agreement rippled through the crowd, and Mrs. Hargrove stood, her voice trembling but resolute. "I've seen too many lives disrupted by this entity. If we are to face it, we must do so with all our strength."

Her words hung in the air, stirring a mixture of inspiration and unease. "Yes," I nodded. "But we also need to share our experiences, gather every scrap of information about what this figure represents. If it feeds on fear, we can use that against it."

Hunter raised an eyebrow, the faintest hint of a smile breaking through his worry. "Are we planning to serve it a lovely dinner of our collective anxieties?"

"Perhaps with a side of bravery," I shot back, unable to resist the levity that hung in the air. Laughter broke out among the crowd, a much-needed balm to our frayed nerves.

"Let's call a town meeting," I continued, my voice steady. "We need to pool our knowledge, all the strange happenings, anything that connects to this figure. The more we understand, the stronger we'll become."

As the townsfolk began to disperse, excitement buzzed in the air, but I caught a flicker of doubt in Hunter's eyes. "You know it won't be that easy, right? Knowledge doesn't always equate to action."

I smiled softly, appreciating his practicality. "True. But action without knowledge is reckless. If we're going to act, let's do it with our eyes wide open."

He chuckled, shaking his head as we stepped outside into the cool night. The salt-tinged breeze tousled my hair, bringing with it the sounds of the ocean crashing against the cliffs. "You always did have a way with words."

As we walked toward the center of town, I couldn't help but feel the energy around us shifting. The air felt charged with possibility, and for the first time in a long while, the weight of our burdens felt lighter. We reached the town square, a gathering spot that had seen countless celebrations and sorrows over the years.

Hunter paused, looking around. "You really think we can convince them? After everything?"

I turned to him, meeting his gaze. "I think we can convince them to try. Sometimes, that's all it takes—a flicker of hope, a shared purpose."

The next few days were a whirlwind of planning and preparation. We held meetings in the town hall, where the townsfolk gathered to share their stories and experiences. Old man Jasper spoke of the time he'd seen the figure on the beach, its eyes glinting like shards of glass. A young mother recounted how her daughter had spoken of a shadow that lurked just out of reach, a constant reminder of fear even in her dreams.

With each tale, the knot of fear began to unravel, threads of shared experience weaving us into a stronger fabric. We were no longer isolated individuals, haunted by our own nightmares. Instead, we became a community, a force against the darkness.

One evening, as we finalized plans, I felt a shift in the air, the chill creeping in with the encroaching twilight. "Are you sure this is going to work?" Hunter asked, his tone laced with a seriousness that pierced through my optimism. "What if the figure is waiting for us to make our move?"

"It might be," I admitted, my heart pounding. "But we can't hide forever. If we stand still, it'll consume us. This isn't just about fighting it; it's about reclaiming our lives."

He sighed, running a hand through his hair. "You're right. I just... I wish we had more time to prepare."

"There's never enough time, is there?" I replied, feeling a strange calm wash over me. "But that's life. We have to seize the moment."

The night of the gathering arrived, a convergence of determination and apprehension. The town square buzzed with energy as people set up lanterns and organized seating. It felt surreal to witness our small town transformed into a beacon of defiance. As the first stars began to twinkle in the darkening sky, I took my place at the front, my heart racing in tandem with the rhythm of the waves crashing against the cliffs.

The crowd hushed as Hunter and I stood side by side, and I took a deep breath, channeling the warmth of the lanterns into my words. "Tonight, we stand together against the shadows that have loomed over us for far too long. We have all felt its presence, the way it festers in our minds, feeding off our fear. But tonight, we refuse to be afraid."

A wave of applause and cheers erupted, filling me with a surge of confidence. I could see the determination etched in their faces, the unity sparking like electricity in the air. "Let's share our knowledge and our strength. Together, we can turn the tide!"

As I spoke, I felt a strange sensation, a prickling at the nape of my neck. Glancing over my shoulder, my heart sank. The figure, shrouded in darkness, lingered at the edge of the square, watching with eyes that glimmered like cold steel. My voice wavered, but I pressed on, rallying the townsfolk to stand firm.

"Do not let it sway you!" I shouted, feeling the energy shift again, this time with a sense of foreboding. "We know what we're fighting for!"

Yet as I spoke, the figure took a step forward, the shadows swirling around it like a storm. The townsfolk gasped, a wave of fear washing over the crowd, but I refused to let panic take hold. "Stay together!" I urged, holding my ground as adrenaline surged through me.

Suddenly, the figure lunged, and chaos erupted. People screamed, and I could feel the weight of dread crashing down around us. I grabbed Hunter's arm, and we began to retreat back, trying to keep the townsfolk organized.

"Focus on the light!" I shouted, pushing the crowd to the front where the lanterns blazed brightly. The flickering flames seemed to shimmer defiantly against the encroaching dark, a fragile yet vital barrier.

"Look to each other!" Hunter called out, his voice steady even as the figure advanced. "Remember the stories! Draw strength from them!"

The townsfolk rallied, hearts ignited by memories of hope and defiance. As the figure drew closer, a strange clarity washed over me.

This wasn't just about confronting a shadow; it was about reclaiming our stories, our lives. The air hummed with the energy of determination, and I felt an unexpected strength surging from within.

"Together!" I cried, igniting the fire within us all. "Let's show this shadow it cannot break us!"

The figure advanced, cloaked in shadows, its very presence sending a shiver through the crowd. The energy shifted, vibrating with an unsettling tension as gasps rippled through the townsfolk, a collective breath held in trepidation. "Stay together!" I shouted, my voice piercing through the veil of panic that threatened to engulf us. "Don't let fear divide us!"

As I stepped forward, I could feel Hunter at my side, his presence a reassuring anchor. Together, we faced the oncoming darkness, hearts pounding in synchrony. The figure twisted, its form shimmering like a mirage in the moonlight, an embodiment of our deepest fears. "You think you can defy me?" it hissed, its voice a slithering whisper that slithered into our ears. "I thrive in your doubt, your despair."

"Not tonight!" Hunter retorted, his voice a low growl, filled with the kind of conviction that could move mountains. The light from our lanterns flickered defiantly, illuminating the faces of the brave souls around us, each reflecting a resolve that I had never seen before.

"Remember why we're here!" I implored, raising my arms, urging everyone to join me. "We stand for our families, for our children, for the lives we have built!"

The figure paused, uncertainty flickering in its glassy eyes, and for a heartbeat, I felt a surge of hope—a momentary crack in its facade of terror. Encouraged, I pressed on, summoning every ounce of courage I could muster. "We know your secret! You thrive on fear, but we are not afraid anymore!"

Suddenly, the figure let out a bone-chilling laugh that echoed through the square, cutting through the night like a knife. "You may think you understand me, but you are merely playing into my hands. Fear is a living thing, and it feeds on your belief."

The air thickened with tension, and a palpable sense of dread washed over the crowd as the shadows around the figure began to ripple, coiling and twisting like serpents ready to strike. "It's time to show you what true fear looks like," it taunted, stepping closer, its form distorting with every heartbeat.

"Focus on the light!" Hunter urged, his voice a clarion call that rang clear amidst the chaos. "Draw from each other! Use your stories, your strength!"

With a collective intake of breath, the townsfolk formed a circle, each one holding their lanterns high, their flames flickering defiantly against the encroaching dark. The light danced and swayed, casting warm golden hues against the deepening shadows, illuminating not just our surroundings but also the steely resolve in our hearts.

"Tell it your story!" I shouted, turning to the crowd. "What are you fighting for?"

An elderly man stepped forward, his hands trembling but his voice steady. "I'm fighting for my wife. She deserves to live without fear!"

His declaration sparked a ripple through the group, and one by one, others joined in, each voice weaving a tapestry of resilience. "I'm fighting for my children's laughter!" cried a young mother. "I want them to feel safe!"

"I'm fighting for my home!" shouted a burly fisherman, his hands calloused but steady. "This town is my blood!"

As the chorus of declarations grew, the figure shrank back, the shadows around it flickering uncertainly. "You think your stories hold power?" it spat, but the tremor in its voice betrayed its growing fear. "I am eternal. I will consume you all!"

Hunter's hand tightened around mine, and I felt the electricity of determination surge between us. "Together!" he shouted, and the townsfolk echoed his rallying cry, their voices swelling into a wave of defiance.

The shadows hesitated, and I seized the moment. "Our strength lies not in the absence of fear, but in our refusal to let it control us!" I shouted, my heart racing. "We stand united, and we will fight!"

The light from our lanterns pulsed, a beacon against the encroaching darkness, and for a moment, it felt as if the very air was charged with possibility. The figure wavered, its edges flickering like a flame on the brink of extinguishing.

But just as victory seemed within reach, the ground beneath us trembled. A deep rumble resonated from the earth, and the lanterns flickered ominously, shadows stretching toward us like desperate fingers. "Foolish mortals!" the figure shrieked, its voice a cacophony of rage and despair. "You think you can sever the ties of fear? You will all pay for this defiance!"

Suddenly, a crack split the ground, a jagged fissure that threatened to swallow us whole. I stumbled back, heart racing as I grabbed Hunter's arm, panic setting in. "What's happening?"

"Stay together!" he yelled, pulling me closer to him as the townsfolk rallied once more, their voices steadying the rising tide of chaos.

The figure surged forward, and the darkness wrapped around me like a shroud, cold and suffocating. "You are mine!" it roared, its form twisting grotesquely, threatening to consume us all.

But the lanterns burned brighter, their flames reaching out like fingers of light, pushing back against the shadows. I could feel the collective strength of the town pulsing around me, a living entity of hope and courage.

Then, with a sudden burst, the ground heaved violently, and I was thrown to the side, landing hard on the cobblestones. I gasped, struggling to rise as the chaos unfolded around me. I could see Hunter, standing resolute at the forefront, his eyes ablaze with determination, his stance unyielding against the figure's onslaught.

"Fight!" he shouted, and the townsfolk rallied once more, their lanterns thrust forward like swords of light.

As I regained my footing, I looked around, heart racing as the shadows writhed and danced, each flicker of flame illuminating the fear etched on the faces of the people I loved. In that moment, a deep-seated fury welled up inside me—a fierce protectiveness that pushed away the fear threatening to take root.

But just as I was about to join the fray, the ground beneath me quaked once more, and a deafening crack echoed through the night. A fissure tore open wider, swallowing one of the lanterns whole, plunging a section of the crowd into darkness. "No!" I screamed, horror crashing over me.

From the depths of the shadowy void, an arm reached out, clawing at the air, and I froze, paralyzed by dread. The townsfolk began to falter, the glow of our collective courage flickering in the face of despair. "We can't let it take anyone!" I shouted, fighting through the panic clawing at my chest.

Just then, a scream pierced the air, and I turned in horror to see a figure being dragged toward the abyss. Hunter's voice cut through the chaos, rallying the townsfolk. "Hold the line! We can't let it win!"

I reached for the nearest lantern, my heart racing as I fought through the panicked crowd. "We can save them!" I cried, determination flooding my veins. But before I could take a step forward, the shadows surged, and the figure laughed—a sound that reverberated with dark glee.

As I glanced back, I saw Hunter struggling against the tide of darkness, his expression fierce and unwavering, but the shadows were closing in. The air crackled with energy, fear swirling around us like a storm. And in that moment, as the darkness threatened to consume us, I realized the truth: our fight was just beginning.

With one last surge of courage, I called out, "Together! We're not done yet!" But even as I said it, a wave of darkness crashed over me, and I felt myself being pulled into the depths of the void, the light of our hope flickering like a candle in the wind.

And then everything went black.

Chapter 18: Into the Abyss

The night descended rapidly, an inky curtain falling over the landscape as the figure loomed closer, shrouded in darkness. Each ominous step echoed through the stillness, sending a ripple of anxiety down my spine. It was as if the very shadows conspired to hide this intruder's intent. Hunter tightened his grip on my hand, his warmth a stark contrast to the chilling air around us. Together, we plunged deeper into the woods, our hearts pounding in tandem with the rustling leaves, the world around us fading into a blur of twilight greens and grays.

The path was narrow, overgrown with brambles and vines that seemed to reach out like grasping fingers, but we pressed on, driven by a mix of fear and curiosity. Every instinct told me to turn back, to flee the encroaching darkness and the lurking presence behind us. Yet something in Hunter's unwavering gaze urged me forward, an unspoken promise of safety amidst the chaos. With each step, the scent of damp earth and danger thickened in the air, wrapping around us like a cloak.

We reached the entrance to the old mines, its gaping maw black and foreboding. The rusted sign, barely legible in the dim light, whispered of long-forgotten tales and lives once vibrant. "Closed for safety," it read, but the irony was not lost on us; we were about to enter a realm where safety was a distant memory. Hunter led the way, his silhouette framed against the jagged edges of the mine's entrance, and I hesitated for a moment, the weight of the world pressing down on me.

"Are you sure about this?" I asked, my voice barely above a whisper, the sound swallowed by the echoing stillness.

He turned, his blue eyes glinting like shards of ice. "We need to know what we're up against. Whatever's lurking out there is tied to this place." His voice was steady, the resolve in his words lending me the courage I needed to follow him into the abyss.

As we crossed the threshold, the cool air inside the mine enveloped us, a stark contrast to the warmth outside. The light from Hunter's flashlight sliced through the darkness, illuminating crumbling walls lined with traces of history—rusted tools, shattered lanterns, and piles of debris that spoke of lives interrupted. It was a tomb of forgotten hopes and dreams, a haunting reminder of the past.

We ventured deeper, our footsteps muted against the damp earth, the silence punctuated only by the distant drip of water and the soft hum of memories lingering in the air. I could almost hear the echoes of laughter and the clang of metal on metal, the vibrant pulse of life that once filled these tunnels. But that vibrancy had long been extinguished, replaced by an unsettling stillness that prickled at my skin.

"There's something about this place," I murmured, glancing over my shoulder as if the shadows themselves were listening. "It feels alive... but in a way that makes my skin crawl."

Hunter nodded, his expression serious. "It's more than just the mine. It's the history tied to Firestone Bay. The people who lived here... they left pieces of themselves behind."

As we navigated the twisting tunnels, I began to understand what he meant. The remnants of lives once lived were scattered everywhere, fragments of a world hidden beneath the earth. It was both fascinating and unnerving, each discovery tugging at my heartstrings. What had brought them here? What had driven them to abandon their homes and lives?

We reached a chamber, its walls etched with symbols that flickered to life under the beam of our flashlight. The air crackled with energy, a palpable tension that set my nerves on edge. I stepped closer, captivated by the intricate designs that spiraled across the stone, each curve and line telling a story I could only begin to grasp.

"Look at this," I said, tracing my fingers over a particularly complex symbol. "It looks like some kind of... map?"

Hunter leaned in, squinting at the markings. "Or a warning. Whatever happened here wasn't just an accident. There's something sinister about it." His voice dropped to a low whisper, laden with gravity. "It's like they were trying to tell us something."

My breath hitched in my throat as an unsettling realization crept in. The shadows around us felt thicker, as if the walls themselves were closing in. It wasn't just the past we were uncovering; we were unearthing a darkness that had been buried for too long. The stories etched in the stone beckoned us closer, their warnings wrapping around us like a tightening noose.

"Do you think it's possible to break whatever curse holds this place?" I asked, the tremor in my voice betraying my bravado.

Hunter hesitated, a flicker of doubt crossing his features. "It's going to take more than just understanding. We need to confront whatever lives down here. If there's a connection between us and the past, we have to be ready to face it."

My heart raced, a mix of fear and determination igniting within me. I knew then that there was no turning back; we were intertwined with the fate of Firestone Bay and its dark history. The chilling truth lay ahead, waiting to be revealed, and I could either cower in the shadows or step boldly into the light of understanding.

Before I could respond, a soft sound echoed in the distance, drawing our attention. It was a voice, faint and ghostly, calling out from the depths of the mine. My heart stopped, the chill in the air deepening as I grasped Hunter's arm, our eyes locking in shared terror. Whatever had lurked in these tunnels was awakening, and we were about to find out just how closely our fates were entwined with the secrets buried beneath the surface.

The echo of our footsteps reverberated through the tunnel, a rhythmic thump against the stone that felt almost like a heartbeat, reminding me that we were very much alive in a world that had long forgotten. Each breath I took was heavy with the scent of damp earth and something acrid that lingered in the air, a reminder of the mine's storied past. I could almost imagine the lives that had traversed these very paths, the miners who had braved the darkness for the promise of silver and gold, their dreams lost to time just like the shadows that danced along the walls.

"Do you think they ever imagined we'd be here?" I mused, my voice breaking the oppressive silence. "I mean, did they ever wonder what would become of their stories?"

Hunter paused, the beam of his flashlight catching the flicker of dust motes swirling in the dim light. He turned to me, his expression thoughtful. "Maybe they hoped someone would care enough to remember. Or maybe they wanted to be forgotten, to leave behind a mystery that would keep people guessing."

"Guessing, huh?" I chuckled, trying to mask the unease curling in my stomach. "Well, if it's a mystery we're uncovering, I hope it doesn't involve any supernatural curses or angry spirits." I tried to lighten the mood, but my attempt fell flat in the thick atmosphere.

"Who knows? Maybe we'll find the answer to why I've been so unlucky with dates," he shot back, a sly grin breaking through the tension. "I've heard that if you stand in the right spot, the spirits give advice on love life."

His playful banter lightened my heart momentarily, but the chilling whisper of the unknown lingered in the air, wrapping around me like a shroud. We continued deeper into the mine, our surroundings growing increasingly claustrophobic, the walls inching closer as if they were alive and breathing.

"Look at this," Hunter said, shining his light onto a wall adorned with faint markings. I stepped closer, squinting to decipher the scratches and engravings. They were crude yet intricate, like the etchings of a child's imagination colliding with desperate artistry.

"What do you think it means?" I asked, my curiosity piqued.

"It looks like some sort of message, perhaps a warning," he replied, his brow furrowed as he traced the lines with his finger. "But without knowing the language, it's hard to tell."

I stepped back, feeling the weight of history press against my chest. "What if it's a warning for us? We shouldn't be here, Hunter. Maybe we should turn back."

"Not until we understand what we're dealing with," he said firmly, a steely resolve in his voice. "We have to dig deeper—figuratively and literally."

As if to punctuate his words, a low rumble echoed through the tunnel, sending a cascade of dust from the ceiling. I stumbled, grasping the edge of the wall for balance. "What was that?"

"Just the mine settling," he said, though his eyes darted nervously. "Let's keep moving. I'm sure it's fine."

I couldn't shake the feeling that the very walls were listening, waiting to reveal their secrets—or perhaps to keep them hidden. The air grew heavier, charged with anticipation, as if the mine were aware of our presence, judging our worthiness to uncover its truths.

We forged ahead, the narrow path leading us into a wider chamber that opened up like the maw of some ancient beast. The flashlight's beam illuminated the walls, revealing more markings, this time accompanied by remnants of objects—old lanterns, fragments of tools, and what looked like rusted chains hanging from the ceiling.

"Charming decor," I muttered, trying to keep my nerves at bay. "Do you think they used these for dramatic flair or as part of some bizarre art installation?"

"More likely for something far less glamorous," Hunter replied, his tone grave. "This place feels like it's steeped in sorrow. It's as if the very stone remembers the pain of those who worked here."

I felt a shiver race down my spine at his words. "Let's just hope we're not about to stumble upon a spirit seeking revenge for all those missed anniversaries."

"Or an overzealous foreman with a penchant for chains," he quipped, the flicker of humor in his eyes momentarily distracting me from the oppressive atmosphere.

Our laughter echoed through the chamber, mingling with the remnants of history that clung to the walls. But the moment was short-lived as I noticed something out of the corner of my eye—a shimmer at the far end of the chamber. My heart raced, curiosity outweighing caution.

"What is that?" I whispered, pointing towards the glow that seemed to pulse like a heartbeat.

"Let's find out," Hunter said, his expression a mix of intrigue and trepidation.

As we approached, the air grew cooler, a gentle breeze sweeping through the chamber, stirring the dust around us. The glow intensified, revealing a series of stones arranged in a circle, their surfaces covered in intricate symbols that mirrored those on the walls. In the center of the circle lay a small, ornate box, its surface gleaming with an otherworldly light.

"This is... strange," I said, glancing at Hunter, who seemed equally captivated. "What do you think it is?"

"I don't know, but it feels important," he replied, his voice barely above a whisper. "We should be careful."

I knelt beside the box, my fingers hovering over its surface, unsure whether to touch it or to retreat. "Should we open it?"

"Absolutely not!" Hunter exclaimed, the humor vanishing from his eyes. "What if it's a Pandora's box situation? We could unleash something awful."

"Or we could find something that helps us understand this place," I countered, feeling a strange pull toward the box.

Before he could respond, a sudden jolt of energy surged through the air, crackling like static electricity. The symbols on the stones began to glow brighter, illuminating our faces in an ethereal light. I gasped, instinctively reaching for Hunter's hand as the temperature dropped sharply, an otherworldly presence filling the space.

"Did you feel that?" I breathed, my voice trembling.

"I did," he replied, his expression shifting from curiosity to alarm. "This isn't just a box. It's a focal point... for something."

The energy in the chamber swelled, and I could feel the air thickening, the shadows twisting into ominous shapes. My heart raced as the glow from the stones pulsed rhythmically, almost as if it were responding to our presence. The whispers from the walls intensified, merging into a cacophony of voices, a tapestry of past lives intertwining with our own.

"What do they want?" I whispered, my eyes wide as the atmosphere thickened with anticipation.

"I don't know, but I have a feeling we're about to find out," Hunter said, his grip tightening around my hand as the glow enveloped us, pulling us into its depths, igniting a chain of events that neither of us could foresee.

The glow from the stones enveloped us, a living pulse that seemed to resonate with the very heartbeat of the earth beneath our feet. It was mesmerizing, drawing me in with the promise of secrets and answers. Yet, beneath that allure lurked an undercurrent of danger, a reminder that not all mysteries were meant to be unraveled. Hunter's grip tightened around my hand, grounding me as I felt the walls of the chamber begin to vibrate with a low hum, reverberating through my bones like a distant drumbeat.

"Okay, so maybe touching it wasn't the best idea," I murmured, half to myself, half to Hunter, as the energy crackled around us, rising and falling in intensity. My heart raced, uncertainty mixing with a strange thrill. "What if it does unleash some ancient curse? I always knew this mine had a dramatic flair."

"Not the time for jokes," he replied, his voice taut with tension. "If this thing has been dormant for years, who knows what's about to wake up?"

I swallowed hard, glancing at the ornate box, its surface glimmering invitingly under the light. "What if it's a key, though? A key to understanding what happened here and why we're connected to it?"

"Or a key to a trap," he countered, his eyes flicking toward the shifting shadows around us. "Let's not pretend we're in some fairy tale. This is real, and whatever is bound to that box might not be friendly."

Just then, the glow intensified, casting eerie reflections on our faces. A low, resonant voice began to weave through the air, melodic yet chilling, like the sound of wind chimes caught in a storm. The words were indistinct, but the tone carried an urgency that made the hairs on my arms stand on end.

"What are they saying?" I asked, the words tumbling from my lips before I could stop myself.

"I can't tell, but it feels like they're warning us," Hunter said, shifting closer, as if trying to shield me from the unseen presence.

The energy around us swirled, whipping into a vortex that danced at the edges of our vision. The symbols on the stones seemed to come alive, their meanings shifting like a kaleidoscope, and suddenly, the air thickened, weighing heavily upon my chest. I stumbled back, clutching at my heart, my breath catching in my throat.

"Breathe," Hunter said, his voice steadying me, but I could see the concern in his eyes as he scanned the chamber. "Whatever this is, it's reacting to us. We need to figure out what it wants."

"I feel like it wants us to leave," I gasped, shaking my head. "This is all too much. Maybe we should just go."

But before I could fully voice my fears, the box sprang open with a sudden rush of energy, revealing a small, intricately designed pendant nestled within. The pendant shimmered with a soft light, pulsating in rhythm with the symbols around us. A gentle hum filled the air, soothing yet commanding, beckoning us closer.

"What do you think it is?" Hunter whispered, his voice a mixture of awe and apprehension.

"Honestly? I have no idea. But it feels... important," I said, drawn inexplicably to its beauty. "Maybe it's a map? Or a talisman? Something that could explain why we're connected to this place."

"Or a ticking time bomb," he warned, but the intrigue in his eyes told me he was just as curious as I was. "Maybe we should touch it together. Safety in numbers, right?"

"Or a great way to end up cursed," I replied, half-joking. The air was electric, charged with possibilities that threatened to spiral out of control. But my curiosity outweighed my caution, and I took a deep breath, nodding.

We both reached for the pendant, our fingers brushing against its smooth surface. The moment we made contact, a surge of warmth spread through me, flooding my senses with a rush of visions. I saw flashes of faces, of miners laughing, their lives intertwining with our own. I felt their hopes, their dreams, and a profound sorrow that echoed through the ages.

"Do you see this?" I gasped, pulling my hand back, overwhelmed. "It's like... memories. Memories trapped in this place."

Hunter's expression mirrored my astonishment. "And we're part of them," he murmured, his brow furrowing in concentration. "What if this pendant is the key to breaking the curse? To releasing them?"

A shudder ran through the chamber, and the whispers intensified, swirling around us like a tempest. The symbols on the stones flickered, and for a heartbeat, it felt as though the very fabric of time was unraveling. Shadows danced wildly on the walls, and a figure began to materialize from the darkness—its features obscured, but its presence undeniably menacing.

"Who dares disturb the rest of the forgotten?" The voice resonated, echoing through the chamber like thunder, demanding and fierce.

Hunter and I exchanged panicked glances, my heart racing as the apparition solidified before us. "Uh, just a couple of curious kids who got lost?" I offered weakly, trying to mask my fear with humor, but it fell flat.

"Curiosity has its price," the figure intoned, its voice dripping with an ancient wisdom that sent chills down my spine. "You have awakened what was meant to stay buried."

"Wait! We didn't mean any harm!" Hunter protested, stepping forward, the pendant still clasped in his hand. "We just wanted to understand. We're tied to this place somehow. Please, let us help you!"

The figure regarded us with hollow eyes, a gaze that seemed to pierce through to our very souls. "Help is a fragile concept. What you seek may lead to your undoing."

"Can't we at least try?" I pleaded, feeling the weight of history pressing down on me. "If there's a way to break this curse, we need to know. These lives matter."

The shadows shifted around the figure, swirling like smoke, and for a moment, I thought I saw a flicker of something—perhaps hope?—before it vanished, leaving only darkness and silence in its wake.

"Did that just happen?" I asked, my voice shaking, staring at the space where the figure had been.

"Let's hope so," Hunter replied, his brow furrowed in concentration. "But I have a feeling it's not done with us yet."

Before I could respond, the ground beneath us trembled violently, sending us both sprawling. The stones around us began to crack, fissures snaking through the walls like veins of lightning. Dust rained down, and I instinctively reached for Hunter, our hands intertwining as panic surged through me.

"We need to get out!" I shouted, my voice barely audible above the cacophony.

But as we scrambled to our feet, the chamber groaned ominously, and a roar echoed through the mine, shaking the very core of the earth. The energy that had once felt inviting now thrummed with a deadly intensity.

"RUN!" Hunter yelled, his eyes wide with urgency.

We raced back toward the tunnel, the glow of the stones dimming behind us as the walls began to close in. The whispers morphed into a cacophony of screams, urging us to escape as we sprinted into the darkness. But the shadows chased us, relentless and hungry, ready to reclaim what had been disturbed.

As we dashed through the twisting passages, I glanced back, heart pounding with dread. The darkness surged forward, and just as we reached the exit, I felt a cold hand wrap around my ankle, pulling me back into the abyss.

"Hunter!" I screamed, grasping for anything that would anchor me to safety, but the void was closing in, and I was slipping away.

Chapter 19: Bloodlines

The mine's entrance loomed like a gaping maw, the air around it thick with the earthy scent of damp stone and echoes of ancient labor. As I stepped closer, a shiver crept down my spine, a premonition of the secrets waiting to be unearthed. The sunlight was a mere whisper behind me, swallowed whole by the shadows that danced at the mine's threshold. I turned to Hunter, his profile stark against the fading light, a steady presence that grounded me amidst the encroaching darkness.

"Ready?" he asked, his voice a low rumble that cut through the silence. I nodded, though my heart raced like a caged bird. This place, with its crumbling walls and rusted tools, felt alive with the weight of stories untold—stories of our families, their intertwined destinies, and the sins we could not escape.

Together, we stepped into the blackness, the sound of our footsteps swallowed by the oppressive quiet. As we descended deeper, the walls narrowed, the air grew cooler, and I could almost hear the whispers of those who had come before us, their regrets lingering like an unwelcome draft. It was a labyrinth of history, and with each turn, I felt the tension coil tighter around us, urging us onward.

The mine opened up into a cavernous chamber, illuminated only by the flickering light of our flashlights. The walls were lined with crude carvings, depictions of figures engaged in what appeared to be rituals. I stepped closer, my breath hitching as I recognized the symbols. They were the same as those in the old journal we had found—the one that had linked our families through generations.

"Look at this," Hunter murmured, gesturing to a figure in the center. "That has to be..."

"The Elder," I breathed, the realization sinking in like a stone in water. The figure was unmistakable, a representation of power and darkness. "Our ancestor. He was the one who... orchestrated it all."

Hunter's jaw tightened, and I could see the tension in his shoulders as he ran a hand through his hair, the gesture both familiar and comforting. "We can't let his legacy define us. We have to break this cycle."

I turned to him, meeting his gaze. There was a fierce determination in his eyes, a fire that mirrored the chaos swirling inside me. "But how? These secrets run deep, Hunter. It's not just about us. It's about everything our families have done."

The weight of our heritage pressed down like the very rock above us, threatening to collapse under the burden of truth. But the more I stood in this hollow place, the more I felt the urge to confront the darkness—not just for ourselves but for the families we represented. As if reading my thoughts, Hunter reached for my hand, his grip firm and reassuring. "Together," he said, a promise woven into the very fabric of the air between us.

Just as I was about to respond, a low rumble echoed through the chamber, and dust began to rain down from the ceiling. My heart thudded in my chest, a frantic beat against the stillness. "What was that?" I asked, panic creeping in.

"Stay close," Hunter commanded, his eyes scanning the shadows as he led me further into the cavern. I followed, adrenaline coursing through my veins, a cocktail of fear and resolve fueling my every step.

In the corner of the chamber, a glint caught my eye. I moved closer, kneeling to examine the source of the light. A small, ornate box lay half-buried in the dirt, its surface intricately carved with the same symbols from the walls. "Hunter, look at this!" I called out, excitement bubbling beneath the surface of my fear.

He knelt beside me, our shoulders brushing, and together we pried the box from its resting place. It felt heavy in my hands, a weight that belied its size. "What do you think it is?" he asked, peering closely.

"Only one way to find out," I said, a teasing smile breaking through the tension. I flipped the clasp, and the lid creaked open, releasing a cloud of dust that swirled in the beam of our flashlights. Inside, nestled on a bed of velvet, lay a set of ornate pendants, each one radiating a sense of power.

"Do you think they're...?" Hunter's voice trailed off, and I nodded, a shiver racing down my spine as I picked up a pendant shaped like a serpent, its emerald eye glimmering with a life of its own.

"Heritage," I whispered, understanding dawning on me. "This is our bloodline. It's a part of the magic that binds us."

As I held the pendant, warmth spread through my fingertips, a connection that felt both thrilling and terrifying. But it was more than just an heirloom; it was a weapon—a chance to fight against the darkness that had tainted our families for far too long.

"Do you think it'll help us?" Hunter asked, his brow furrowed.

"I think it might," I replied, my voice steadying. "But we need to be careful. We can't let it consume us like it did the Elder."

Just then, a shadow flickered at the edge of the cavern, a movement that sent my heart racing once more. "Did you see that?" I whispered, my grip tightening around the pendant.

Hunter nodded, his expression darkening as we both turned to face the source of the disturbance. The air grew heavier, charged with an electricity that made the hairs on my arms stand on end. "Stay behind me," he instructed, and I felt a rush of both irritation and admiration.

"Please, I'm not a damsel in distress," I shot back, stepping up beside him. "We're in this together."

The tension hung thick as the shadow approached, its shape coalescing into a figure cloaked in darkness. I felt the pull of recognition as it stepped into the light. It was not a ghostly apparition but a living embodiment of everything we feared.

"Hello, dear descendants," the figure drawled, a sly smile creeping across its face. It was a face I had seen in old family portraits—the same cold eyes that once filled me with dread. The betrayal of bloodlines was not merely a ghost from our past; it was a legacy that had come to haunt us in the flesh.

Hunter's hand slipped to my waist, a silent assurance as I braced myself for whatever revelation awaited us. The air crackled with the electricity of our shared history, the shadows of betrayal coiling tighter around us as we faced the embodiment of our darkest fears.

The figure stepped forward, its features now illuminated by the flickering light of our flashlights. I recognized the sharp angles of the face, the way the smile twisted into something that felt almost predatory. My breath caught in my throat. "You!" I spat, the word tasting bitter on my tongue.

"Ah, so you do remember dear old Uncle Walter," the figure purred, his voice silky smooth yet laced with something cold. He leaned against the cavern wall, the shadows enveloping him like a second skin. "How lovely to see my legacy has not been forgotten."

"What are you doing here?" Hunter demanded, his protective stance next to me unyielding. The tension in the air was palpable, a thick layer of unspoken history wrapping around us like a noose.

"Isn't it obvious?" Walter chuckled, a sound that echoed off the stone walls, raising goosebumps on my skin. "I'm here to reclaim what's rightfully mine. This mine, these secrets—they belong to me and to our bloodline. Not to you, and certainly not to the likes of you," he sneered, directing his disdain at me.

"Your bloodline? You mean the one steeped in betrayal?" I shot back, my voice steadier than I felt. "You're a parasite, living off the suffering of others."

His laughter rang hollow, bouncing off the cavern walls as he pushed himself upright. "Oh, how dramatic. But isn't that what our families have always done? Feed off each other, take what we can without a second thought?" His eyes glittered with malice. "You're so naive if you think you can change that."

"Change is what we're here for," Hunter interjected, stepping forward, the warmth radiating from him a shield against the encroaching coldness. "You may have your twisted vision of legacy, but we won't let you drag us down with you."

Walter's eyes flickered with annoyance before his lips curled into a smirk. "You think you're some kind of hero, don't you? A knight in shining armor rescuing the damsel?" He waved a hand dismissively. "You don't even know what you're up against."

"Try us," I retorted, feeling a rush of defiance coursing through me. The power of the pendants felt like a warm pulse in my palm, urging me to stand my ground. I caught Hunter's eye, and in that moment, we shared an unspoken pact—whatever this creature was, we would face it together.

With a mocking bow, Walter gestured around the cavern. "You really have no idea of the forces at play, do you? I have spent years learning to harness the darkness that runs through our veins. You're just children playing with toys."

"You're wrong," Hunter said, his voice low and steady. "We're not here to play. We're here to end this."

"End it?" Walter laughed, the sound grating against my nerves. "You really believe you can erase the past? You're tethered to it, darling. Just like I am."

I felt the weight of his words settle over me, pressing down like a shroud. "No. We're here to break the cycle," I insisted, even as doubt crept in like a thief in the night.

"Oh, how charming. And what do you propose to do? Use those shiny little pendants?" He eyed them with a mix of interest and contempt. "You think they hold power? They're merely trinkets, remnants of a forgotten time."

With a sudden resolve, I stepped closer to Hunter, letting our shoulders touch for support. "They might be trinkets, but they're our trinkets. We'll wield them better than you ever could."

Walter's expression darkened, the mirth fading like a sunset swallowed by night. "You're making a grave mistake, child. This mine is my domain, and you've trespassed into a world you cannot comprehend."

Before I could respond, he lunged toward us, shadows swirling like smoke around him. My heart raced as I instinctively pulled Hunter back. "Get ready!"

Hunter didn't hesitate, reaching for my hand as we dodged to the side, adrenaline pumping through our veins. "We can't let him corner us," he muttered, his eyes darting around the cavern, searching for an escape route.

"Look for something we can use!" I shouted, scanning the walls as Walter's figure shifted and flickered, merging with the shadows like a living nightmare.

Just then, I noticed something glinting on the ground—a shard of metal, perhaps from a long-forgotten tool. I snatched it up, feeling its cool weight in my palm. "Hunter! This might help!"

With a fierce determination, I advanced, wielding the shard like a sword, my heart pounding with each step. "Stay away from us, Walter!" I shouted, my voice echoing in the cavern.

Walter paused, a flicker of surprise crossing his features. "You think you can threaten me with a scrap of metal?"

"It's not the metal," I replied, feeling the surge of power from the pendant still hanging around my neck. "It's the intent behind it."

Hunter stepped beside me, his presence bolstering my confidence. "We're not afraid of you, Walter. We will confront the darkness you represent. We'll bring light to our family's legacy."

For a moment, we were locked in a standoff, the air crackling with unspoken tension. Walter's smirk faded, replaced by a cold fury. "You're foolish to think you can change anything. The darkness is a part of us; it always will be."

"Then we'll have to be the light that drives it away," I said, adrenaline propelling my words. I lifted the shard higher, a beacon of defiance against the weight of our history.

Walter lunged again, but this time, I was ready. I stepped aside and swung the metal shard toward the ground, striking the stone with a force that reverberated through the air. Sparks flew, and with a burst of energy, the pendants began to glow, bathing the chamber in an ethereal light.

"What is this?" Walter snarled, stumbling back as the light pushed against him like a wall.

"It's our strength," I replied, a thrill coursing through me. "Our determination to break free from the shackles of our bloodlines."

With each pulse of the pendants, the shadows receded, revealing the chamber in all its crumbling glory. The carvings on the walls shimmered, the figures now alive with the light of our resolve.

I felt Hunter's hand tighten around mine, our bond solidifying with each flicker of brilliance. "Let's finish this," he said, his voice low but unwavering.

As we advanced together, the power surged, creating a barrier between us and the darkness that had threatened to consume our families for generations. With every step, I could feel the weight of our ancestors' choices shift, the air thick with the promise of a new legacy waiting to be forged.

The glow from the pendants flared brighter, illuminating the cavern in a wash of vibrant light that seemed to pulse in time with my racing heart. Walter staggered back, his expression morphing from arrogance to a flicker of something akin to fear. It was a sight that sparked a wicked thrill within me—seeing the embodiment of our family's darkness suddenly diminished by the very legacy he thought he controlled.

"What's happening?" Walter spat, his voice edged with panic. "You think this light can protect you?"

"Not just protect us," I countered, the conviction in my voice surprising even myself. "It can free us."

Hunter squeezed my hand tighter, the warmth radiating from him mixing with the newfound energy coursing through my veins. "We'll make sure this ends tonight, Walter. You may have twisted our heritage into something monstrous, but it's time to reclaim it."

The walls of the cavern began to shimmer, the shadows retreating further under the assault of the light we wielded. In that moment, I saw more than just carvings; they morphed into a tapestry of our lineage, each story woven with threads of pain and resilience. With each pulse, I felt the weight of our ancestors' failures—and their hopes—flow through me.

"Foolish children," Walter sneered, though there was an edge of desperation to his tone now. "You think this ancient power is yours to wield? It belongs to those who are truly worthy."

"Worthy?" I scoffed. "You mean to those who've turned their backs on everything good in this world?"

A flicker of anger flashed in his eyes, and in that instant, the air shifted. The shadows around him twisted and surged like a living entity, coiling around him like tendrils seeking to break free. "You underestimate the power of bloodlines," he hissed, his voice suddenly layered with an otherworldly timbre.

Before I could respond, the shadows lunged toward us, a mass of darkness that threatened to swallow the light whole. I yanked Hunter closer, our shoulders pressed together as we braced ourselves against the onslaught.

"Together!" he shouted, and we lifted the pendants high, channeling the light into a concentrated beam. It cut through the shadows, illuminating the cavern with a brilliance that felt almost alive.

"Enough!" Walter roared, the shadows around him dissipating momentarily, revealing the man beneath the darkness. "You cannot defeat what has been etched in blood. You're merely pawns in a game far older than you can imagine."

"Maybe," I said, my voice steady despite the chaos. "But we refuse to be pawns any longer. We're rewriting our story, starting now."

In a moment of clarity, I recalled the journal's passages about breaking curses. "Hunter, remember what we read about the ancestral bond? We need to channel our lineage, not just ours, but all of those who suffered because of him."

His eyes lit with understanding, and he nodded. "Yes! The light isn't just ours; it's every choice made in our name, every act of kindness and courage."

We closed our eyes for a heartbeat, allowing the light to wash over us, connecting us to the cavern's ancient roots and the stories embedded in its walls. I felt the strength of my ancestors surge, and suddenly, the pendants pulsed in unison, releasing a radiant energy that spiraled outwards, enveloping us in a cocoon of warmth.

Walter's face contorted with fury as the light wrapped around him, restricting his movements. "You think this will bind me? You have no idea what you're doing!"

"Actually, I think we're just starting to figure it out," I shot back, my heart pounding with newfound confidence. The air crackled, the power surging and intertwining with the shadows, creating a brilliant spectacle of light and dark.

Just as I thought we had him, Walter's laughter echoed, dark and twisted. "You've awakened something far more dangerous than you realize! You've unleashed the true nature of this mine!"

Suddenly, the ground shook beneath us, a deep rumble that reverberated through the cavern like a warning bell. The walls trembled as dust and debris rained down, and I struggled to keep my balance.

"Hold on!" Hunter shouted, gripping my arm tightly. We stumbled backward as the chamber began to collapse, the shadows swirling chaotically around us, a tempest fueled by Walter's malevolence.

"Fools!" he cried, his voice laced with glee. "This is just the beginning! You will pay for this—your bloodline is forever tainted!"

The chamber's ceiling cracked, and chunks of rock began to fall, creating a chaotic dance of destruction. "We have to get out!" I yelled, panic creeping into my voice as the walls seemed to close in on us.

Hunter nodded, pulling me toward the mine's exit. "This way! We can't let him win!"

As we sprinted through the cavern, the light from our pendants flickered in response to the chaos around us. I glanced back at Walter, who was engulfed in shadows, his form twisting as he struggled against the energy we had unleashed. For a moment, I felt a pang of sympathy—he was a prisoner of his own making.

But there was no time for pity. We barreled toward the exit, the echoes of Walter's rage chasing us like a storm. Just as we neared the threshold, a deafening crack split the air, and a massive boulder fell between us and the light, blocking our path.

"Hunter!" I shouted, fear gripping my chest.

He pushed against the boulder, but it wouldn't budge. "We can't give up!" His voice was a fierce promise, but the weight of the rock was unforgiving.

With a surge of adrenaline, I took a step back. "If we can't go over it, let's go under!"

"What?" he questioned, eyes wide with confusion.

"Just trust me!" I said, sinking to my knees and feeling around the edge of the boulder. It was cold and unyielding, but I sensed a crack beneath it, just wide enough to fit through if we could leverage our strength.

"Now!" I yelled, and together we heaved against the stone, pushing with everything we had. The ground trembled again, but this time it was in our favor. The boulder shifted slightly, creating a narrow opening.

"Get in!" I urged, shoving Hunter forward. He squeezed through, and I followed, the darkness encroaching at my back. Just as I slipped through, a scream pierced the air—a raw, primal sound that echoed off the walls and sent chills down my spine.

I turned to see Walter's form morphing, the shadows swirling violently as he was consumed by the very darkness he had wielded. "This isn't over!" he howled, the echo of his voice lingering in the air like a curse.

With a final push, I tumbled through the narrow escape just as the cavern collapsed behind us, sealing Walter within the mine's depths. I lay on the ground, gasping for breath, the adrenaline still coursing through my veins.

"Is it... over?" Hunter panted beside me, his face pale but resolute.

"I don't know," I admitted, my heart racing as I looked back at the now-still entrance, the dust settling like a tomb over the darkness.

As we caught our breath, a low rumble echoed through the ground beneath us—a distant warning or a call to arms? I couldn't tell.

Then, from the shadows, a new figure emerged, stepping into the light of our pendants. My heart dropped, fear coiling tightly in my chest as I realized we were not alone.

Chapter 20: The Breaking Point

The air in the dimly lit room was thick with the scent of betrayal, and I could feel it clinging to my skin like an unwelcome shroud. I stood frozen, the weight of the revelation crashing over me like a tidal wave. Hunter, standing beside me, was oblivious to the storm brewing in my heart. His presence was a lifeline I desperately wanted to cling to, yet I felt the chasm between us widening with every passing second. My thoughts spiraled as I replayed the moment—the words, the expressions, the unmistakable intent hidden behind what had once felt like a safe alliance. It was astonishing how quickly trust could crumble, reduced to mere dust in the wake of one person's treachery.

"Can you believe this?" I muttered, the sharpness of my voice slicing through the tense silence. Hunter's brows furrowed in confusion as he turned to face me. The intensity of his gaze momentarily anchored me, grounding me in the present, but the storm within still raged.

"What do you mean?" he asked, and I could hear the underlying worry in his tone. The faint lines on his forehead deepened, etched there by the burdens we both carried.

I took a deep breath, searching for the right words. "I thought we had a plan, that we were on the same side. But it turns out someone we trusted has been pulling the strings all along. They want to keep us in the dark, away from the truth." My hands trembled as I spoke, my voice trembling with the realization that the person I had once confided in had become a puppeteer of deceit.

Hunter's jaw tightened, and his eyes flashed with anger. "Who? What do they want?"

I hesitated, the name sitting heavy on my tongue. It felt like betrayal layered upon betrayal. "It's Ella. She's been feeding information to our enemies, ensuring we never find the answers we seek."

Hunter's face morphed from concern to disbelief, his expression hardened as if I had just struck him. "Ella? But she's been with us since the beginning. She's one of us."

"She was," I corrected, bitterness creeping into my voice. "But now she's become part of the very darkness we're trying to fight against. It's as if she's taken everything we built and shattered it with her bare hands."

Silence enveloped us, the kind that pressed against my chest, making it difficult to breathe. I could see the gears turning in Hunter's mind, a flurry of emotions flickering across his face. In that moment, I wanted nothing more than to bridge the gap that had suddenly formed between us, yet I felt powerless. I could sense the invisible threads of our connection fraying, the warmth of his trust slipping away as reality settled in.

"Why would she do this?" Hunter finally asked, his voice low and contemplative.

"Power," I replied, my heart racing as I formulated my thoughts. "Or maybe she thought she could control the situation. It doesn't matter. What matters is that she's jeopardizing everything we've fought for."

Hunter raked a hand through his hair, frustration etched across his features. "We need to confront her. We can't let her dictate our fate."

Confrontation hung in the air like an uninvited guest. The idea of facing Ella made my stomach churn, but I knew it was necessary. I didn't want to run from the truth anymore, no matter how painful it might be. Yet, beneath the bravado, I felt the quaking uncertainty of what we might find—a confrontation that could spiral into chaos.

"Do you really think we can reason with her?" I asked, my voice barely above a whisper.

"I don't want to reason with her," Hunter shot back, the fire in his eyes igniting my own. "I want to expose her for what she is. We can't let her walk away scot-free."

His anger was fierce and intoxicating, a spark that momentarily flickered in the shadows enveloping us. I could almost feel the warmth of his resolve merging with my own, urging me to take a step forward, to embrace the uncertainty.

Yet doubt loomed larger, feeding on my insecurities. "What if she turns it against us?" I whispered, images of chaos flaring through my mind—spreading lies, sowing discord, making our struggle that much harder.

Hunter took a step closer, closing the distance between us, and I could feel his warmth, the familiar scent of him—fresh cedar and something unmistakably him—wrapping around me like a blanket. "We'll figure it out together," he promised, his voice a low rumble that sent a thrill through me. "No more secrets. No more shadows. We confront her, and we take control of our own narrative."

There was a fierce determination in his words, a promise that we would face this challenge together. In that moment, I found strength in his unwavering gaze, igniting a flicker of hope amidst the chaos.

"What if she tries to turn us against each other?" The question slipped from my lips, heavy with the weight of my fears.

"Let her try," he replied, a slight smirk breaking through the storm in his eyes. "I trust you. I trust us. And if she tries to drive a wedge between us, it will only show how weak she really is."

The resolve in his voice washed over me, filling the cracks in my confidence. I wanted to believe in our alliance, to trust that our bond could withstand even the fiercest storms. But as we prepared to face Ella, I knew the battle ahead would not just be against her deception; it would be a fight to reclaim the pieces of ourselves we had almost lost along the way.

With a deep breath, I nodded, my heart steadying. "Then let's do it. Together."

And as we stepped into the unknown, hand in hand, I felt the spark of hope flicker alive once more, a tiny flame in the vast darkness. It was time to confront the betrayal and reclaim our truth, no matter the cost.

We stepped into the stark light of the hallway, the atmosphere heavy with unspoken tension. The once-vibrant space felt muted, like a theater after the curtain falls—echoing with the aftermath of a performance fraught with conflict. Hunter's determination ignited something in me, a flicker of the tenacity I had almost lost. Yet, doubt lingered at the edges of my mind like a haunting melody, a reminder that even the strongest alliances could falter in the face of deceit.

"Let's go," Hunter said, his voice firm but not without warmth. He offered his hand, and I took it, our fingers intertwining in a silent vow. With every step toward Ella, I could feel my heart pounding—a relentless drumbeat underscoring my trepidation.

As we approached the small, dimly lit room where we had often gathered to plan our next move, I hesitated, the familiar echoes of laughter and camaraderie now replaced with an unsettling silence. "What if she tries to twist our words against us?" I asked, fear creeping into my voice like shadows at dusk.

"Then we twist them back," Hunter replied, a hint of a smile tugging at the corners of his mouth. "We'll outsmart her. We've done it before."

I appreciated his confidence, but the thought of facing Ella felt akin to walking into a lion's den with a steak tied around my neck. With a final deep breath, I nodded, determination settling over me like a comforting blanket.

The door creaked as we entered, revealing Ella perched at the edge of the table, her expression inscrutable, like a cat poised to pounce. "Well, look who finally decided to join me," she said, her tone dripping with saccharine sweetness. "I was beginning to think you two had lost your nerve."

Hunter stepped forward, his posture rigid. "We know what you've been up to, Ella."

She feigned innocence, raising an eyebrow, but her eyes flickered with something I couldn't quite place—defiance, maybe, or perhaps a glimmer of fear. "Oh? And what exactly do you think you know?"

I crossed my arms, stepping beside Hunter. "We know you've been feeding information to our enemies. You've been playing both sides."

Ella laughed, the sound sharp and brittle, shattering the fragile air around us. "You think you're so clever, don't you? But you have no idea what you're really up against."

Hunter clenched his jaw, and I felt the tension radiating from him. "We're not afraid of you, Ella. We're done playing your games."

"Games?" she echoed, her voice dripping with mockery. "This is not a game, darling. This is survival. And if you two are too naïve to understand that, then you deserve what's coming."

My heart raced as I processed her words. There was something darker lurking beneath her facade, a sinister intent wrapped in the guise of self-preservation. "What do you mean?" I asked, stepping forward. "What's coming?"

A wicked smile crept across her lips. "You'll see soon enough. But don't worry; I'll make sure it's a spectacle worth watching."

Hunter's eyes darkened with anger, the protective instinct I admired igniting within him. "If you think we're just going to stand by and let you destroy everything we've built, you're gravely mistaken."

Ella shrugged, her confidence unshaken. "Do you really believe you can stop me? You're like children playing dress-up in a world you don't understand. You have no idea the lengths I'm willing to go to protect myself."

The words hung in the air, thickening the tension until it felt almost suffocating. "You think this is about you?" I challenged, my voice stronger than I felt. "This is about us, about the people we care about. You're not invincible, Ella. You're just as vulnerable as the rest of us."

She narrowed her eyes, and for the first time, I saw a flicker of uncertainty dance across her features. "You really think you can turn the tables on me?"

"Watch us," Hunter said, stepping closer, determination radiating from him like an electric current.

With a swift motion, Ella reached for something beneath the table, and instinctively, my heart dropped. I knew that whatever she had, it wouldn't be good. "I suggest you both take a step back," she warned, her voice cold and lethal.

I glanced at Hunter, and in that brief moment, our silent communication spoke volumes. Whatever Ella planned to pull, we needed to be ready.

"What do you have, Ella?" I asked, trying to buy us time as I took a step toward her. "You're bluffing. We know you're scared."

Her eyes flickered with anger, but beneath that façade, I saw a hint of fear that bolstered my confidence. "You think you can intimidate me? I'll have you both regret ever crossing me."

Without warning, she lunged, a flash of movement that sent adrenaline coursing through my veins. Hunter acted on instinct, his reflexes honed by the chaos we had faced together. He grabbed my arm, yanking me back just as Ella's hand shot forward, revealing a sleek, silver device that crackled ominously with energy.

"What is that?" I gasped, my heart racing.

"It's a little something I've been working on," she replied, a manic glint in her eye. "An insurance policy, if you will. The moment you cross me, it'll be lights out."

Hunter pulled me closer, his grip firm and reassuring. "You're not going to use that, Ella. You don't want to go down this road."

She hesitated, uncertainty flickering in her expression for the briefest of moments. "You think you understand me? You don't know what I've lost, what I've sacrificed to be where I am. You're just obstacles in my path."

"And you think that makes you strong?" I challenged, emboldened by the rising tide of anger within me. "All it shows is that you're scared. You're terrified of losing control."

Ella's expression twisted, and I could see the struggle within her as she fought to maintain her composure. It was a fleeting victory, but it was enough to shift the power balance, if only slightly.

"Stop," she hissed, her voice low and dangerous. "You don't know what you're doing."

"Maybe we don't," Hunter replied, "but we won't let you dictate our fate any longer."

The room pulsed with tension, and in that moment, the roles had shifted. Ella was no longer the puppet master, and for the first time, I felt the weight of our choices settle around us, tangible and electric. This was our turning point, and with it came the realization that the battle wasn't just about confronting Ella. It was about reclaiming our own power and redefining the narrative we had almost allowed her to write for us.

As we stood there, the air charged with unspoken possibilities, I knew one thing for certain: we were no longer playing her game. The time for fear had passed, and now it was our turn to seize the reins of our fate.

The tension in the room hung like a thick fog, the air charged with unspoken threats and electric potential. Ella's hand still gripped the silver device, her eyes darting between us, gauging our reactions, trying to reclaim the upper hand. I could sense Hunter's readiness, an almost palpable aura of defiance radiating from him, making me feel braver than I had moments before.

"Ella," I began, striving to sound more assertive than I felt, "you've made your choices clear. But what about the consequences?"

She hesitated, a flicker of uncertainty breaking through her bravado, and I seized the moment. "You don't have to do this. We can find another way. You don't have to isolate yourself like this."

"I'm not isolating myself!" she snapped, anger and desperation intertwining in her voice. "You both just don't understand the stakes."

Hunter stepped closer, his presence unwavering. "Then explain them. Help us understand why you're willing to sacrifice everything."

Ella's gaze shifted, a fleeting look of conflict passing over her features. "You think this is just about me? It's about survival, and sometimes you have to make sacrifices to keep your head above water."

"Sacrifices?" I echoed, incredulity lacing my tone. "Like betraying us? Like playing both sides?"

"Like doing what it takes to ensure I'm not the one who ends up on the chopping block," she shot back, her composure faltering. The mask she wore cracked slightly, revealing a glimpse of the fear that lurked beneath.

"Then what do you need from us?" Hunter pressed, his voice steady, trying to pull her from the brink. "We can't help you if you keep us in the dark."

Ella looked at us, the flicker of vulnerability intensifying in her gaze. "You don't know what I've seen, what I've done to survive in this world," she murmured, her voice dropping to a near whisper. "People like us—we don't get to just walk away. Not without consequences."

"What do you mean 'people like us'?" I asked, intrigued despite myself. "You think you're the only one who has faced challenges?"

Her laughter was a harsh, humorless sound. "No, but I have made choices—choices that haunt me. If you only knew the lengths I had to go to stay alive..."

The moment hung suspended between us, the possibility of connection battling against the animosity we had built. But before I could press further, she straightened, the steel returning to her spine. "But enough of this. If you think you can play this game, you're mistaken. I have something you want."

"Ella," I warned, sensing the shift in her demeanor, "don't—"

"Shut up!" she screamed, the room vibrating with her fury. "You want the truth? I've got it. But it's not free. You'll have to trade something valuable."

Hunter and I exchanged glances, a silent understanding passing between us. This wasn't just about trust anymore; it was a negotiation steeped in danger. "What do you want?" Hunter asked, his tone shifting from anger to cautious curiosity.

Ella smiled, and it felt like the sun slipping behind a cloud. "I want to see how far you'll go for each other. You claim to have this unbreakable bond, but do you really? Are you willing to sacrifice everything for love?"

"I'd do anything for her," Hunter replied without hesitation, his gaze unwavering.

"Would you?" Ella taunted, leaning forward, her eyes glinting with mischief. "What if it meant turning against everything you believed in? What if you had to choose between her and your own life?"

My heart raced, the room narrowing down to a single point of focus. "That's not a choice anyone should have to make," I said, my voice steadier than I felt.

"But it's a choice you might have to face," she replied, her smile widening, satisfaction gleaming in her eyes. "You see, there are forces at play beyond your comprehension, and I can either guide you through them or watch you stumble in the dark."

Hunter's grip on my hand tightened, a silent pledge of solidarity. "What do you know?" he demanded, his voice low and dangerous.

"I know you're playing a losing game," she replied, her tone almost teasing. "And I know there are others watching, waiting for you to make a mistake. You'll have to decide quickly, or you might find your time is up."

The implications of her words twisted in my stomach, fear and urgency mixing into a potent cocktail. "You're threatening us?" I asked, incredulous.

"I'm warning you," she corrected, the sharp edge of her voice cutting through the tension. "But if you want to play along, be my guest. I have something more valuable than you know—something that could change everything."

"What is it?" Hunter pressed, frustration lacing his voice. "Just tell us!"

Ella's smile widened, and she took a step back, placing the device on the table between us. "You want answers? Fine. But first, you must prove your worth. This—" she gestured to the device, "can reveal truths. It's your key, but it demands a sacrifice."

"What kind of sacrifice?" I asked, instinctively stepping closer, drawn by the curiosity laced with dread.

Ella leaned back, her expression enigmatic. "One that weighs heavy on the heart. You'll have to decide what you value most. Your loyalty to each other, or the information that could change your fate."

A heavy silence enveloped us, the weight of her ultimatum sinking in. Hunter's fingers intertwined with mine, and I could feel the heat radiating from him, a silent reassurance against the chilling implications of her words. "We're not afraid of sacrifice," he said, the confidence in his voice unwavering. "We just need to know what you're hiding."

Ella's laughter echoed in the small room, a sound filled with both amusement and madness. "Oh, sweet naïveté. You'll soon learn that love can be the most dangerous weapon of all."

In that moment, a sense of dread crept over me, a premonition that whatever lay ahead would be more perilous than anything we had faced thus far. Ella's eyes glinted with a wicked light, as if she were savoring the moment like a cat toying with a cornered mouse.

"Let's see just how much you're willing to gamble for the truth," she said, her voice a silken whisper that promised chaos.

Before I could respond, a sharp noise broke through the tension, echoing from somewhere outside the door. A thunderous crash followed by shouting. Panic surged within me, eclipsing everything else. I turned to Hunter, my heart racing as dread filled my gut.

"What was that?" I gasped, the walls of our fragile world starting to close in around us.

Hunter's expression shifted from anger to alarm, his grip tightening around my hand. "We need to get out of here—now!"

But as we turned toward the door, a figure appeared in the doorway, silhouetted against the flickering lights. The moment froze, and my blood ran cold as recognition washed over me. The newcomer's smirk promised a different kind of chaos, one that was all too familiar and far too dangerous.

"Did I interrupt something?" the figure purred, and just like that, the game had changed once more.

Chapter 21: The Heart of the Matter

The air crackled with tension, a palpable energy that felt almost electric as I stood shoulder to shoulder with Hunter. We faced the looming figure that had haunted our every step, the specter of a shared past clawing its way back into our lives with all the ferocity of a storm. Shadows danced in the flickering light, twisting and shifting as the figure moved, its features obscured, but the malice in its presence was unmistakable. Every heartbeat echoed like a battle drum, urging me forward, urging me to reclaim my voice and my power in a world that had tried to silence me.

"Do you think you can just walk in here and take everything away from us?" I shouted, my words slicing through the oppressive atmosphere. The sound of my own voice surprised me, strong and unwavering, as if it was the very embodiment of my determination. I felt Hunter's presence beside me, solid and reassuring, igniting a fire within me that had long been extinguished by fear.

The figure laughed—a low, haunting sound that sent shivers racing down my spine. "You think this is about you? About the two of you?" Its voice was smooth, dripping with contempt. "This is far bigger than your little lives. This is about legacy, about the sins of your families that should have never been forgotten."

"Enough with the theatrics!" Hunter stepped forward, his fists clenched at his sides, a protective stance that both calmed and emboldened me. I could see the determination etched into his features, the way his jaw tightened, a stark contrast to the storm brewing in my chest. We had faced demons before, but this was different. This was personal, a twisted game of revenge that sought to tear us apart at the seams.

As the figure lunged, I instinctively moved closer to Hunter, ready to fight. The moment felt surreal, like a scene ripped from the pages of a book, where good clashed against evil. I could feel the warmth radiating from Hunter, his presence a beacon of strength as we battled against the unseen threat. Every blow we exchanged was a reminder of what we had fought through together, a testament to our growing bond, forged in the fires of shared adversity.

In the midst of the chaos, as fists flew and shadows clashed, a strange clarity washed over me. I realized the figure's true motives weren't just about vengeance against our families; it was a misguided attempt to rewrite history, to pull us into a web of hatred spun from a past neither Hunter nor I had lived through. This was an obsession, an echo of old grievances that had festered and grown, morphing into something monstrous.

"You think your families are innocent?" the figure spat, dodging another of Hunter's blows. "They built their empires on the suffering of others. You should have been taught that."

"Maybe, but we're not our families," I shot back, the truth igniting my resolve. "We're not responsible for their choices. We have our own lives to live, our own paths to forge." Each word was a declaration, a rallying cry that resonated within me as the memories of our shared laughter and dreams filled my mind.

Hunter caught my eye, a flicker of surprise crossing his face, followed by a knowing nod. "You're right," he said, his voice steady. "We've spent too long letting their mistakes dictate who we are. It's time to break free from that legacy."

As if my words were a catalyst, the figure faltered for a brief moment, a shadow of doubt flickering across its face. That tiny crack in its armor was all the opening we needed. Fueled by our shared conviction, we surged forward, fighting not just against our enemy but against the chains that had bound us to our families' pasts.

The confrontation turned into a dance of strength and strategy, each of us pushing the other to new heights. My fists were driven by a fierce desire to protect the life Hunter and I had built, one that thrived on the promise of new beginnings rather than the shadows of old grudges. Each strike was more than just a physical blow; it was a defiance against a history that threatened to suffocate us.

The figure's face contorted in frustration as it attempted to regain control, but we pressed on, unyielding in our resolve. "You think you can change the course of destiny?" it yelled, desperation creeping into its voice.

"Destiny is what we make it!" I shouted back, feeling the weight of the truth in those words. Each punch, each kick, was a step toward liberation—not just for us, but for everyone who had ever been held captive by the sins of the past.

As the dust began to settle and the air thickened with the remnants of our struggle, I saw the figure stumble. The mask of invincibility began to crack, revealing a depth of pain and hurt that had driven its obsession. In that moment, I understood—this battle was never just about defeating an enemy; it was about finding common ground, about understanding that even the darkest souls were shaped by their own tragedies.

"We're not enemies," I said, my voice softer now, cutting through the remnants of hostility. "We don't have to continue this cycle of pain."

The figure paused, hesitating as if my words had struck a chord deep within. Hunter stood beside me, a solid anchor, our combined strength radiating a hope that felt almost tangible in the smoky air. "You can choose to break this cycle," he added, his tone firm yet compassionate.

In that charged silence, I realized the true battle was not just against the figure before us, but against the fears that had held us captive for too long. With every passing moment, I felt the chains that had bound us begin to crumble, revealing the path to a future unfettered by the weight of our families' legacies.

The tension in the room shifted as the figure hesitated, caught between its rage and the unexpected vulnerability I had exposed. I could see the flickering shadows of doubt in its eyes, a crack in the armor of its furious facade. "You think words can change anything?" it sneered, but the tremor in its voice betrayed a deeper uncertainty. "This isn't just about revenge; it's about justice. Your families deserve to suffer for what they've done."

"Justice?" Hunter countered, his voice like granite, unwavering. "Justice doesn't mean dragging innocent people into your vendetta. If you truly seek justice, you should start with the truth."

For a moment, the room was thick with a silence that felt almost sacred. I could feel my heart thudding in my chest, a steady reminder of the urgency pressing down on us. This confrontation had morphed from a mere battle of strength to a moral reckoning, the stakes rising higher with each exchanged word. The figure was caught in the grip of its own narrative, a tale woven from years of hatred and unresolved grievances.

"Your families don't deserve redemption," it hissed, edging forward with the wild energy of a cornered animal. "They've hurt too many people. They've silenced too many voices."

"Maybe so," I replied, my voice stronger now, "but we're not them. Hunter and I are not the architects of their sins. We can't pay for their mistakes." My conviction rang clear, mingling with the echoes of the past that threatened to smother our present. "But we can forge a different path."

Hunter took a step closer, his eyes locked onto the figure with an intensity that could have burned through steel. "This isn't just about you versus us. It's about a choice. You can choose to continue this cycle of pain or find a way to break free." His voice softened, and there was an undeniable compassion that cut through the anger that had ruled this moment.

The figure paused, its hands trembling slightly as it considered our words. In that fleeting moment, I saw the threads of rage begin to unravel, revealing the tangled emotions beneath. Was it regret? Loneliness? Perhaps a desperate longing for resolution, for closure?

"Don't you see?" I pressed on, taking a step forward, my heart racing with the possibility that we could sway this being's hardened heart. "Your fight doesn't have to be against us. It can be against the pain itself. Together, we can unearth the truth and lay it to rest."

For the first time, the figure faltered, its defiance wavering as the weight of our words settled over it like a heavy cloak. I could see the conflict warring within it, the desire for vengeance colliding with an inkling of understanding. "You think this is simple?" it finally spat, but the venom was laced with uncertainty. "You think you can just wave a magic wand and make everything okay?"

"No," Hunter replied, a gentle resolve in his voice. "But we can take the first step. We can work towards understanding, towards healing."

It was then that the figure visibly shifted, the energy in the room transforming from hostile to contemplative. The harsh lines of its anger softened, and for a moment, I felt a fragile connection—an echo of shared humanity in the midst of a chaotic struggle.

"What if I choose to let this go?" it murmured, its voice tinged with the faintest glimmer of hope. "What if I want to break free from this rage?"

"Then do it," I urged, emboldened by the shift in the atmosphere. "Choose freedom over vengeance. Together, we can uncover the truth of the past without dragging each other into the darkness."

The figure took a deep breath, its shoulders sagging under the weight of years spent in the throes of bitterness. The lines of battle etched into its face seemed to smooth out, replaced by an expression that was almost... vulnerable. "What if the truth is too painful to face?"

"Then let us face it together," I said softly, my heart pounding with the weight of my words. "You're not alone in this. We can carry that burden as a team."

A silence hung between us, heavy with the gravity of the moment, as the figure considered my offer. In that stillness, I could sense the potential for change, for redemption that had long been buried beneath layers of hurt.

Finally, the figure stepped back, dropping its clenched fists. "Maybe... maybe I've been wrong," it admitted, the bravado evaporating like morning mist. "Maybe all I've known is revenge, and it's led me nowhere but deeper into this abyss."

"Then let's help each other out of it," Hunter said, his voice steady and inviting. "We can be more than just our families' mistakes. We can be the ones who finally break this cycle."

With that, something shifted in the air. The oppressive weight of anger began to lift, replaced by an overwhelming sense of possibility. The figure nodded slowly, a tentative acceptance flickering in its eyes. "Okay. Let's try."

As the last remnants of tension dissipated, I felt the world around us begin to breathe again. The shadows that had once felt like chains now danced lightly on the walls, almost as if the very fabric of reality was welcoming our newfound alliance.

But as we stood there, surrounded by the debris of our confrontation, I couldn't shake the feeling that the path ahead would not be without its challenges. Old wounds had not yet healed, and the shadows of the past were still lurking just beneath the surface, waiting to rise again.

Still, for the first time, I felt a glimmer of hope. Perhaps we were on the brink of something transformative, a journey that could reshape our destinies. The battles we had fought were not just against a singular foe, but against the scars left by our families' histories.

And in that realization, I knew we had taken the first step toward a brighter future, together.

It was time to forge our own legacies—free from the chains of the past.

The figure stepped back, its breath coming in short, ragged gasps, the fight visibly draining from its posture. A moment of uneasy silence settled over us, thick as molasses. "You really believe we can change this?" it asked, the bravado leaking from its voice, revealing a hint of vulnerability that sent a ripple of uncertainty through me.

"Absolutely," I replied, surprising myself with the steadiness of my tone. "You don't have to be a prisoner of your past. We can work through this together." I looked at Hunter, whose expression mirrored my determination, a silent pledge of unity between us.

But the figure shook its head, a bitter laugh escaping its lips. "You think it's that easy? You think just saying some nice words can erase years of hurt? Years of betrayal?"

"Nice words?" Hunter interjected, a hint of playful sarcasm creeping into his voice. "I don't know about you, but my words are top-notch. They're practically certified by a panel of experts. It's practically a miracle they haven't started charging me for public speaking."

I couldn't help but stifle a laugh, the absurdity of the situation breaking the tension momentarily. "I think your comedy career is going to have to wait, Hunter," I said, nudging him with my elbow, grateful for the lightness that seeped into the air around us. "Let's focus on the matter at hand."

The figure's expression softened, caught between anger and something else—something almost like longing. "Maybe... maybe it's easier to hold onto hatred. It's familiar, like an old blanket you can't bring yourself to throw away."

"Familiar or not, that blanket is full of holes," I said, feeling bold. "It won't keep you warm, and it definitely won't protect you from the cold." The figure's eyes flickered with recognition, and for the first time, I saw a glimmer of hope flash across its face. "You can let go," I urged. "You can choose a different path. Just take a step back and breathe."

"Easier said than done," it replied, but there was a quiver in its voice that suggested it was considering my words, wrestling with an internal struggle that mirrored our own. "What if I don't know how? What if it's too late for me?"

Hunter stepped forward, his intensity radiating warmth. "It's never too late. You don't have to figure it all out right now. Just take that first step, and we'll figure it out together."

The figure hesitated, and I could feel the weight of the moment hang in the air like a tightly strung bow. The transformation of anger to uncertainty crackled between us, creating an almost magnetic tension that pulled me closer. "What's stopping you?" I asked softly, my heart racing as I tried to bridge the distance between us.

And then, just as the figure seemed ready to drop its defenses, the air shifted. A low rumble echoed from the depths of the shadowy corners of the room, and suddenly, the walls around us seemed to pulse with a life of their own. The temperature plummeted, and I shivered as a gust of wind howled through the space, swirling around us like a ghost released from its chains.

"Do you feel that?" Hunter asked, his eyes widening in realization.

The figure's face contorted with fear, panic settling in as it turned to look behind it. "No! Not now! Not again!" it cried, the sudden dread in its voice slicing through my heart.

"What's happening?" I demanded, the words barely escaping my lips as the air thickened, an ominous presence coiling around us like smoke.

"It's not over! The past doesn't let go that easily!" The figure stepped back, its resolve crumbling as shadows began to coalesce into something darker, more dangerous.

Hunter pulled me close, our shoulders touching, and I could feel his heartbeat racing alongside mine. "Whatever is happening, we have to stay together," he urged, determination igniting in his eyes. "No matter what comes next, we face it as one."

But before I could respond, the shadows coiled tighter, rising from the ground like a tidal wave, swallowing the light and darkening our surroundings. I felt an icy grip on my throat, a palpable reminder of the fears we thought we had just begun to confront.

"Why won't you just let me go?" the figure cried out, desperation spilling from its lips as it stood before the encroaching darkness. "You don't understand! This is my burden!"

Suddenly, the shadows twisted and reformed, taking the shape of monstrous figures, each one an embodiment of pain and resentment. Their hollow eyes glimmered with malice, their forms flickering like flames about to extinguish. It was as if every past grievance had risen to the surface, echoing with the voices of those long gone.

"No!" I shouted, stepping forward instinctively, feeling the weight of the shadows pressing down on me, yet refusing to back down. "You are not defined by these shadows. None of us are!"

"Can you even hear yourself?" the figure barked, shaking its head in disbelief as it pointed at the monstrous forms. "They are manifestations of everything I've held onto! You think words can change that?"

"It's not just words," Hunter replied, his voice steady despite the chaos around us. "It's action. We can't let these shadows control us any longer. We've fought too hard to let fear win!"

The shadows hesitated, their forms wavering, the flickers of light breaking through. For an instant, I thought we might have a chance to push back against the darkness. But then, as if sensing our defiance, they surged forward with a ferocious howl, ready to consume everything in their path.

"Run!" I screamed, grabbing Hunter's hand as we turned to flee. But the figure remained rooted in place, staring into the depths of the chaos with an expression of horror. "You can't leave me!" it cried, fear twisting its features into a mask of despair.

"No! We can't leave you!" I shouted back, fighting against the instinct to escape. "You're part of this too! We can fight this together!"

But before I could reach out, the shadows lunged, engulfing the figure in a storm of darkness, its scream swallowed by the cacophony of rage. I felt a surge of desperation as I pulled Hunter back, unwilling to let the shadows take us as well.

"Hold on!" Hunter shouted, gripping my hand tightly as we were swept away, the world around us blurring into a haze of terror and despair. Just as we stumbled back, I caught a glimpse of the figure's eyes—filled with a haunting mix of fear and yearning.

And then it was gone, consumed by the shadows, leaving only the howling wind and the echo of its cries behind. The darkness rushed in, threatening to swallow us whole as we turned to run, unsure if we would escape this nightmare or become part of its legacy.

Chapter 22: Rebuilding

The sun dipped low on the horizon, casting a warm golden glow across Firestone Bay, as if the sky were painting a tender portrait of rebirth. I stood at the edge of the shore, the cool ocean breeze tousling my hair and mingling with the salty scent of the sea, a perfume that felt like freedom. The rhythmic sound of waves lapping against the shore resonated in my chest, a steady reminder that life continues, regardless of the chaos that had engulfed us just weeks before.

Beside me, Hunter's silhouette cut a striking figure against the sunset, his dark hair catching the last rays of light, creating an almost halo effect around him. There was a comfort in his presence, an unspoken promise that together we could navigate whatever came next. Our shared laughter echoed across the water, a sound I had almost forgotten amid the turmoil, and I marveled at how quickly joy could resurface when hope was given a chance to breathe.

"Do you remember the last time we stood here?" Hunter asked, breaking the comfortable silence that hung between us like the warm breeze.

I smiled, my heart fluttering at the memory. "You mean when you nearly got us both swept away by that rogue wave? I thought I was going to have to swim for my life."

"Hey, I was just trying to impress you with my adventurous spirit," he replied, grinning. "Though, in hindsight, maybe I should have kept my bravado to less wet and wild activities."

I chuckled, shaking my head. "Next time, just stick to your charming conversation skills. They work wonders."

Hunter's gaze turned serious as he looked out over the water. "It's hard to believe how much has changed since then. We were so naive, thinking the worst was behind us."

His words carried a weight that settled in the air between us, but I wasn't ready to succumb to the shadows of our past. "We've come through it, Hunter. Together. That's what matters now."

The vulnerability in his eyes told me he understood, even if the memories still haunted him. We both carried the scars of our experiences, but they no longer defined us. Instead, they shaped our resolve. The darkness that had threatened to swallow us was now a flickering shadow in the rearview mirror of our lives. We could rebuild, and we would.

"Let's make a promise," I said, turning to face him, the waves crashing behind me like a chorus. "No matter what happens, we'll always find our way back to each other. We'll keep moving forward, one step at a time."

"I promise," he replied, his voice steady. "I'd follow you anywhere, you know that."

I reached for his hand, intertwining our fingers as if sealing our pact. There was a spark between us, electric and alive, and it ignited a sense of courage within me. Together, we would reclaim our lives from the remnants of fear, breathing life back into the dreams we had almost forgotten.

As we wandered along the shoreline, the setting sun painted the sky in hues of orange and purple, a brilliant tapestry that felt like a celebration of our victory. We stopped to collect smooth pebbles, their surfaces polished by the relentless waves, each one a testament to the resilience of nature. I marveled at how each stone held its own story, weathered and beautiful, just like us.

"What do you think we should do first?" Hunter asked, tossing a pebble into the surf and watching as it skipped across the surface before disappearing into the depths.

"Let's start with the community," I suggested. "We should organize a gathering, something to bring everyone together. They need to know they're not alone in this."

"I like that idea," he said, a spark of enthusiasm lighting up his features. "A celebration to remind everyone of what we've fought for."

As we brainstormed, an idea began to take shape. The bay needed a festival, a way to commemorate our resilience and the bonds we had forged. We could invite local musicians, food vendors, and artists—each one a piece of the vibrant tapestry that made Firestone Bay unique. The festival could serve as a reminder of our strength, a declaration that we would not be defined by our past but would embrace the future.

"Let's call it the Rebirth Festival," I suggested, feeling a swell of excitement at the thought of bringing our community together.

"Perfect," Hunter replied, his eyes brightening. "And we can use the old pier as a focal point. It needs a little love, but it'll be the heart of the celebration."

The very idea of revitalizing the pier sent a thrill down my spine. It had stood through storms and calm, much like the people of Firestone Bay. It symbolized hope, resilience, and our shared history. If we could bring it back to life, we could mirror that effort in our community.

We spent the afternoon plotting the details, losing ourselves in the excitement of our plans. With each idea exchanged, the tension that had once lingered in the back of my mind began to dissipate, replaced by a sense of purpose. We would gather the townspeople, ignite their passions, and weave together a tapestry of stories—our stories—of courage and survival.

As dusk settled over the bay, the first stars twinkled to life in the sky, shimmering reflections of our renewed hope. I felt a sense of warmth radiating from within, filling the empty spaces left by fear and uncertainty. We had emerged from the darkness, and now, we were stepping into the light, hand in hand, ready to embrace whatever came next.

But even as the warmth enveloped me, a whisper of unease lingered at the edges of my mind, reminding me that while the battle might be over, the war for our future was just beginning.

The following days felt like a whirlwind of color and sound, as preparations for the Rebirth Festival consumed Firestone Bay. Hunter and I dove into the project with a fervor that surprised even us. What had begun as a mere idea blossomed into a communal effort, uniting everyone in a tapestry of shared determination. The air hummed with excitement and laughter as neighbors who once exchanged polite nods became collaborators, sharing recipes, stories, and ideas like old friends.

I often found myself at the local community center, transformed into a makeshift headquarters, adorned with streamers and chalkboards filled with lists of tasks. Each time I walked in, the air was thick with the scent of fresh paint and the sound of hammers echoing as people worked tirelessly to restore the old pier. We were driven by something deeper than the festival itself; it felt like we were stitching together the fabric of our town, mending the frayed edges of our collective heart.

Hunter was a relentless force of nature. He effortlessly coordinated volunteers, his enthusiasm contagious as he rallied the town's youth to help with everything from painting signs to designing booths. "Just think of it as a giant group project, but with fewer people slacking off," he quipped one afternoon, grinning as he handed out paintbrushes like a proud teacher. I couldn't help but laugh, my heart swelling at the sight of him immersed in our plans, his passion radiating like the sun.

But amidst the joyful chaos, a storm brewed quietly on the horizon. I began to notice small shifts in the air—a tension that flickered like shadows at the edges of our laughter. Whispers of dissent circulated, an undercurrent of skepticism that some felt the festival was too soon, too hopeful. They questioned whether the wounds of our past could truly heal, or if we were merely bandaging over something far more profound. I could see it in their eyes, the remnants of fear lingering just below the surface, and it worried me.

One evening, while decorating the community center with twinkling lights that promised warmth and celebration, I overheard a hushed conversation between two women who were arranging a table of baked goods for the festival. "What if it's just a distraction?" one murmured, glancing around as if the very walls had ears. "What if we're only delaying the inevitable?"

I felt a chill race down my spine, the weight of her words settling heavily on my chest. The last thing I wanted was for the festival to be a shallow celebration, masking deeper issues that needed addressing. I needed to confront this growing unease, to remind our community of the strength we had displayed through adversity.

That night, as I lay in bed, Hunter's presence beside me was a comforting anchor. The soft sound of his breathing, steady and reassuring, helped drown out the echoes of doubt. I turned to him, my thoughts tumbling like the waves outside my window. "Do you think people are worried this festival is just a band-aid over our scars?"

He shifted slightly, his brow furrowing in thought. "It's natural to feel that way. Change can be terrifying, especially when you've just come out of something dark. But we can't let fear dictate how we move forward. We have to embrace the light, even if it feels fragile."

His words struck a chord deep within me, igniting a flicker of resolve. "Then let's make the festival a celebration of our resilience," I proposed, excitement bubbling in my chest. "We should highlight the stories of everyone in the community—what we've overcome, the strengths we've found. We can invite people to share their experiences, their journeys. It's not just a party; it's a reminder of who we are."

Hunter nodded, a grin spreading across his face. "I love it. A storytelling corner! We can set up a stage for open mic sessions, a place for people to speak their truth. Everyone has a story worth sharing, and it could help bridge that gap."

Fueled by our newfound determination, we spent the next day planning every detail. We contacted local musicians, secured a few brave volunteers willing to share their stories, and spread the word about our vision. Each conversation sparked enthusiasm, igniting a fire in the hearts of those who had been hesitant. The idea of sharing our journeys became an anthem of unity, an opportunity to embrace vulnerability together.

As the festival day approached, the atmosphere buzzed with anticipation. Banners hung from the old pier, colorful and vibrant, as laughter danced on the wind like the notes of a familiar song. The scent of grilled food wafted through the air, mingling with the sweet aroma of freshly baked pies, a tantalizing promise of the delights to come.

I found myself at the center of it all, watching as families set up picnic blankets, children raced about, their laughter ringing clear like silver bells. Hunter was off securing last-minute details, his energy seemingly endless, while I greeted the vendors and checked in with performers. Everything was coming together beautifully, and yet, as I moved through the crowd, I sensed an undercurrent of tension still simmering beneath the surface.

In the late afternoon, as the sun cast a warm golden glow over Firestone Bay, I took a moment to step away from the festivities, seeking a breath of fresh air. The water sparkled under the sun, a tranquil facade that belied the tumultuous emotions brewing in my chest. I leaned against the railing of the pier, letting the breeze wash over me, but my moment of peace was interrupted by the approach of familiar footsteps.

I turned to find a few of the more skeptical townsfolk—the same women I'd overheard discussing their doubts. Their expressions were guarded, shadows flickering in their eyes like remnants of a storm. "Can we talk?" one of them asked, her voice barely above a whisper.

A knot formed in my stomach as I nodded, inviting them to join me at the edge of the pier. I could feel the weight of their hesitation, the unspoken fears that loomed like dark clouds overhead. They stood in a loose circle, the sun behind them creating a halo effect that contrasted sharply with the heaviness they carried.

"I don't want to be a wet blanket," one woman began, her hands clasped nervously, "but what if this festival ends up being a farce? What if we're just pretending everything's fine when we're still dealing with the aftermath?"

Her words hung in the air like a heavy fog, and I felt the stirrings of frustration begin to bubble within me. "But isn't that the point? We're here to acknowledge what we've been through and to show that we're not alone. This festival is a celebration of our resilience, not a denial of our past."

Another woman chimed in, her voice shaking slightly. "But what if the stories we share only serve to reopen wounds? What if it all becomes too much?"

I took a deep breath, forcing myself to remain calm. "We're not asking anyone to ignore their pain or pretend it doesn't exist. We're inviting them to share it, to find strength in vulnerability. Healing isn't linear; it's messy and complicated, but it's also powerful."

The sincerity in my words seemed to resonate with them. I watched as the tension in their shoulders eased, just a fraction, and hope flickered in their eyes like the glint of sunlight on the water. "What if we made it a safe space?" I suggested. "A place where everyone can express themselves without judgment? We can create a platform for healing, not just a celebration."

Gradually, they nodded, their expressions shifting from skepticism to tentative agreement. As we stood together, the sun dipped lower in the sky, painting everything in shades of gold and crimson, and I realized that the festival was not just a reflection of our triumph but a collective embrace of our journey forward. We were ready to step into the light, together, one brave story at a time.

The sun began its slow descent over Firestone Bay, drenching everything in a soft, warm glow that felt almost magical. The festival was now in full swing, laughter blending with the tantalizing aromas wafting from food stalls lining the pier. I moved through the crowd, the energy around me palpable, each smile and cheer weaving a tapestry of connection that filled my heart with joy. This was the community I loved—a mosaic of stories, each more vibrant than the last, coming together to form something beautiful.

Hunter was at the center of the action, rallying the local musicians and ensuring everything was running smoothly. His enthusiasm was contagious, and I couldn't help but admire how effortlessly he brought people together. "Can you believe we actually pulled this off?" he shouted over the music, a grin spreading across his face. "I mean, it's like we've created our own little slice of magic."

"It's more than magic," I replied, watching as families gathered to listen to a band of teenagers playing upbeat tunes. "It's a celebration of us—the resilience of Firestone Bay."

With a renewed sense of purpose, I made my way to the stage where local storytellers were beginning to share their tales. A middle-aged woman stepped up, her hands shaking slightly as she gripped the microphone. "I was here when the darkness came," she began, her voice steadying as she looked out at the crowd. "I lost my husband, but I also found strength I never knew I had. Sharing our stories helps us heal, helps us remember that we are never alone."

A wave of emotion washed over me as she spoke, and I could see the faces of the audience soften, drawn into the warmth of her words. The fear that had once threatened to swallow us whole was now being transformed into shared understanding. Each story felt like a thread in the fabric of our community, stitching together our pasts into a future filled with promise.

As the sun dipped below the horizon, casting long shadows across the festival, I felt an arm slip around my waist. I turned to find Hunter beside me, his expression a mixture of pride and tenderness.

"I can't believe how far we've come," he said, his voice low enough that it felt like a secret shared between us.

"It's just the beginning," I replied, leaning into him. "We have so much more to do."

With the sun setting, the stage lights illuminated the area, creating a warm, inviting glow. A local band began to play a lively tune, and couples started to dance, the rhythm pulsing through the crowd like a heartbeat. I felt a tug at my heart, a desire to join them, to lose myself in the music and the moment. Hunter must have sensed it too, as he took my hand and led me toward the dance floor.

"Shall we?" he asked, his eyes sparkling with mischief.

"Only if you promise not to step on my toes," I teased, the lightness of the moment wrapping around us like a cocoon.

He chuckled, pulling me close as the music swelled. We twirled and swayed, the world around us fading into a blur. The connection between us felt electric, a dance not just of bodies but of souls. I caught sight of friends and neighbors, all around us lost in the joy of the evening, and it struck me how far we had come. The love we had fought for flourished in the most unexpected of places.

As the night deepened, a hush fell over the crowd, signaling the beginning of the storytelling segment. One by one, brave souls took to the stage, sharing their truths, their losses, and their victories. Each tale echoed in my heart, carving out a space for hope amidst the shadows of fear.

Then, from the corner of my eye, I noticed a figure lurking at the edge of the festival grounds. The shadows clung to him like a shroud, and my heart quickened. There was something familiar about the way he stood, as if he were waiting for the right moment to strike. I glanced at Hunter, who was engrossed in the storyteller, and felt a jolt of apprehension.

"Hunter," I whispered, trying to keep my voice steady. "Do you see that guy over there?"

He turned, his brow furrowing as he followed my gaze. "What guy?"

"The one near the trees. He looks out of place." My pulse raced, the sense of unease creeping back in like an unwelcome chill.

Hunter squinted, his expression shifting from amusement to concern. "Stay here. I'll check it out."

Before I could protest, he was weaving through the crowd, his tall frame cutting a determined path toward the figure. I stood rooted in place, anxiety knotting in my stomach as I watched Hunter approach the man. He spoke to him, gesturing as if trying to coax him into the light, but the stranger simply turned, half-shrouded in darkness, and retreated into the shadows of the trees.

"Hunter!" I called out, my voice rising above the music. I pushed through the crowd, desperation fueling my steps.

I reached him just as the stranger disappeared completely. "What did he say?" I panted, my heart racing.

"Nothing. He didn't even acknowledge me." Hunter looked troubled, scanning the area with narrowed eyes. "It felt wrong. I think we should—"

Suddenly, the sound of shattering glass cut through the night, sharp and jarring. Gasps erupted from the crowd as people turned toward the source of the noise, a stall that had just been knocked over. In the chaos, the tension in the air shifted dramatically.

"Stay close," Hunter ordered, his voice low and urgent. We maneuvered through the throng, hearts pounding, adrenaline surging through our veins.

As we reached the stall, a sense of dread unfurled within me. Broken glass glittered like shards of stars on the ground, and a few people were kneeling, helping the vendor who looked shaken and disoriented. "What happened?" I asked, kneeling beside them.

"Someone just... charged through," the vendor stammered, gesturing wildly. "They were yelling about the curse! Something about it returning!"

The word hung heavy in the air, a thunderclap amidst the laughter and music of the festival. The mention of the curse sent a ripple of fear through me, reminding me of the darkness we had fought so hard to banish.

Before I could process it, a loud crack split the night, like a gunshot, and the lights flickered ominously. Panic rippled through the crowd, and people began to scatter, fear etched on their faces. I turned to Hunter, my heart racing. "What's happening?"

"I don't know, but we need to find everyone and get out of here!"

Just as we turned to make our way through the fleeing crowd, a shadow emerged from the chaos, the same figure I'd seen earlier. He was moving toward us, his face obscured, but his intent was clear. My heart pounded in my chest as I realized he was not just an observer—he was here for a reason, and the festival's celebration was about to take a dark turn.

As he drew closer, the atmosphere shifted, a storm brewing in the depths of my gut. I could feel the impending danger pulsating through the air, and just before I could grab Hunter's hand, the figure lunged forward, and everything went dark.

Chapter 23: A New Dawn

The vibrant hues of dawn spilled across Firestone Bay like a painter's brush against a canvas, the sky a tapestry of soft pinks and golds. I took a deep breath, savoring the salty tang of the ocean mixed with the sweet scent of wildflowers that grew along the coastal path. Each step felt lighter than the last, our intertwined fingers a silent promise of unity against the challenges we had faced. Hunter glanced sideways at me, his eyes gleaming with a mix of mischief and affection, and my heart did that delightful fluttering thing it had perfected around him.

"Do you think we'll ever be boring?" he teased, a lopsided grin spreading across his face. "You know, like that couple down the street who just mows their lawn on weekends and debates the merits of mulch?"

I laughed, a sound bright enough to chase away any lingering shadows. "I doubt it. I'm pretty sure we'll always be too busy plotting our next grand adventure—or, you know, figuring out how to keep our plants alive."

He snorted, his laughter rich and contagious, as we stepped over a gnarled tree root that sprawled across the path. "Well, I could always turn to a life of crime. I hear garden gnomes are a hot commodity."

"Only if you promise to wear a striped shirt and a beret. A dashing criminal like you deserves a signature look." I elbowed him playfully, relishing the ease that had settled between us, a warmth that had once seemed impossible.

The scenery shifted as we meandered toward the cliffs, where the rugged edges met the crashing waves below. Sea birds cawed overhead, riding the morning breeze, their freedom echoing in the very essence of our surroundings. The world felt alive, brimming with possibilities, much like the bubbling excitement that surged within me.

"Do you ever wonder how we got here?" I asked, my voice quieter now as I leaned against a weathered railing overlooking the sea. The rhythmic roar of the waves below matched the pounding of my heart, the water shimmering like liquid diamonds. "I mean, who would've thought the guy who nearly pushed me into the tide would end up holding my hand?"

Hunter's expression softened, and he took a moment to gather his thoughts. "It's funny, isn't it? I used to think you were just this cute girl who didn't belong in my world. And then, here we are—two misfits who found their way through all the chaos."

The sincerity in his tone washed over me, and I felt the edges of my smile deepen. "Misfits, huh? Is that what we're calling it now?" I challenged, raising an eyebrow. "What do you think the town would say? 'Look out, here come the love-struck hooligans!'"

"Exactly," he replied, his voice taking on an exaggerated gravitas. "We should totally get T-shirts made. 'Firestone Bay's Premier Misfits—Best at Causing Trouble and Breaking Hearts.'"

"Just our luck, we'd have to fight the T-shirt shop owner for the rights." I shook my head, my laughter blending with the sounds of the waves. But beneath the humor lay a bittersweet truth; we had emerged from the wreckage of our tumultuous beginnings, finding solace in each other, and it felt surreal.

As we resumed our stroll, a shift in the air pricked at my senses. The sun climbed higher, casting longer shadows, and I felt the stirrings of apprehension mingling with our lighthearted banter. It was a reminder that the past, while no longer a weight upon my heart, still lurked in the corners, ready to pounce when least expected.

"Do you ever miss it?" I ventured, breaking the comfortable silence. "The thrill of the chase? The mystery of it all?"

Hunter paused, his brows furrowing slightly. "You mean the drama? The uncertainty?" He rubbed the back of his neck as if searching for the right words. "Sometimes, I think I miss the adrenaline, but not the chaos. That part nearly broke us."

"True." I nodded, biting my lip as I mulled over his words. "It's just... sometimes I wonder if we'll ever truly be free of it."

His gaze locked onto mine, and I could see the weight of his thoughts mirrored in his eyes. "Freedom isn't just about letting go of the past. It's about deciding who we want to be moving forward." He squeezed my hand, a grounding gesture that sent a ripple of warmth through me. "Together."

I considered his words as we reached the cliffs. The wind whipped through my hair, and I closed my eyes for a moment, letting the ocean's roar drown out my fears. Together. That single word carried more weight than any promise, a bond forged through fire.

"Okay then," I said, my voice steady as I opened my eyes to the vast horizon. "Let's make a pact. No more running away from what scares us. Let's face it head-on, whatever it is."

He raised an eyebrow, his playful smirk returning. "Even if it means confronting rogue garden gnomes?"

"Especially the gnomes," I declared, a giggle escaping me. "And the nosy neighbors. And whoever keeps stealing my mail!"

With a hearty laugh, Hunter leaned in, brushing his lips against my temple. "Deal. Just promise me one thing."

"What's that?"

"Promise we'll always remember to laugh—even in the face of chaos."

I nodded, warmth blooming in my chest. "Always."

As the sun continued to climb, bathing us in golden light, I felt a renewed sense of purpose. We would navigate whatever came our way together, hand in hand, misfits against the world, ready to carve out our own path beneath the ever-expanding sky.

The sound of laughter echoed around us as we rounded a bend in the path, where the scent of fresh coffee wafted from a small café nestled by the beach. I had always thought of this place as a hidden gem, a secret spot where locals gathered to sip steaming cups and share stories. With Hunter by my side, the familiar surroundings felt charged with new possibilities, like the beginning of an uncharted adventure.

"Coffee?" he asked, his eyes sparkling with mischief. "Or should we go for something a bit more adventurous? I hear the barista has a new concoction that involves seaweed."

I scrunched my nose, unable to suppress a grin. "Seaweed? Really? Are we aiming for a gourmet experience or a food challenge?"

Hunter laughed, the sound warm and inviting. "Isn't a bit of culinary risk what life's all about? Plus, we could add it to our list of 'things that went horribly wrong' for our future memoir."

"Let's save that for when we're older and need to spice up our lives," I shot back playfully. "I'm not quite ready to put seaweed in my morning routine. Let's stick with the classics."

As we stepped inside, the café welcomed us with its cozy charm. The walls were painted a soft seafoam green, adorned with nautical-themed artwork that captured the essence of Firestone Bay. A bell jingled above the door, and the barista, a cheerful woman with a tousled bun and a bright apron, waved at us from behind the counter.

"Good morning! What can I get for you lovely people?" she called out, her voice brimming with enthusiasm.

"Two coffees, please," I said, leaning on the counter. "And one of those oversized muffins that looks like it could double as a doorstop."

Hunter nodded in agreement, a hint of mischief in his gaze. "Make that two muffins. We'll need the fuel for our day of reckless decision-making."

"Two muffins it is!" the barista replied with a wink, already reaching for a plate.

We settled into a sunlit corner table, and I felt a wave of contentment wash over me as I took in the cheerful atmosphere. The warmth of the morning sun filtered through the window, casting a golden glow around us. I watched as Hunter leaned back in his chair, his gaze fixed on the waves beyond the glass. There was something comforting about the way he carried himself, a silent assurance that everything was going to be okay.

"Do you think it's weird that I'm already daydreaming about what our first anniversary might look like?" I asked, tracing the rim of my coffee cup with a finger.

He raised an eyebrow, feigning seriousness. "Isn't that a bit ambitious? What if we decide to go our separate ways next week? We might end up on opposite sides of the world, fighting for the last piece of seaweed muffin."

"Please, like I would ever abandon you in a seaweed muffin crisis," I shot back, unable to contain a laugh. "But seriously, what do you see for us? A cozy dinner? A spontaneous trip? Or are we destined for a reality show where we navigate the wilds of our relationship?"

He considered my question, the corner of his mouth quirking up in that delightful way that made my heart race. "I like the idea of an adventure. Maybe we could take a road trip down the coast, just the two of us, blasting our favorite songs and stopping at all the ridiculous roadside attractions."

"Sounds perfect," I mused, feeling a flicker of excitement. "But if we find a giant ball of yarn, I'm totally stopping for a picture. No questions asked."

"Agreed. But I get to pick the next roadside attraction, and it better not involve anything remotely related to seaweed." He raised his coffee cup in mock toast, and I clinked mine against his, laughter bubbling between us.

Just then, the door swung open, and a group of locals entered, their chatter filling the room. My heart sank as I recognized one of them—a woman with striking red hair and a confident stride. Chloe. The very name conjured memories that felt like a fist tightening around my chest.

"Look who it is," Hunter whispered, his voice low, but I could hear the tension simmering beneath it.

"Great," I murmured, forcing a smile as she caught my eye. "Just what we need—our past walking in with its bright hair and self-assured attitude."

"Act natural," he advised, a hint of amusement in his tone. "Remember, we're misfits. We're supposed to be unpredictable."

As Chloe approached, her gaze flickered between us, a mixture of surprise and curiosity lighting her features. "Well, well, if it isn't the dynamic duo," she said, her tone dripping with sarcasm. "Didn't expect to see you two lovebirds together. How's the romance?"

"Better than the last time you asked," I replied, trying to keep my voice steady, but the words came out sharper than I intended. "We've moved past the 'I can't stand you' phase."

Chloe chuckled, her laughter echoing like the tinkling of wind chimes, but it held an edge. "I guess miracles do happen. Who would've thought you two would make a cute couple? Must be something in the bay air."

Hunter shifted in his seat, the tension rising. "We're happy, Chloe. That's what matters."

"Happy? Is that what you call it?" She leaned closer, her gaze assessing. "Just make sure you're not setting yourselves up for another train wreck. You know how it goes in this town—things have a way of spiraling out of control."

I felt the warmth of the café drain away, replaced by an uncomfortable chill. "We're not worried about train wrecks, thanks. We've got our own plans."

Her expression softened momentarily, and for a fleeting second, I saw a glimpse of the girl I once considered a friend. "Just remember, it's a small town. Rumors travel fast. One wrong move, and everyone will know."

With that, she turned on her heel, her group following her like a parade of shadowy figures. I let out a breath I hadn't realized I was holding, the tension dissipating, but the words lingered like a haunting melody in the back of my mind.

"That was... fun," I said, attempting to inject levity into the moment. "Not the welcome wagon we were hoping for."

Hunter leaned forward, concern etched on his face. "You okay? I could've tossed a muffin at her. I hear that's a popular way to settle disputes around here."

"Tempting, but let's not escalate things too quickly. I'd rather not have a pastry war on our hands." I took a sip of my coffee, trying to shake off the unease that clung to me. "I guess it's just a reminder that the past doesn't always fade away neatly. It has a way of sneaking back when you least expect it."

He reached across the table, his hand warm and reassuring. "We'll deal with it, together. No matter what comes our way. Just remember, you've got me in your corner, seaweed muffins and all."

I smiled, a genuine warmth blooming within me as I squeezed his hand. "Thanks, Hunter. Just don't forget to pack those muffins for our road trip. They might come in handy against any potential muffin-wielding enemies."

His laughter filled the café, a sound that drowned out the echoes of the past, and I knew, despite the shadows that lingered, we would face whatever challenges lay ahead with determination and a dash of humor.

With the warm sunlight spilling through the café windows, I felt a renewed sense of hope. The brief encounter with Chloe, though uncomfortable, had ignited something deeper within me—a fierce determination to protect what Hunter and I had built. I didn't want the echoes of past relationships or unkind words to unravel the tapestry we were weaving together.

As we finished our coffee, Hunter leaned back in his chair, a thoughtful expression on his face. "So, what's next for our intrepid duo? A beach day? A hike? Maybe a trip to the local library to search for more recipes involving seaweed?"

"Are you really obsessed with that seaweed muffin idea?" I asked, feigning exasperation while trying to suppress a smile. "I'm starting to think you have some hidden ambition to become a gourmet chef."

"Hidden? Hardly," he chuckled, glancing at the barista as she cleaned the counter. "But I am dedicated to living life to the fullest—even if it means risking my taste buds on whatever concoction that woman comes up with next."

"Or we could go for a walk along the shore," I suggested, my gaze drifting to the shimmering ocean outside. "Feel the sand between our toes and maybe collect some shells for the grand project of 'making our apartment feel slightly less like a cave.'"

"Sounds like a plan." He rose, offering me his hand, and I took it, feeling the familiar spark of connection. The moment we stepped outside, the sea breeze enveloped us, invigorating my senses and washing away the remnants of our earlier encounter.

The shoreline stretched before us, a sandy expanse framed by gentle waves that lapped at the shore, leaving behind delicate seashells like forgotten treasures. We walked side by side, our footsteps mingling with the whispers of the tide. I could hardly contain my excitement as I spotted a particularly beautiful conch shell partially buried in the sand.

"Look at this one!" I exclaimed, bending down to pick it up. The shell felt cool and smooth in my palm, a perfect specimen of nature's artistry. "It's like finding a piece of the ocean itself."

"Nice find! Now we just need a few more, and we'll have enough to start our own shell collection or, better yet, a small museum." Hunter grinned, and I laughed at the idea, but it was tempting.

As I slipped the shell into my pocket, I glanced up to find Hunter gazing at the horizon, his expression shifting from playful to serious. "What's on your mind?" I asked, sensing the change.

He hesitated, a shadow crossing his features. "I've been thinking about what Chloe said back at the café. About rumors. It's easy to brush them off, but sometimes... sometimes they have a way of spiraling out of control."

"Rumors are like wildfires," I replied, trying to lighten the mood. "If we ignore them, they might fizzle out. But if we give them too much attention, they could spread."

"Exactly." He sighed, running a hand through his hair, tousling it in a way that made my heart flutter. "I just don't want anything to threaten what we have."

I stepped closer, wrapping my arms around his waist. "Nothing can tear us apart unless we let it. We're stronger together, remember?"

He nodded, a flicker of warmth returning to his gaze. "You're right. It's just... the thought of losing you scares me."

"Let's not dwell on that. Instead, let's focus on the fun stuff—like planning our first big adventure together. What if we drove up the coast, stopping at every quirky diner we can find?"

"Now that's the spirit!" He grinned, the tension melting away as he looked back toward the ocean. "Maybe we'll even find a diner famous for its—dare I say—seaweed salad."

"Hunter!" I gasped, mock horror in my eyes. "That's taking things too far!"

We laughed, the sound mingling with the rhythm of the waves. The tension from earlier faded, replaced by the easy camaraderie that defined our relationship. I felt lighter, ready to embrace whatever came our way.

But just as I was settling back into that warmth, a shadow loomed on the horizon. Squinting against the sun, I spotted a figure standing a little farther down the beach, their posture rigid and unyielding. Something about the way they stood sent a shiver down my spine.

"Hunter?" I said, my voice low, a flicker of unease creeping in. "Do you see that?"

He turned to follow my gaze, his brow furrowing. "Yeah, I see it. Looks like someone is just... standing there. You think it's one of those rogue beachgoers, or are we about to have a run-in with a real-life mermaid?"

"Please, let it be a mermaid," I replied with a nervous laugh, but the unease lingered, tightening my stomach. The figure didn't move, just stood there, as if waiting for something—or someone.

As we approached, I realized it was a man, tall and imposing, dressed in dark clothes that contrasted starkly against the beach's vibrant colors. He turned slightly, and even from a distance, I could see his features were sharp, his eyes scanning the shoreline with a hawk-like intensity.

"Something's off about him," I whispered to Hunter, who nodded, his demeanor shifting to one of alertness.

"Stay close," he murmured, stepping protectively in front of me. The carefree afternoon had taken a sharp turn into uncertainty, the lightness of our laughter replaced by a heavy tension in the air.

Just then, the man turned fully to face us, and I froze, my breath hitching in my throat. There was something unsettling about his gaze, as if he had been watching us long before we had noticed him.

"Looking for something?" he called, his voice low and smooth, but there was an underlying edge that sent chills racing down my spine.

Hunter stepped forward slightly, placing himself between me and the stranger. "We were just enjoying the beach," he replied, trying to keep his tone casual, though I could feel the tension radiating off him.

The man smiled, but it didn't reach his eyes. "I see. It's a beautiful day for a walk... or for finding lost things."

"What do you mean by that?" I asked, trying to sound braver than I felt.

He tilted his head slightly, his expression almost amused. "You might want to be careful about what you wish to find. Sometimes, lost things aren't meant to be found."

With that cryptic remark, he took a step back, his silhouette stark against the sunlit sea. My heart raced as I exchanged a glance with Hunter, the earlier lightheartedness dissipating into a heavy dread.

Before I could utter another word, the man turned and strode away, leaving only the sound of the waves crashing against the shore. As he disappeared into the distance, I felt an icy knot form in my stomach, the weight of his warning hanging in the air like a dark cloud threatening to overshadow our newfound happiness.

"What just happened?" I whispered, more to myself than to Hunter.

"I don't know, but we need to keep our guard up," he replied, his grip tightening on my hand. The warmth of the sun felt distant now, overshadowed by an unsettling chill that hinted at the chaos that might yet unfold.

Chapter 24: The Promise

Firestone Bay was a place where the salt-laden breeze mingled with laughter, and the scent of sun-warmed sand lingered long after the tide retreated. Each summer, the town came alive, transforming into a vibrant tapestry of colorful umbrellas dotting the shoreline, children darting between the waves, and the sweet sound of music spilling from beach bonfires as dusk fell. It was in this intoxicating atmosphere, wrapped in the warmth of familiarity and the thrill of the unknown, that Hunter chose to reveal the depths of his heart.

I could hardly believe the moment unfolding before me, the soft glow of the golden hour painting the sky in rich hues of orange and pink. Hunter's expression, a mix of vulnerability and determination, held me captive. He dropped to one knee on the sun-kissed sand, a sharp contrast to the softness of the ocean waves lapping at our feet. In that heartbeat of eternity, the world around us melted away. The raucous laughter of my friends faded into a gentle murmur, the laughter blending with the distant cries of seagulls wheeling overhead.

"Jenna," he began, his voice steady yet filled with the raw emotion of someone baring their soul. The way my name slipped from his lips made it feel like an incantation, binding us together in that sacred space. "You've become my greatest adventure, my safe harbor. Will you promise to face whatever comes next with me?" His hands, rough yet tender, held a small velvet box, and the weight of that promise hung in the air, shimmering like the evening stars preparing to peek out from the twilight.

I felt the corners of my mouth twitching, caught between disbelief and joy. Every shared secret, each whispered dream, surged to the forefront of my mind—those late-night conversations beneath the stars, the playful banter that had solidified our bond, and the way his presence had effortlessly woven itself into the fabric of my life. How could I ever have thought I could live without this?

With a shaky breath, I knelt beside him, my heart racing like a wild stallion. "Are you serious? You want to take on this rollercoaster with me?" The teasing glint in my eyes was met with the fervor of his unwavering gaze, full of the steadfastness I had come to rely on.

"Absolutely," he replied, laughter spilling from his lips like sunshine breaking through a storm. "Life with you is the only ride I want to be on."

My laughter mingled with the ocean's symphony, a sound that echoed the joy we both felt. As I opened the small box, a glint of silver caught the fading light, revealing a ring that seemed to dance with the rhythm of the waves. It was simple yet elegant—a band with a small sapphire nestled among sparkling diamonds, a perfect representation of us: steadfast, vibrant, and a little unpredictable.

"I love it," I breathed, the words tumbling from my lips as if propelled by the sheer gravity of the moment. "But Hunter, this is so much... I mean, are we really ready for this?"

"Ready or not, life has a way of throwing us into the deep end," he said, a soft smile curling at his lips. "But I want to dive in with you."

With shaking fingers, I slipped the ring onto my finger, feeling the weight of my own promise—this commitment to adventure and love, to laughter and, yes, even to the tears that would surely come. My heart soared at the realization that we were crafting our own story, one that would be written in the ink of shared experiences and unyielding support.

The world began to seep back into focus. Cheers erupted from our friends, their excited voices wrapping around us like the waves crashing onto the shore. I glanced over to see Melissa jumping up and down, her sandy hair dancing in the wind, while Ryan clapped Hunter on the back, his laughter booming in delight.

In the midst of our celebration, however, a small, nagging feeling twisted in my gut. Life had never been just sunshine and rainbows for us. Challenges loomed on the horizon like distant storms gathering in the sky, and I could feel their presence, the weight of what we had yet to face pressing against my chest.

"Do you think we're ready for this?" I asked softly, glancing at Hunter, who was still beaming with pride.

"Ready or not, I don't want to face it without you," he assured me, his voice resolute. "Whatever storms come, we'll weather them together. You and me against the world."

I leaned into him, letting the warmth of his body wash over me, a shield against the creeping uncertainty. The waves rolled steadily, a reminder of life's rhythms, the way it ebbed and flowed. Each moment we shared, each promise exchanged, was a testament to our bond, an unbreakable thread that wove through our hearts.

As the sun dipped below the horizon, casting the world in shades of dusk, I felt a surge of hope. We were embarking on this journey hand in hand, hearts aligned with a fierce determination to embrace every twist, every unforeseen detour that awaited us. This was our moment, our promise—a commitment not just to each other, but to the life we would build together, come what may.

The laughter of our friends echoed around us, a jubilant chorus that seemed to bounce off the waves crashing against the shore. Their excitement wrapped around us like a warm blanket, providing a cocoon of support as Hunter and I stood in our own little bubble of bliss. My heart danced with exhilaration, a feeling of being utterly alive and filled with the magic of the moment. Yet, just as quickly as joy surged through me, a thread of apprehension tugged at the edges of my mind.

As Hunter rose to his feet, pulling me into a warm embrace, I couldn't help but feel the enormity of what lay ahead. Yes, we had made a promise, but life had a way of complicating even the simplest vows. A sudden gust of wind swept through the beach, sending a flurry of sand into the air, momentarily blinding me. It felt like nature itself was trying to remind us that unpredictability was part of the journey we'd just embarked upon.

"Welcome to your new life as my fiancée," Hunter teased, his smile wide and genuine, the spark in his eyes rekindling the warmth that surrounded us. I laughed, swatting playfully at the sand sticking to my arms. "Is there a handbook for this?"

"Just follow your instincts and try not to get buried in paperwork," he replied with a mock-seriousness that made me giggle.

But the laughter that rolled off our lips began to fade, replaced by a strange quiet that settled over the gathering. I turned to see Melissa standing with her arms crossed, a frown etched across her face, her brows knitting together in concern. Ryan, too, had fallen silent, his usual exuberance dimmed as he glanced between us, clearly sensing the shift in the atmosphere.

"Everything okay?" I asked, an unease creeping into my tone as I approached them.

"Yeah, we're just... surprised," Melissa admitted, her voice slightly strained. "I mean, you just got engaged, Jenna. That's huge. Are you sure you're ready for this?"

Her words struck like a sudden chill on a warm summer day. "What do you mean? Of course I'm ready!" I retorted, my voice sharper than I intended. I felt the weight of her gaze, the concern written all over her features, and I struggled to rein in the defensiveness creeping into my tone.

"I just want to make sure you've thought this through," she said carefully, her eyes softening. "I mean, you're young. You both are. What if you decide you want to travel or explore a bit more? A ring doesn't magically mean you have to settle down right now."

The moment hung between us, heavy with unspoken fears and the echoes of our own ambitions. I exchanged a glance with Hunter, who remained quiet but attentive, his eyes filled with understanding. "I want to explore with him," I finally said, my voice steadier than I felt. "We're not throwing our lives away. We're building something together."

"Right," Ryan chimed in, attempting to bridge the divide. "It's like a partnership, you know? You're not just signing a contract; you're agreeing to the journey."

"Exactly!" Hunter's enthusiasm burst forth, a vivid color in the otherwise muted conversation. "Life's an adventure, and I'd much rather have Jenna beside me, navigating the twists and turns than going solo."

As he spoke, I felt my heart swell with renewed confidence. There was truth in his words; a life without the thrill of shared experiences felt hollow. But in the midst of the swirling joy, a small doubt crept in, the kind that whispered sinister possibilities: What if the world outside of Firestone Bay grew too enticing?

Just then, the sky above us darkened, clouds rolling in like an unexpected interruption to our idyllic evening. The wind picked up, sending a shiver through the gathering. The joyful atmosphere turned tense as our friends instinctively huddled closer together.

"Looks like a storm is coming," Ryan observed, his brows furrowed as he pointed toward the horizon, where dark clouds loomed ominously.

"Let's not let a little rain dampen our spirits!" Hunter exclaimed, clapping his hands together. "Let's take this party indoors!"

Cheers erupted as we gathered our things, but I could feel the weight of apprehension lingering in the air. The prospect of a storm outside felt almost like a premonition of turbulence ahead, and I found myself clutching Hunter's hand tightly as we made our way toward the beach house, the familiar path now appearing darker and more foreboding than before.

Once inside, we settled into the cozy living room, the soft glow of candles flickering against the walls, casting playful shadows that danced to the rhythm of the wind. As our friends filled the space with chatter and laughter, I couldn't shake the feeling that the impending storm mirrored the uncertainty swirling in my heart.

Hunter slid his arm around me, pulling me closer as we sank into the plush couch. "Hey," he whispered, his breath warm against my ear, "are you okay? You've gone quiet."

"I just... I don't want to disappoint anyone," I admitted, the vulnerability in my voice revealing more than I intended. "What if we're not ready for this? What if we're just kids playing house?"

"Kids playing house can still build a castle," he said, his tone playful yet reassuring. "You and I have always been a little unpredictable, but I wouldn't have it any other way."

His words sparked something inside me, a flicker of defiance against the doubts that threatened to snuff out my excitement. "You're right," I said, straightening my shoulders. "We'll figure it out as we go."

Just as I felt that rush of certainty, a crash of thunder rattled the windows, followed by a sudden downpour, the rain drumming loudly against the roof. The sound drowned out the conversations, and all eyes turned toward the windows, where sheets of rain blurred the outside world into a gray canvas.

"Looks like we're stuck here for a bit!" Melissa chirped, attempting to lighten the mood, though her voice carried an edge of concern.

"Perfect time for a toast!" Hunter declared, lifting a glass of lemonade. "To love, to adventure, and to whatever storms may come!"

With that, the tension broke, and laughter filled the room once more, the storm outside becoming a mere backdrop to our celebration. But as I clinked my glass against Hunter's, I felt a shiver of foreboding pass through me. In that moment of joyous camaraderie, a question loomed large: What if the real storms were waiting just beyond the horizon, preparing to test the very promises we had made?

The wind howled outside like an unruly child, whipping raindrops against the windows in a frantic dance that echoed our internal chaos. Inside the cozy beach house, laughter flowed freely, wrapping around us like a warm embrace, but my thoughts remained a whirlwind of uncertainty. The celebratory atmosphere buzzed with energy, yet the tempest outside seemed to echo the very conflict brewing in my heart.

Hunter leaned closer, his arm draping around my shoulders as if to shield me from the storm, though I knew the real tempest was the one we had just stepped into. "You okay?" he asked, his voice low enough to keep our conversation private amidst the clamor of our friends.

"Yeah, I'm great. Just pondering the complexities of our future," I replied, forcing a smile, but inside, I felt like a ship at sea, unsteady and vulnerable against the crashing waves of doubt.

He chuckled, that infectious laugh that made my heart leap, but I could see the flicker of concern in his eyes. "Complexities? Sounds like you're already a married woman. Don't you think you're jumping the gun a bit?"

"Who said anything about marriage?" I retorted playfully, shoving him lightly. "I'm still figuring out if I want to share my fries with you, let alone my life!"

Our banter lightened the atmosphere between us, but beneath the surface, I sensed an undercurrent of unease. I watched as our friends shared stories and laughter, their faces illuminated by the flickering candlelight, blissfully unaware of the storm outside and the one brewing within me. It was a perfect moment, yet the shadows seemed to creep closer, reminding me that storms often heralded change, sometimes unwelcome.

Ryan sidled up to us, brandishing a deck of cards. "Alright, it's time for some party games! Who's in?" he announced, his voice cutting through the tension like a knife.

"Count me in!" Hunter said, his eyes lighting up. "Jenna, you're playing, right?"

"Absolutely! Just keep your competitive spirit in check, okay?" I replied, feigning sternness. But deep down, I knew Hunter's drive to win was only one of the many qualities I adored about him.

As the card game unfolded, laughter erupted in waves, each hand played punctuated by playful jabs and good-natured ribbing. The storm outside raged on, but within those four walls, we created a world filled with joy and connection. I felt the tension in my chest loosen slightly with every smile exchanged, every burst of laughter shared. Yet still, I couldn't shake the feeling that the laughter would soon be interrupted, as if the universe had a way of pulling the rug out from under us just when we thought we had our footing.

With every shuffle of the cards, a nagging feeling persisted—what if our carefree moments were just the calm before the storm? Hunter leaned closer, whispering something witty about my inability to shuffle cards properly. I shot him a glare, but deep down, his presence anchored me amidst my swirling thoughts. I craved that stability, but it was the uncertainty of our future that kept me awake at night, tossing and turning as I weighed the possibilities.

As the game progressed, Hunter continued to catch my eye, that mischievous glint sparkling like the candles' flames. He was genuinely lost in the moment, completely absorbed in the friendly competition, and I envied his ability to let go. I wanted to be like him—to embrace life's unpredictability with open arms. But just as I was beginning to settle into that thought, an unexpected crash of thunder rattled the house, shaking me from my reverie.

Our laughter faltered, eyes darting toward the windows where rain lashed violently against the glass. The light dimmed, flickering as the power threatened to give in to the storm's fury. I felt a shiver of apprehension wash over me, and just as I opened my mouth to suggest we move to a safer area of the house, the lights flickered once, twice, then went out entirely, plunging us into darkness.

A chorus of startled gasps rose around the room, the sudden void amplifying the storm's roars outside. "Everyone stay calm!" Ryan called out, his voice rising above the din. "It's just a little weather! I've got a flashlight somewhere!"

"Who needs a flashlight?" Hunter quipped, breaking through the tension with his trademark humor. "We have each other! How romantic!"

A few nervous chuckles broke the silence, but I could see the uncertainty etched on faces as they navigated the unfamiliar territory of darkness. I squeezed Hunter's hand, feeling his warmth seep into me, grounding me even as the storm raged on outside.

"Are you scared?" he whispered, his breath warm against my ear.

"A little," I admitted, my heart racing. "But mostly, I'm worried about what else is lurking out there."

Before he could respond, a sharp crack of thunder boomed overhead, vibrating through the floorboards like an earthquake. The sudden sound set off a flurry of panicked voices, confusion rippling through the group.

"Let's head to the kitchen!" Melissa suggested, her voice edged with anxiety. "It's probably the safest place with no windows."

Hunter and I followed the others, weaving our way through the chaos. As we moved toward the kitchen, I couldn't shake the feeling that the storm was more than just a passing inconvenience. Something about the energy in the air felt charged, electric, like a warning waiting to be deciphered.

Once we reached the kitchen, I pulled out my phone, the soft glow illuminating our faces. We huddled together, shadows stretching across the walls like dark specters lurking just beyond our vision. I could feel the tension in the room rising, hearts pounding in unison as we waited for the storm to subside.

"This is ridiculous," Ryan said, attempting to lighten the mood. "What are the odds that our first storm as a group happens to be a full-on weather event? I'd like a refund on my tickets, please!"

Hunter chuckled but suddenly fell silent, his gaze fixed on the kitchen window. "Guys," he said slowly, the light from my phone revealing the worry in his eyes. "Look outside."

We all turned toward the window, breath catching in our throats. Just beyond the glass, the storm revealed something sinister—dark shadows skittering just out of reach, barely visible in the flickering light. It was as if something was moving within the chaos, lurking in the corners, waiting for the right moment to strike.

"What is that?" Melissa breathed, her voice barely above a whisper, panic creeping into her words.

Before anyone could respond, a loud crash echoed from outside, followed by a figure darting past the window, shrouded in darkness. The hairs on the back of my neck prickled, and for a moment, fear gripped me like a vice.

"Did you see that?" I exclaimed, my heart racing. "Something's out there!"

The group erupted into murmurs, each face etched with shock and disbelief, and just as quickly, the lights flickered back to life. But the warmth they provided felt hollow compared to the tension that had settled over us. Hunter and I shared a wide-eyed glance, both of us aware that whatever awaited us outside was more than just a storm. It was a foreboding promise of change, of challenge, and it had only just begun.

9 798227 970886